DEATH ON COVERT CIRCLE

Secret Sleuth, Book 4

Patricia McLinn

Copyright © 2020 Patricia McLinn
Print ISBN: 978-1-944126-70-4
Ebook ISBN: 978-1-944126-69-8
Audiobook ISBN: 978-1-944126-95-7
Print Edition

www.PatriciaMcLinn.com

Cover design: Art by Karri

Death on Covert Circle

Also by Patricia McLinn

Secret Sleuth series

Death on the Diversion

Death on Torrid Avenue

Death on Beguiling Way

Death on Covert Circle

Death on Shady Bridge

Death on Carrion Lane

Death on ZigZag Trail

Death on Puzzle Place

Caught Dead in Wyoming series

Sign Off

Left Hanging

Shoot First

Last Ditch

Look Live

Back Story

Cold Open

Hot Roll

Reaction Shot

Body Brace

Cross Talk

Air Ready

Holiday Bullets

Cue Up

The Innocence Series

Proof of Innocence

Price of Innocence

Premise of Innocence

DAY ONE
MONDAY

CHAPTER ONE

ORANGE JUICE.

That's what entangled my friend, Clara Woodrow, and me in a murder.

Not a lot of people can say that.

Clara apologized again for our detour to the Jolly Roger grocery store, even though I'd agreed to it. "Ned's so easygoing about most things and he does love his orange juice. He's coming in really late tonight from his business trip, then he has meetings starting early tomorrow morning, poor baby. This way he'll have his orange juice before he goes."

Pre-detour, we'd been headed to my house from a meeting at the Torrid Avenue Dog Park.

I'd approved stopping at the Roger, as the store was commonly called, despite it eating into time I'd mentally assigned to writing, as I tried to write my first novel, something no one else in Haines Tavern knew about.

Something no one else *anywhere* knew about.

This was not the first time I'd let my assigned writing time be overrun by other activities, though it was the first time orange juice was the culprit.

"I read a wonderful book on oranges once that said orange juice for breakfast is widely considered an American habit, though, in fact, people in other countries drink it for breakfast. And sometimes all the rest of the day. They also do things like clean floors with oranges," I said. "Half an orange in each hand, down on their knees, scrubbing."

I had time to expand on my memories of the book *Oranges* by John McPhee, because the Roger was some distance down the rolling highway.

The Roger sat well back from the highway at a rising point in its endless up and down existence, tucked back on a solitary loop of a road called Covert Circle, which leads nowhere except the grocery store, a bank branch on one side of it, and a cut-rate (pun intended) hair place on the other.

It was as if the buildings were outcasts, pushed firmly beyond the invisible yet widely understood borders of Haines Tavern, Kentucky.

Heck, the townspeople allowed the dog park, with its attendant noise and smells, and the jail, ditto, to be built closer to the center of town than the Roger. That should tell you where it ranked in their estimation. They'd shop there for convenience, but they weren't proud of it.

To hear the people of Haines Tavern talk, they exclusively patronized Shep's Market, the generations-old store near the center of town. Yet I ran into a higher percentage of people I knew at the Roger than at Shep's.

Still, if we'd been in town, I'd wager Clara would have opted for Shep's Market. But Roger's represented a far shorter detour than Shep's to prevent Ned from being orange juice-less—and, thus, according to him, breakfastless—tomorrow morning.

If we'd been coming with the dogs from the park, I'd have stayed in Clara's SUV, running the AC full blast, because it was far too warm for furred beings to stay in a sun-soaked vehicle. But we'd left our dogs at my house for this meeting with parks officials about adding an agility area.

Clara and I had been elected to represent users of the dog park in a close-run election.

In other words, Donna, the dog park's czarina, said someone was needed to attend this meeting. No one volunteered. No one she approved of, anyway. She assigned us.

We'd report at the park this evening.

"A whole book on oranges?" Clara asked. "You have to give me the title of that one, too, Sheila."

"The title's simple—*Oranges*. But you don't have to read every book I mention. No one will expect you to have read every book out there."

Since she'd begun an online course to train as a virtual assistant for authors, Clara had been on a maniacal book binge, in addition to readings for the course and doing assignments.

"Not every book. But a lot more than I have. And you recommend such wonderful books. Not like what they made us read in school. So depressing. Turned me off reading for years. I still wouldn't be reading if it weren't for you and your great-aunt's books."

The topic of my Great-Aunt Kit, particularly the sub-topic of her books, tiptoed us right up to the edge of a precipice I did not want to go over. The landing would be on an unforgiving bed of sharp, protruding rocks known as secrets.

Kit's secrets. My secrets. Our secrets.

"Gee, look. Don't see that every day in Haines Tavern," I said in a brilliant and subtle change of subject.

I was aided by there actually being something unusual to look at as we approached the Roger.

It was one of those SUV limousines. Not the super long ones like kids rent for prom, but the kind executives get driven around in so they don't ever have to stop being important. It had an extra section between the front and back doors, plus a raised roof over the passenger compartment. As we got closer, I saw Range Rover branding.

It also had bright orange safety cones set around it, keeping all plebian vehicles well away from its glistening surfaces.

The likely cone-setter was a barrel-chested suit-wearing man slowly walking around the vehicle with a cloth in one hand, attending to the glisten.

As Clara's path took us close to the limo, the man turned and glared at her dog-toting, Kentucky dust-wearing, not of this decade SUV, as if daring us to bring the vehicular mutt any closer to his pristine purebred.

I had an urge to grab a grocery cart, pass right between the cones, and ram the side of the limo-SUV.

Good thing I was still inside a moving vehicle. Made it much easier to withstand temptation.

Clara parked with an aplomb I would never achieve in an SUV, we got out, and without discussion met at the front bumper, which started us on a route toward the limo-SUV, rather than to the main doors.

"Who do you think it belongs to?" Clara whispered, tipping her head toward the vehicle that, in a pinch, could probably hold all the dogs from the dog park.

I suppressed a grin at the glisten-attender's reaction to that scenario.

"No idea. Can't see a celebrity popping into the Roger, even if they did find themselves in North Bend County. Were there any special events scheduled?"

She lifted a shoulder, then had to re-seat her purse strap, which had dropped off her shoulder. "I never pay attention to the stuff they do here."

We'd need to adjust our path eventually or we'd run right into the vehicle, but rather than angling away, we kept straight on for now, but with a right-angle turn in our near futures.

The driver continued his circuit. He opened the farthest back door on the driver's side, giving us a view inside. Not his intention, I suspected, but a bonus from our angle.

A desk was pushed way back from the leather chair-like back seat, probably to let its occupant exit. Computing devices and a screen sat on the desk. On the passenger side of the compartment, another desk with similar tools was set up in front of a somewhat more spartan rear-facing seat.

"Definitely not a celeb," I murmured to Clara, as we made the right angle turn under the watchful eyes of the guy in the suit, who dusted already dust-free surfaces.

"No," she agreed mournfully. "No glitter in sight. All work and no play. Plenty of comfort, though. They sure have more leg room than if they faced each other."

"Could accomplish the same thing with two passengers sitting side by side. I bet this is to keep the hierarchy fully enforced, with the underling in the rear-facing seat."

"Smart," she said admiringly. "I mean you, not the rear seat limo person."

We grinned at each other as we entered the store and encountered Petey.

It was more common to see him out in the parking lot, even when winter had been its coldest, than inside.

Petey operated as a cross between a cart wrangler and a Wal-Mart greeter.

He'd called me by name the first time I'd shopped at the Roger. I still don't know how he'd known. He called everybody by name. And even the most curmudgeonly soon learned his name and used it in return.

I'd guess his age at north of seventy. He came up to my shoulder. He never failed to smile and say hello.

Except now.

A blonde woman wearing the store uniform with a pin on her black vest that read *Hi, I'm Jacqueline Yancik, Assistant Store Manager, How Can I Help You?* put her hand on his arm in a consoling gesture, then hurried after a knot of people congregated where register lines emptied out under a wall holding stiff photos of the store's management team.

Petey turned toward us—or more likely the exit door—with his head down.

"Petey, what is all this? Who's here?" Clara asked.

He looked up, produced a grimaced version of his usual smile. "CEO. Rod Birchall.

"CEO of the Jolly Roger chain? Here? Why?"

"Don't know. Yelled at the guy with him. Yelled at me. Yelled at her." His head-jerk indicated the departing assistant manager. "Probably yelling at somebody else now."

As badly as this unpleasantness appeared to have put Petey off his stride, he still pulled a cart—a small one in response to Clara's gesture—free from the line and presented it to her. But without a smile. And then he walked past us and out through the automatic door.

"Apparently the CEO of Jolly Roger came to Haines Tavern to yell at people," I summarized. "Clara, let's get the OJ and get out of here before he yells at us."

She side-eyed me with a glimmer of mischief. "Don't you want to hear what he's yelling about first? See a big CEO up close and personal?"

CHAPTER TWO

I'D SEEN MORE than a few in the years I'd spent in Manhattan, being known to the world by a different name and as the author of a book that became a movie, won awards and set records in each medium. The catch being that I hadn't actually written the book. My great-aunt had.

A fact very few people knew. Of those few people one lived in Haines Tavern. Me.

People here knew me as Sheila Mackey. With no literary identity attached.

For myself, I would have skipped getting a closer viewing of this CEO. Or any other CEO.

Too many of them reminded me of sea lions.

They're smart and can be fun to watch from a distance. A long distance. Because up close you realize they're noisy, have been known to snatch away small pets, and stink of putrid fish. Considering their diet, that's not surprising—the sea lions' diet, not the CEOs'.

But who was I to deny Clara the opportunity to experience a CEO? After all, everyone should go see sea lions in person. Once.

Besides, I might have an opportunity to ask if his was the brilliant mind behind associating a chain of grocery stores with piracy by naming them Jolly Roger. Way to make customers think they're getting a good deal.

"Sure."

Since Clara had already started wheeling the cart after the knot of people Petey had indicated and the assistant manager had joined, it was a foregone conclusion, but I voiced my agreement to make it official.

In addition to the assistant manager named Jacqueline, the knot included a woman I'd seen in passing at the dog park—she and her terrier mix often were leaving as I arrived with Gracie, my collie—but had never officially met.

Not only did I not know her name, I didn't know her dog's name, which made her next-best to a total stranger to me.

"Do you know her?" I asked Clara, indicating the woman by shifting my eyes.

"No. Shh."

Also part of the knot were three store employees in red vests, seven people I took for customers, a gangly young man in a white dress shirt and slacks with one arm wrapped across his waist as if his stomach hurt and a phone in his other hand, and, finally, the obvious CEO.

Obvious not only because he was the focus of the group and because his pristine white shirt and suit pants had been tailored by masters you've never heard of because they would never be so gauche as to advertise, but because he had the thrust-out chest, lifted head, and minimalist chin of a sea lion.

Though that might have been a coincidence.

Also, he was the one talking.

"…making this the most convenient and best choice for all shoppers in…"

At the CEO's pause, the gangly young man stepped forward, whispering.

The older man spoke loudly, as if that wiped out being fed his line by whisper. "…North Bent County. Since—"

"Bend, not Bent," corrected a voice from my left.

"—I took over, we've improved by leaps and bounds in record time, but we won't be satisfied with improvement. Our aim is perfect."

A woman with white wings to her dark, upswept hair and glasses on the tip of her nose, which facilitated looking over them at him in disapproval, slid into a crack in his discourse.

"You are far from perfect. You have London broil on sale at this store." Her clear, precise voice stirred memories of a high school English teacher.

"Glad you like your local Jolly Roger." If his non-responsive answer hadn't already given it away, his turned-away head as he scanned the aisle signs would have made it clear he wasn't paying attention.

"I do not like Jolly Roger at all at the moment. You have not improved, but rather, regressed. The London broil that I desire is no longer available. The employees at the meat counter, who have previously supplied exactly what I desired, informed me they can no longer cut it to my specifications. They tell me that rules from corporate headquarters have been handed down limiting the varieties of meat that can be cut at the stores, hamstringing the butchers, as it were. Further, I have ascertained that you are the party responsible for this change and others equally unwelcomed."

"Hamstringing butchers," Clara repeated under her breath. "That's good."

Still not looking at the woman, the CEO glanced toward the store employees and his gangly assistant, who wasn't as young as he'd first seemed. "This is the entrenched thinking we have to overcome, since we know meat production is far more profitable when we centralize it."

Seemed to me he was faulting the woman for not being happy to sacrifice getting London broil the way she liked it as long as it improved the Jolly Roger's bottom line … and, presumably, its CEO's annual bonus.

Yeah, that's what most consumers want first and foremost—to fatten stores' and CEOs' bottom lines.

"You're not producing meat. You're cutting it," grumbled a man standing across the group from the teacher, a man in his early forties, dressed in worn jeans, sneakers, and a white shirt, with the sleeves rolled back on powerful forearms.

The CEO, named Rod Birchall according to Petey, paid no attention. Not to the man, not to the woman voicing the complaint. He seemed to think the matter was settled.

She didn't, which was clear from her expression.

"Your profit relies on having customers, which you will not have with these changes," the woman said.

"Plenty of pre-packaged meat available," the assistant said with nervous heartiness.

As if he hadn't spoken, Rod Birchall said, "All the cuts you could want are here. All of them. We offer more choices than ever before—"

"Not true." Again, the woman's support came from the man on the opposite side of the group.

His right hand was raised slightly. At first, I thought he'd formed a fist. But the position of his hand was more elongated. More like a tennis racquet grip? No, that wasn't quite right, either. Yet there was something familiar...

The CEO interrupted my musing. "More choice than ever before and—"

"No. Prepackaging limits a purchaser's choices." Giving up on reading the man's grip, I read his face. *Not* a satisfied customer. "A lot of times you're selling mostly white meat."

White meat? But the woman had talked about red meat—London broil. Not to mention, her complaint centered on whether meat could be cut to a customer's specifications in the store, not white vs. red.

I might have been distracted by the non-sequitur, but the teacher-ish woman wasn't. She took control again.

"Indeed, there is no choice at all, in effect, because your packages offer only meat that is far too thin. Pork chops you can be seen through—no wonder people say it's dry. It is like trying to cook tissue paper. That is its flavor, as well. In addition, the supposed London broil in your packages, which could not be sliced to serve, because it would be like trying to slice a pancake."

"Some people do like it thin and—" started Jacqueline, the assistant store manager.

Birchall talked over her, as CEOs tend to do. "Statistically, shoppers prefer thin."

"None of those shoppers eat at my table," the London broil woman said curtly. "Are you going to return to having customers inform the butcher how they want their meat cut?"

"No," Birchall said. "Machines are more efficient and cost less. Butchers are remnants of past centuries. Should have moved aside for more efficient and cost-effective means years ago."

Didn't seem to me to be a good strategy to irritate and dismiss people who knew how to handle cleavers. On the other hand, this guy seemed determined to irritate everybody, including customers.

And he wasn't done. "We can't have butchers taking all day with customers. Centralizing meat-cutting provides better use of man-hours. More efficient."

"Prices haven't dropped to reflect any supposed efficiency," said the vaguely familiar man, a muscle beside his eye jumping.

Rod Birchall gave him a hard look and I'd swear the odor of putrid fish wafted past us.

"It's more efficient and cheaper for the entire chain." This CEO was not the first person I'd encountered who seemed to think repeating something was the same as making a valid point. He wasn't any less annoying for not being original.

"Not for the customers," the woman said.

He didn't even pretend to have listened. "Not to mention it makes the best sense for a store like this—a convenience, rather than a full-service store, like the one in…"

This time the gangly assistant's whisper was audible and identifiable. "Stringer. Two stores."

"The two stores in Stringer."

"If we wanted convenience, we'd pick up things at the gas station," said the terrier mix's owner from the dog park. "This place isn't as convenient at the gas station market *and* doesn't have all the things I need. It's the worst of both worlds."

"Then go to our big store—*two* big stores in Stinger."

The assistant winced.

When Birchall smiled, the center of his top lip didn't lift along with the corners, reminding me of a jack-o'-lantern. Only not as human.

"If I'm going that far, I'm going to stores with better products, more choice, lower prices, *and* without house brands they cram down my throat. In the meantime, this *convenient* Roger doesn't carry half the items I want. You've got to stop having your checkout clerks ask if we found everything we were looking for, because when we tell them what all we couldn't find it's slowing down the lines even worse than usual."

"Talk to your store manager." He looked toward the assistant manager.

"Kurt Verker," she supplied. "As I started to say before, he, uh, he had to leave. He wasn't feeling well. He'll be so sorry to have missed your visit."

The oldest of the red vests, a woman, coughed. The other two appeared caught between horror and a growing fear they'd burst out laughing.

"Even when he *is* here, he's not much use," the dog park woman said. "Promises to special order and call when it comes in, but he never calls and when I ask him about it, he says he couldn't get it—*them*. Any of the *many* things I've asked for. When I confront him, he mumbles on about rules from corporate and not enough room."

"That's true," Jacqueline, the assistant manager, said quickly. "We need to have enough room on the shelves to stock a carton's worth or we don't get a product." Considering the way the assistant manager tried to walk a tightrope between her customers and the CEO, she needed one of those super-long floppy balancing poles.

"You have plenty of room for more and more house brands," the dog park woman said. "We're not stupid, you know. We know stores make more money selling house brands than national brands."

"Our brands are a value offer," Birchall said, "giving you the same product for a lower price point—"

"That would be great if they *were* the same product. But most of your house brands are junk. We want the brand names that have proven their worth over years, not some jumped-up imitator."

"Our brands are superior—"

"They're *not*. Your lemon concentrate has seeds in it for heaven's sake. I want the brand I've been using for years and don't need to strain first. If I you don't offer it here—"

"If we don't offer it, it's because that brand name product doesn't sell in sufficient numbers to deserve space on the shelves. Blame your fellow shoppers."

"Bull," said the man in jeans.

The assistant store manager made an abortive gesture that might have been an instinctual plea to him not to antagonize the CEO. Whether the man interpreted it that way or not, he did not elaborate on the single word.

But the woman from the dog park kept to her point. "My fellow shoppers don't have a choice. You don't *stock* the product in this store."

"Because it doesn't sell," Birchall said triumphantly, turning away from her and starting off.

"Are you serious?" She immediately answered her own question. "Yes. Seriously stupid. It *can't* sell when you won't stock it."

She said the end louder, because he was walking away, on a path toward the produce section. He waved one hand overhead without stopping.

The knot divided.

With an apologetic smile over her shoulder, the assistant manager, along with Birchall's assistant, and the trio of employees wearing red vests, caught up with the CEO, their body language conveying reluctance in various dialects.

And I didn't think the reluctance was entirely explained by the fact they were moving closer to the home of Brussels sprouts and turnips.

Most of the grumbling group of customers left. But the man, the possible teacher, and the woman from the dog park headed in the same direction as the Roger employees.

Maybe they craved Brussels sprouts and turnips, but I doubted it.

Clara and I looked at each other.

"Do you need to get home right away?" she asked.

I blithely threw my writing time under the bus. "No. And this guy has me on the edge of my metaphorical seat to see how much worse he can get."

"I *know*. Let's go."

We followed in the wake of the remaining group.

CHAPTER THREE

AT THE CUSTOMER service desk, Birchall stopped abruptly, causing a chain reaction of stops for the employees, the three customers, then Clara and me. He reached over the counter and held up a bright blue object.

"You. What is this?"

It must have been an optical illusion that the other employees shrank away from the assistant manager, because I'd swear no one moved. But as clearly as if they'd extended their digits, they were all pointing to her as the one responsible for answering.

"A … uh, stapler?" she said.

"Of course, it's a stapler, you cretin. You must have read the memo." He pointed the butt end of the stapler at her in accusation. "Well, did you?"

"I, uh, I'm sure I did. I read them all, sir."

"Then you weren't capable of comprehending it. The stapler is to be on the left side of the desk. *Left*. Not over here on the right. And never—*never*—are you to use another brand. Always a Jolly Roger brand stapler—"

"Good heavens," I muttered to Clara. "They have house brand staplers."

"And they write memos about where to place them on the desk," she muttered back.

"—at the customer service desk. All—"

"It kept breaking," said the older woman in the red vest. But softly enough for the rest to pretend they hadn't heard.

"—materials used at the Customer Service desk or the registers or anywhere else customers can see are to be Jolly Roger brand. You."

He waved toward the man who certainly seemed to be his assistant. Hard to believe Birchall didn't know his name.

Or couldn't be bothered to use it.

The man hurried to his side, an effort made more difficult because the CEO strode off without waiting for him. Birchall snapped, "Write it down."

"Write, uh … what?"

"Stapler. Wrong kind. Wrong place. Disregarding memo. No excuse."

"Yes, sir."

Frowning as he looked from side to side, the CEO waved a finger at his assistant. "I have a brilliant thought. Check if switching to thicker meat would lower meat production costs because it takes fewer cuts. We might get rid of more overpriced butchers."

At least the woman with the upswept hair would be happy…

"If it saves us money and we can market it as premium with a premium price, even better."

…or not.

"You." This time Birchall pointed at Jacqueline. "Your sales are lower than they should be. You haven't met projections for eight months."

"I've only been here four, but—"

"I don't care if you've been here five minutes. You're responsible. Hit those projections or you'll be gone. Can't have dead weight dragging down my numbers."

"Sir, we sent in a report to the district manager, you, and the entire executive team. Those projections are not reasonable. We couldn't reach them without posting nearly forty-percent growth year over year. We have stiff competition from a local store that's an institution in Haines Tavern—"

"What does a tavern have to do with it?"

"Haines Tavern is the town's name. And—"

"Doesn't matter, doesn't matter. Crush any local competition. Put them out of business. Problem solved."

The assistant whispered something I didn't hear.

The CEO's brows snapped together. He focused fully on the assistant manager for the first time—with a scowl.

"This is the store where a rinky-dink local's running the same specials before ours? How do they know what's going to run next? Somebody's got to be telling them. Are you the traitor?"

She paled. "As I said I've only been here a few months, I don't even know—"

"Make a note," Birchall snapped to the assistant. "Management of this store has two weeks to track down the leak or they're out."

The assistant store manager sucked in a breath. She wasn't the only one. Several of us reacted to his harsh threat, especially in front of an audience. The teacher clicked her tongue. I wished it were a precursor to taking this man by the ear and dragging him to the principal's office.

"And you haven't fully implemented the multi-tier promotion plan we sent. Do it. Now. Should have been done weeks ago."

"Sir, in my memo, I included customer comments showing it doesn't work for our customer base. I recommended—"

"Just do it. Don't try to think and for God's sake don't recommend."

"We'll lose customers." She spoke more strongly. Perhaps she felt she had nothing to lose, not with the two-weeks-and-out threat. "The service we could offer was already suffering before this latest round of personnel cutbacks. And—"

I'd read about the Jolly Roger chain cutting a lot of store-level jobs, while leaving the corporate workforce intact.

"—you heard what people said about—"

"So what if you lose customers or stores, as long as we'll make more money."

"Isn't that the strategy tried in Idaho before the chain you ran went bankrupt?"

Good for Jacqueline.

Though if she thought that would dent his self-satisfaction, she was disappointed. On the flip side, his barely seeming to hear her lessened the chances she'd committed employment suicide.

He'd reached the produce section, stopping to gaze around him with his hands on his hips and his stern disapproval seemingly focused on the pints of blueberries.

"The failure was implementation," he told the blueberries. "Lazy workforce wouldn't follow the program. Like you. Couldn't get good people. But the board here saw the brilliance behind it and brought me in to make it work here. Are *you* on the board?"

"Of course not."

"I didn't think so. But you better get *on board* or you'll be gone."

His assistant made a sound possibly intended as an admiring chuckle at his brilliant play on words. Birchall didn't show any sign of hearing and the assistant cut it off.

From the corner of my eye, I caught stealthy movement. Two employees behind the deli counter side-stepped to get out of view. A third abandoned her post behind a tray stacked with paper-wrapped samples outside the deli and disappeared past an end cap.

I respected their decision-making.

If I'd been Jacqueline, I'd have wanted to smack the CEO for his disdain.

I wasn't her and I still wanted to smack him.

But it seemed to fuel her. "The customers' reactions to the Dynamic Price Reduction Program—"

"Enough about customers. They have to be led. They don't run our stores."

The customers behind him stirred. It might only take one comment to spark a rebellion. I bet we could chase him back to his posh SUV in seconds.

A muscle in the assistant manager's jaw throbbed. "My customers don't like the complicated sales. With X number of items on sale for Y days and a different set of four items on sale for three days. Then weekend specials sometimes being for Friday through Sunday, but other times just Saturday and Sunday."

"Our data shows dynamic price reductions keep consumers engaged."

"It keeps them confused, not engaged."

Birchall's assistant huffed.

But the CEO did not appear to pay any attention as he gazed around.

Jacqueline kept on anyway. "We have a fair percentage of older customers here and they don't like sales with variable rules. They also don't like the digital coupons that have to be loaded onto smart phones—not all of them have smart phones."

I was sure individual customers didn't like the coupons for those reasons, but it struck me as an unfair generalization. I couldn't help but think of Petey the cart guy whizzing through his photos and videos on his phone to share his grandchildren's brilliance with all lookers. Or my Great-Aunt Kit, who I swear could show Bill Gates a thing or two, especially about word processing programs.

"So they load them on their loyalty card using their computer."

"A lot don't register for the card and not all of them have computers."

"Internet cafés—"

"In Haines Tavern? Have you seen an internet café here? They're not going to take the time. And they don't care for all the variables. They might clip paper coupons, but they're not going to use digital coupons."

"Then they pay full price. Even better."

Before anyone could respond, he strode off, having turned his attention to a younger demographic.

A woman with a cherubic little girl with blonde curls, had come around the corner of the last aisle and stopped abruptly, staring at the group clustered in the produce section.

CHAPTER FOUR

NOT ONLY WAS the girl a pre-school cutie, but she was strapped into the grocery cart seat—not something I often see. And what held her was not the thin, twisted store belt, but a padded shoulder harness connected to the back of the seat, supplemented by straps hooked to the sides, limiting lateral movement.

No hanging sideways over the edge until her head was upside down for this kid.

I'd thought it was quite enterprising of my nephew to assume that position when I'd visited his branch of my family a while back.

Yes, I'd laughed.

Yes, I probably *had* encouraged him, as my sister-in-law stated in her two-pronged scold.

Yes, I could see the potential danger.

Still. Enterprising. My nephew could go far.

This little girl wasn't going anywhere.

Birchall stopped short, with displays of onions and potatoes between him and the mother-daughter pair.

"You. Take a picture. Should have been doing it all along. You're useless. No—Not me alone. Do those later. First, get the kid."

The rumpled assistant had pulled out his phone at the first order, but with the second his mouth opened and he looked around in alarm.

"The kid. The kid. Get the kid for my shot. People like that stuff. Need to get something useful out of this stop."

The assistant loped toward the woman with the little girl.

"You." Birchall pointed at the oldest of the three red vest wearers, a woman with Belinda on her name tag. "Get out of my shot."

She scuttled backward as if receiving an electric shock, while also appearing grateful the shock gave her an excuse to put space between them.

"No." The mother blurted out the word, drawing my attention. Call me shallow, but I zoomed in on her clothes. Not Haines Tavern issue. More like my Manhattan wardrobe ... before I gave most of it away.

Getting out that one word seemed to open the way for more from the woman. "You may not take any pictures of my daughter, especially not with Rod Birchall."

"You. Take care of it," the CEO ordered.

His assistant's urgent and urging tone rose.

So did the mother's.

"No. I said no."

"But—"

Birchall strode to them, elbowing aside the assistant. "Ma'am. You don't understand. A few pictures with your lovely daughter. Then we won't need you and you can be on your way."

"My daughter and I can be on our way *now*, because she's not having her photo taken with you. Ever. If you had your way, she'd be dead."

The assistant recoiled. The CEO didn't.

Impossible to tell if that was the result of stalwartly standing his ground or the impunity of the dense.

"Nonsense." He took hold of the end of the shopping cart and tugged it closer to the strawberries, plastered a smile on his face, and ordered the assistant, "Good background color. Get the picture, you idiot." He added, in nearly the same tone, "Want some chocolate, little girl?"

The assistant fumbled to get the phone up to take a photo.

The girl's face puckered into a cry forestalled only by surprise when her mother yanked the grocery cart back with a shout.

"Your orders have pushed food safety labeling back a decade, you ... you criminal."

The CEO hung on, the cart seesawing between the two adults, with the girl no longer in danger of crying, but appearing on the verge of seesaw-sickness.

"We meet the standards."

"Minimum standards your toadies set. Failing to list ingredients that can kill children like my daughter because it might make the label a line or two longer. You would have killed—"

She turned away, obscuring her next words.

"If people like you didn't scream about the font size—"

"It's illegible as it is now. If you make it smaller it will be as bad as leaving ingredients off. You won't make it the size it needs to be because you don't want to spend a few pennies more on labels."

"People like *you* don't want to spend a few pennies more, but you're willing to dig it out of *my* pocket." He growled at the assistant, "Have you got the shot?"

"I, uh, I don't know. I think it was on video. I might be able to get stills from it. But it might not—"

"For God's sake—Do you or don't you?"

"Yes, yes, yes. I have a shot. I do. I have a shot. Yes."

The CEO pushed off on the cart, adding momentum to his sudden release, and sending it back into the woman's body. She bent forward with a cry.

"*Mommy! Mommy!*"

"Hysterical," Birchall growled. "Both of 'em."

He turned his back on them. As he strode back toward us, he scanned the witnesses, possibly looking for someone he considered worth trying to impress. If so, he didn't find anyone.

For a second I thought the woman intended to ram the cart into his back. I think she thought that, too. But she looked at her sobbing daughter, gave a small cry herself, wheeled the cart around, and hurried away, the child's cries fading with distance.

"You," Birchall pointed at Jacqueline. "Let's wrap this up. You've failed miserably. If you'd had the right kind of shoppers here to greet me the way you were supposed to—"

Clara and I slunk backward as unobtrusively as possible. If this guy was on the hunt for customers he hadn't yet insulted, we did not want to be in the vicinity. She mumbled something about orange juice. I breathed a *yeah*.

"—none of that nonsense would have happened."

"It's a surprise visit," Jacqueline protested. "I had no idea you were coming, much less—"

He turned away. "I'm going in the back room. See what you've screwed up back there. Can't be any worse than this. No. Stay. You and you."

The command—familiar from the dog park, yet never delivered with such disdain there—was addressed to the assistant, who had moved to follow him, and the assistant store manager, who had not.

He snatched a sample from the tray beside the deli as he marched past, ripped off its paper wrapping, then pushed open the double swinging doors. As they thwapped closed, then re-opened a bit from the force, we heard his angry, "Good God," followed by a sound masked by the rubber edges of the doors settling closed.

We heard nothing more.

His report on the back room didn't promise to be a highlight of this visit.

The assistant store manager squeezed her eyes shut.

"*You*," she muttered. "He can't even bother to read a name tag."

The man in the jeans opened his hand from that unpin-downable position as if to pat her shoulder. Or something more? "Are you okay?"

She held up her hand and stepped back. "I'm fine. We'll … He'll be back." She looked at Birchall's assistant. "Won't he?"

Seeming to take the *stay* command literally, he moved only his eyes toward her. "Probably."

CHAPTER FIVE

THE GUY IN jeans said, not making it a question, "That wasn't true about the store manager, just happening not to be here today."

What *was* it about this guy? I associated him with *something*. Something medical? I couldn't pin it down, and I'd swear I'd never met the man. Which made no sense, I know.

The assistant manager smoothed back her hair with both hands. "He was here. He got a phone call and before I knew it, he was saying he had to leave for the day, turning everything over to me. Said he was going and I was in charge. I couldn't imagine what got into him until I got a call saying Rod Birchall was here. God. What a day."

I was surprised she was that candid.

Straightening her black vest, she looked at the trio of red vests. "Uh, you all better get back to work. I'll announce for you if we need you again."

"Let's go," I said softly to Clara, to relieve the woman of our presence.

As it happened, other customers also moved off. Ahead of us, we saw the teacher-type heading out of the store with no purchases, while the dog park woman entered the aisle for pet supplies.

Not long after, Clara spotted a sale sign down the soup aisle and turned in there.

I looked back toward the produce section as I followed and saw only the guy in jeans remained, along with the assistant store manager, and Birchall's unfortunate assistant.

As Clara stowed cans in the cart, she said, "Shep's had even better prices last week, but they were all out of the beef barley soup Ned loves and—Look, that man who was so unhappy with the CEO must be leaving, too. I'd thought he'd staying to give Birchall a piece of his mind when he came back."

She tipped her head and I turned to see the vaguely familiar male customer in jeans stride past the end of our aisle toward the front of the store, possibly heading for the exit.

"Guess this is enough." She placed a final can to the cart.

As we turned back into the main aisle across the store's front, we were half a dozen yards behind the man. Twice that far in front of him, we saw the limo driver. Abruptly, the driver turned right, into an aisle and headed toward the back of the store.

Clara and I discussed Rod Birchall's performance as we worked our way through the store.

We retrieved a bottle of orange juice for Ned, then I picked up a carton of plain yogurt for a chicken recipe I wanted to try, and, finally, started back. A man crossed our line of sight in the wide area in front of display cases of cheese on the back wall.

He wore khakis with a white shirt with the sleeves rolled back. He was medium height and build, with black glasses and dark hair shorter on the sides than the top.

"Look at that," I said to Clara. "Only a guy is ever in a grocery store with no cart and his hands empty."

Clara looked, but then seemed more interested in looking at me. "You do notice the strangest things."

The man disappeared into the ice cream aisle. I suppose it held other things, but I never noticed them.

"Think about it. Are you ever in here without a cart? You automatically took a cart even though we came in only for Ned's orange juice."

"I thought you might want to pick up a few things. Or I might."

I grinned at her. "See? And even if we're absolutely sure we're going to get one thing and one thing only, we'll still almost immediately have a couple more things in our hands. Never nothing."

We found ourselves in the pet aisle with three other customers, though not the woman from the dog park.

Yes, a variety of treats and chews joined the cart.

"Donna said Hattie loves that kind of chew," Clara said, "and I've been wanting to try this new brand of treat, haven't you?"

"Me? Not so much. Gracie? Absolutely. And … there goes another one."

"Another one what? Another treat you want to—"

"No. Plenty of treats. It was another man without a cart or anything in his hands. This time, that assistant guy to the CEO."

"The whisperer? I'm surprised he was brave enough to leave for even a second. I thought he'd stay right outside the door waiting for the Birchall man to return."

"Like a faithful dog?"

"Hah. My *faithful* dog would be off in a shot. LuLu almost was the other day. You know we have a gate in the fence in the backyard, down near the creek?"

"I didn't know that." I'd been in their back yard a few times, but not for fence inspecting.

"Yeah. Double gates, actually, so we can get equipment down to that wild part leading to the creek if we wanted to clean it up. But it's so steep, we haven't tried. Mostly, Ned uses the gates to dump leaves and things. We keep them latched, because I sure don't want LuLu down there. Ticks and burs and all sorts of nasty stuff.

"Yesterday, some kids went by. Friends of this boy who lives four houses down, maybe ten years old, and we didn't think anything of it, figured they were working their way down to the creek. But one unhooked the gate latch as they went by. First I knew of it, I heard Ned hollering."

"At the kids?"

"At them, at LuLu, and for me to help. I got down there and the kids had scattered—I could hear them crashing through the brush but couldn't see them—and Ned was down on his knees, his arm wrapped around LuLu, with a face full of fur as her legs went like crazy as she tried to run off after the boys. And then Ned was just hollering at me."

"At you? Why?"

"Because, first, I told him to let LuLu go so he wouldn't hurt her and he said he wasn't hurting her and I could see he wasn't. She was wagging her tail right in his face. And, second, I was laughing so hard, I couldn't even call to LuLu—"

She interrupted herself to nod her head toward the end of the aisle at the back of the store. I turned and saw the well-dressed woman with her little girl in the cart, heading away from the side of the store where they'd earlier had their encounter with the Jolly Roger CEO. Brave of them to have gone back there.

"—not that it would've done any good," Clara picked up. "I had to get around in front of her and get a good hold on her collar. Even then I almost lost her when Ned let go. We finally got her back enough to close the gate. Oh, look, there goes a *woman* without a cart or anything in her hands." Clara pointed.

Jacqueline Yancik, Assistant Store Manager, How can I help you? walked past the end of the aisle, walking across the front of the store toward produce. We must have missed her outbound trip.

"Employees don't count."

"Then you can't count the assistant guy." At my nod acknowledging her point, Clara added, "Speaking of him and the assistant store manager and all of them, let's go back and see what's happening. Aren't you dying to know if he could be any more awful than he was?"

Further discussion of Rod Birchall occupied us as we started toward the produce section.

Curiosity might have done in the cat, but I was a dog person, so I was safe. Right?

CHAPTER SIX

THE SAME GROUP of three stood in the same relative positions as when we'd left them, apparently each resuming his or her previous position when returning from whatever had taken them out into the rest of the store.

Except the entire tableau had moved closer to the back room.

"He's still not back?" Clara asked.

No one answered directly.

A voice turned androgynous by whispering said something about waiting. That had to be the assistant.

Birchall had been in the back room a long time.

Certainly, he'd been silent far longer than any previous stretch Clara and I had witnessed.

With apparent reluctance and possibly nudged by Clara's question and our return, Jacqueline said, "He has been gone quite a while."

She glanced around, seeming to make eye contact with the guy in the worn jeans for an instant, then trying to make eye contact with the assistant.

But he appeared fascinated with the tips of his shoes. Nice, but not up to CEO standards.

Jacqueline breathed out through her mouth, then walked toward the doors. She paused, possibly for another breath, then pushed the right-hand one open a crack.

"Mr. Birchall?"

He didn't answer.

Not surprising, since she was barely audible.

She opened the door a bit wider and repeated his name into the space.

Nothing.

The third time, she pushed the door all the way open and held it there.

"Mr. Bircha—"

She finished the name, but it was drowned out by the combined intake of breath by the rest of us. Because we'd all seen what, for some reason, she apparently had not.

Rod Birchall's feet stuck out past a tower of cartons that hid most of his body, reminiscent of the Wicked Witch of the East's under Dorothy's tornado-driven house. Except no striped stockings and ruby slippers for him. His socks looked like Bresciani cashmere and his leather oxfords matched the socks.

A white paper wrapper like the one that had covered what he'd grabbed from the sample tray by the deli fluttered against a second wrapper, this one brightly colored.

But what riveted my attention was Birchall's cashmere-hugged calves and his cobbler's top work-enclosed feet, holding a position not seen in live human beings.

✧ ✧ ✧ ✧

THE MOMENTS AFTER were not as chaotic as some might expect.

The CEO's assistant appeared catatonic, cutting one potential source of chaos.

Jacqueline slowly let the door close and remained where she was, with her back to us. The guy in the jeans strode to her, gave her a quick look, perhaps assessing if she was going to remain upright, then pushed the door open wide enough so it caught to stay open.

That revealed all of Birchall's strangely disposed legs and feet, but not his body.

I was torn between gratitude for that and temptation to follow the guy in jeans.

Three things stopped me. The memory of an autopsy. A vision of explaining to the sheriff's department why my footprints were around the crime scene. And a vision of explaining it to Teague O'Donnell.

That last one might seem weird, since Teague was currently working on restoring a retaining wall at the back of my lot, so he was in my employ and I owed him no explanations at all.

He seldom saw it that way.

He was a former cop—detective, in fact—and he landed somewhere between total disapproval and thinking Clara and I were nuts for our investigative efforts.

He thought we should leave it to the sheriff's department, shouldn't interfere, and shouldn't take chances. On the other hand, he'd told one of the deputies that we had good instincts.

Right now, my instincts said not to give him a chance to say I was stupid to have interfered with a crime scene.

I did move to beside Jacqueline at the threshold.

Behind me, Clara had pulled out her phone and was already talking to 911.

In another couple strides, the man in jeans was beside Birchall. He didn't bend down.

"They say to start CPR," Clara relayed from the phone.

"No use. He's dead. He's been bashed in the head."

Beside me, Jacqueline shuddered. She put her hands over her mouth, covering a sound that might have been almost anything, including laughter.

"Are you sure?" Clara asked, clearly relaying the 911 operator's words.

"Yes."

"They're on the way. Don't touch anything. Keep everybody in the store."

Jacqueline surged a step into the back room, as if pushed from behind. I took hold of her arm, wondering if she had lost her balance or was going to be sick.

"Let go." It was the most authoritative I'd heard her.

"You shouldn't go in there. You don't want to confuse the—" I deleted the word *crime* before it could come out. "—scene."

"She's right," the man said. "Stay out of this."

"I can't. I have to secure the other side so none of the employees come along and see… See anything."

"I'll do that. You get the store closed."

Her pull against my hold eased. Instead, she pushed the door, releasing the catch.

As it swung closed, she and I both backed out of its way, back to the produce department side of it.

"Will you two stay here, keep anybody from going in while I go up front and get the store closed?" She looked from me to Clara.

"Yes." I answered for both of us, since Clara was still on the phone with dispatch.

I stood in front of the door, prepared to block anyone trying to get in … or out.

CHAPTER SEVEN

"...HE DIDN'T COME out—Mr. Birchall, the chain's CEO, I mean. But we had no idea, absolutely no idea, something might be wrong."

Jacqueline's voice, recounting the finding of Rod Birchall's body, preceded her coming around the corner into the produce section with three deputies—one behind, one to the left, and one to the right, slightly ahead of her. That last one drew my attention.

Deputy Hensen.

Good news. It was not Deputy Eckles.

Clara and I had encountered both of them before. Neither welcomed our efforts with open arms, but Hensen had a couple positives in his favor—he had a sense of humor and he liked dogs.

Neither attribute, unfortunately, applied to this situation.

"We were all here," Jacqueline was saying when I tuned back into her voice. "The entire time. Watching the doors. No one went in after Mr. Birchall did. No one got past us. Absolutely no one. I swear."

Hensen's eyes twitched, as if they wanted to roll but he'd held them in check by force of will.

Now, why would he find what she'd said eye-roll-worthy?

We—Clara and I—knew Jacqueline had told a lie, purposely or not, because we'd seen her, the assistant, and the guy in jeans out and about in the store. If *any* of them had remained here, surely they'd noticed the others depart and presumably return.

No matter what, each of them had a period of time when they'd been away and could not swear no one had gone in these doors to the back room.

Still, that most likely left one, maybe two people here in front of the door at any given time. Though it would take careful questioning to pin that down.

Besides, while *we* knew she'd lied about them all being here at the same time and for the whole time, Hensen didn't.

So why the twitch to suppress an eye roll?

As if he considered a group watching these doors utterly unimportant when a man had been found dead, apparently murdered, behind them.

"It's got to be a horrible accident," Jacqueline told Hensen.

"Uh-huh." Hensen had spotted Clara and me. He shook his head slowly, somewhere between resignation and grudging recognition, then seemed to catch himself and went expressionless.

Not an eye roll.

Not even a twitch to suppress an eye roll.

Which had been such a specific reaction and not one I'd seen from him before. Why…?

Oh.

Oh.

The group watching these doors *was* unimportant.

But the individuals straying from them were not.

I clutched Clara's arm.

"Ow."

"Shh." She obeyed, but continued prying my fingers from the flesh over her radius, as I leaned in and whispered, "Anyone could have gotten into the back by one of the other doors."

CHAPTER EIGHT

CLARA STOPPED PRYING my fingers, instead, twisting her neck sharply to look at me.

I released my grip and nodded.

"Of course," she breathed. "Of course."

I nodded again.

Hensen had reached us. "I don't even want to know what you two are doing here."

Clara told him anyway. "Shopping." She nodded to the small cart.

"One of the customers stayed with the body," I told Hensen. "Don't know his name. Male, over six feet, dark hair, cut short, light stubble, earlyish forties, white shirt, and worn but clean jeans."

He nodded receipt of the information.

"Stay here." He issued the order to everyone in sight with no indication of a sense of humor or that he liked dogs. He paused only to slip on blue paper booties.

One of his minion deputies stayed at the back of the group. Hensen addressed him. "If you need help, get one of the men getting statements from the customers up front."

He pushed one swinging door open with his shoulder. If he was trying to preserve finger prints I wondered how long it would take them to sort through all the employees who must have pushed since the last time it had been cleaned.

Through the opening, I saw Rod Birchall's lower legs and feet again. Unmoved.

Not that I would have expected *him* to move them. Or even the guy in the jeans to have moved them. But, anyway, they hadn't moved.

The guy in the jeans *had* moved. He was nowhere in sight. Though, in fairness, my sight was somewhat limited, because Hensen hadn't been overly generous with his door-opening.

On the other hand, Hensen didn't react as if he saw anybody live back there in the brief time before the door *thwumphed* closed.

I turned to see Jacqueline straighten from leaning sideways to see into the back room, too. She seemed to relax a bit.

The remaining deputy stepped between Clara and me, taking the prime spot in front of the door, then demoted us succinctly. "Join the others, please."

Clara demoted him right back, holding her position an extra beat and saying into her phone, "Yes, thank you. Deputy Hensen and other people are here now."

A burble of amusement climbed my throat. I didn't let it escape as we joined Jacqueline and the assistant who hadn't moved or said anything since the idea of going in back to see what Rod Birchall was doing had been raised.

I didn't take it personally, but at that moment Birchall's assistant went pale, his mouth pinched, and his lips gray.

"I'm… I'm… I'm… Ah."

The man began to crumple.

I was too far away, Clara even farther, Jacqueline paying no attention.

"Deputy—"

He had good reflexes. He caught the assistant before he hit the floor. But not before a stork-like elbow caught a display of pyramided potatoes.

Pyramids crumble fast when they're made of potatoes. Good thing the Egyptians used other building materials.

Clara, Jacqueline, and I chased potatoes rolling erratically in all directions. I caught one during its wobbly airborne arc, then scooped several from the floor. The deputy lowered the assistant to a seat on the floor, propping his back against the bottom of a refrigerated case holding shrink-wrapped melons in various configurations of halves, quarters, slices, and filets.

I started to pile my finds back onto the remaining ruins of the potato pyramid.

"Don't," Clara said. "They'll be all bruised. They shouldn't be sold. Jacqueline, where should we put these?"

The assistant store manager looked around wildly. "I don't know. I don't know."

"How about on top of those bags of nuts. They'll be protected from any broken potatoes until you get someone to clean up."

"Yeah, yeah. Okay. This is a nightmare. An absolute nightmare."

Figuring she wasn't talking about the potatoes all over aisle one, I decided it was on-topic to ask, "Where's that guy?"

"Guy?"

"The tall one. One of the customers. White shirt and jeans. He waited with you—"

"He wasn't with me."

"—and the CEO's assistant and then—"

"Assistant?"

I tipped my head toward the nervous man, who had come out of his faint, but sat with his knees drawn up and his head in his hands, moaning, and seemingly unaware of anything around him.

Her face scrunched up as if she were about to sneeze. "He's not Rod Birchall's assistant. He's his heir apparent. He's now the acting CEO of the Jolly Roger supermarket chain."

Clara and I looked at each other.

I suspected my face was saying the same thing her face was: *Talk about a motive.*

CHAPTER NINE

"Okay," I said slowly. "He's the new CEO. What's his name?"

"Utton. Foster Utton. Acting CEO."

He did not respond in any way to his name, which put his aware-ness well below that of my dog, Gracie. Her ears reacted not only to her name and numerous other words representing positives in her world—treat, dog park, eat, outside, walk, LuLu, and Murphy led the list—but also to *she*. A bit egocentric, maybe, but far more situationally alert than the new CEO of the Jolly Roger chain.

Skipping over discussion of his suitability for CEO-dom, I stuck with my main point.

"Along with you and Foster Utton, there was a man who went in and said Mr. Birchall was dead and then said he'd stay with the body and you should go secure the store and let the deputies in. You must remember."

She bent for a single potato, then turned and placed it atop the nut bags. "Of course. But I don't know where he is."

Interesting.

I'd have expected her to assume he remained in back. But if she had assumed that, why not say so?

Could she have seen enough of the back room to be certain he *hadn't* waited for the sheriff's department's arrival? But then wouldn't she be more curious?

"I hope nothing's happened to him, too," I said.

Her head came up and she flashed a look at me, but said nothing.

"I mean, if Mr. Birchall was murdered and there's a murderer loose…"

"Murdered? Of course not. He wasn't murdered. It must have been an accident. Or a heart attack. Or—"

"Healthy as a horse," came unexpectedly from the presumptive CEO. He didn't raise his head from his hands, so it was muffled, but no mistaking the words.

"—something," Jacqueline insisted.

"Something he ate," muttered Foster Utton, face still covered.

"But that guy—" Clara broke off at my sharp head shake. She substituted, "What thing he ate?"

Utton gave no sign of hearing her first, aborted comment and I wondered if he'd absorbed that the guy in jeans said Birchall was bashed in the head.

"Something he ate with sesame in it." He raised his head, peering around until his gaze landed on Jacqueline. "That thing he ate as he went in the back room, did it have sesame in it? Flour or seeds or oil. If it had poppy seeds, too, that makes it worse."

She looked at him blankly. "I have no idea."

Clara went to the display, but as she reached for one of whatever was wrapped in white paper, the deputy at the door said, "Don't touch anything, ma'am."

"Of course not, Deputy. No touching. I'll just…" She scooched down so she was eye level with the display, then twisted around to see the back of one misaligned package.

"No ingredients listed at all. It says for more detailed information to contact Jolly Roger—how about *any* information. I see flecks all over the bottom of the tray like they fell off whatever's in the wrappers. Those could be poppy seeds."

"Not being on the label doesn't necessarily mean it's not there," Jacqueline said. "Mass produced food items have to list the top allergens, but there's an exception for fresh made."

"That was part of the complaint by the woman with the little girl, wasn't it?"

Utton stared straight ahead, possibly back in his catatonic state.

Jacqueline said, "Also that things came from corporate that you'd think were mass produced, but they said they weren't, so those items get around the rules."

"It's not illegal." Utton's voice didn't sound like his, though I'd barely heard his voice other than whispers. More like a ventriloquist echoing Birchall. Or a medium channeling him.

A chilling thought.

Before the full chill hit me, however, a line of medical personnel with crime scene techs on their heels came through the produce section.

The deputy on door duty cracked it open and said, "They're here, sir."

Hensen appeared, holding a quiet conversation with the head of each group.

The door deputy also said something to Hensen, whose gaze touched on Clara and me, then passed to Foster Utton.

"Deputy," Hensen said to the Foster-catcher, "please take Ms. Mackey and Mrs. Woodrow to join the group in the housewares aisle and stay with them. Mr. Utton, I understand you've been unwell. Medical personnel will check you out in a moment. Ms. Yancik, I'll be with you in a few more minutes."

She protested, "I'll come back, but I should check on my employees and the store and—"

"All being taken care of. Remain here."

The door deputy went to her side, clearly prepared to do more if needed.

The other deputy stepped back, nodding for Clara and me to precede him.

"Darn," Clara grumbled. "Just when things were getting interesting here."

Then she had another setback when she reached for the handle of the cart and the deputy ordered, "Leave it."

CHAPTER TEN

LOOKING DOWN THE main aisle that crossed the front of the store, we caught sight of a dozen and a half civilians and about half a dozen uniforms in the open area past the registers.

Our deputy ended our efforts to figure out what was happening there by directing us up an aisle selling dishtowels, hot pads, plates, silverware, cooking utensils, and more.

The three red vests sat on the floor, looking slightly scared and entirely bored. A deputy stood a couple yards away.

Maybe our guardian? Our spy, for sure.

As we neared, the three red vests separated into individuals.

A young man and young woman, each in their twenties, then Belinda, the older woman with crow's feet at her eyes and deeper grooves beside her mouth.

Clara sank down next to Belinda. "Horrible thing to happen, isn't it?"

"Yes." Hard to gauge her reaction—if any.

"I don't know why we're being held." The younger woman's name tag read Myghavnn.

What are some parents thinking? Can't they expend their creativity in flower-arranging or painting their faces for sports events? Something normal and relatively unharmful to their progeny.

"We never even talked to him," she said. "Walked around the store a little listening to him go on and—Listening to him. What about all the customers who were yelling at him? Why aren't any of them being persecuted this way?"

"Told you, Myghavnn. They have to talk to everybody." From her tone, Belinda had tired of saying that. Or maybe she was tired of trying to remember how to spell the younger woman's name. She answered one question—she pronounced the name as Meghan.

"We're customers and they're keeping us here, too," Clara said cheerfully. So cheerfully, that those who knew her well would understand she'd have to be kicked out to miss what was going on.

Myghavnn grumbled, "Doesn't help me any."

"Strange this happened at the same time the manager got sick." I hoped to turn her thoughts to a more productive angle—more productive for Clara and me.

"Sick? No way. He was absolutely fine this morning. He bailed. Funked," the guy said. His name tag proclaimed him a thankfully more mundane Josh.

"You're sore he chewed your butt this morning about the olives being shelved with soup overnight." The bite of competition in her words said Myghavnn was more than half pleased Josh received said butt-chewing.

"Like I'm here to watch those guys every second. Besides, it was a few cans and—"

"That's our job, to watch them every second," Belinda said.

"So, the store manager was fine this morning and everything was normal until he bailed." I purposefully used Josh's word.

"Never seen him move that fast." The young man shook his head. "Came out of his office—coming out's weird enough by itself—and blew past Belinda, then nearly knocked three customers over. Had to catch an old—" He swallowed what he'd started to say and substituted. "—lady."

The two younger ones exchanged a look in a moment of solidarity.

The girl giggled. "He did look pretty sick, though. Thought he was going to hurl in front of customers."

Clara's eyes widened. "You think he knew Rod Birchall was coming to Haines Tavern?"

The two younger red-vested employees looked toward Belinda.

She said, "He knew. He's been around so long he has connections from cart jockeys to corporate. That's how he's hung on so long. The only reason he's hung on so long. Somebody called and warned him."

"Who?"

"I don't know. I'm not in his hip pocket. I work hard and do my job. Nothing that's valued in the Jolly Roger chain."

Combined with her attitude toward Jacqueline, I suspected she'd hoped for the assistant store manager job.

Now and then a deputy had passed the end of the aisle, headed toward the main doors or back toward the produce section.

But now the deputy, tall and broad, turned into our aisle and walked toward us.

It took a moment to realize he accompanied Petey, short and narrow.

The same deputy who'd delivered us said briefly to Petey, "Have a seat," then to our watchdog deputy, "Hensen wants to talk to him, too. He was out in the parking lot when the victim arrived."

Interesting. I hadn't thought of Rod Birchall as a victim.

Of course he *was* a murder victim. And I didn't think he deserved being killed. Not many do in my opinion. On the other hand, my brief observation of him hadn't engendered tears at his death.

"What's going on out front, Petey?" Belinda asked.

"Not much. Sorting through the customers. Letting most go. Folks coming in for a prescription or a gallon of milk wouldn't even know a bigshot was here."

He could have included toilet paper, cereal, hamburger meat, and rice. All those were located on the left side of the store, opposite from the produce section.

Only that knot of people who'd been drawn into the discussion around Birchall would have been aware of his presence in the store.

What about the customers who had been part of the knot, though, including the woman from the dog park and the teacherish woman? We hadn't seen either actually leave.

Surely Hensen wasn't limiting himself to the trio of door-watchers.

The recognition that Birchall's killer could have entered the back area through any of several doors, widened the field. But, as a practical matter, how much?

Unless the killer was in back for some other reason and happened to see Birchall and be overcome by a compulsion to bash him in the head—according to the potentially-AWOL guy in jeans, but not officially confirmed—did the field of suspects really grow?

I'd swear the guy in jeans wasn't in back when Hensen went in, but could they have found him since?

"Petey, have they taken anyone out? Like to question them at the sheriff's department?"

Myghavnn jumped at my abrupt question into a silence I hadn't noticed because I was occupied with my cogitations.

Petey, made of sterner stuff, said, "Not that I saw. And I would've seen."

"How are they deciding which customers to let go?"

"Checking the cameras, I guess."

I supposed the store's security cameras could quickly eliminate any customers who came in after the body was found. Also, anyone who didn't go in any of the doors that provided access to the back room, though it would take more checking.

At that moment, our escort deputy came into our aisle with another person for the collection—Foster Utton.

I'd have expected Hensen to keep Utton, as one of the prime suspects, separate from the rest of us witnesses.

But the sleuth in one of Kit's mystery series liked to say suspects were more likely to talk to each other than to him, so he liked to put them together with a way to overhear.

Our guard deputy provided the ears.

The least we innocent good citizens could do was stir the talk.

"How are you, Foster?" Clara's warmth and use of his first name softened him up.

"Those medical people say I'm fine." He didn't seem to believe it. "Feels like my head's being crushed."

She patted his sleeve. "That's stress. Of course you feel that way. Right from the start, with this surprise visit…"

"Had you visited other stores today?" I asked.

"No. We have another after this stop… I guess not now."

"Good news is you don't have to call to cancel," Josh said. Myghavnn punched his arm. "What? It's true. A surprise inspection. Nobody expecting them. So, they don't need to let anyone know they're not going to be there."

As if distracting from Josh's socially awkward attempt at finding a bright side to murder, I asked Foster Utton, "What was Mr. Birchall doing before you came here?"

"Made calls in the car. Had me make calls, too. Nothing out of the ordinary."

"Before that?" I asked.

"I have no idea. I got the call to be ready to go in ten minutes and got down to the car. Made it in five, but he was already there and yelled I was late."

"Was that usual?"

"He yelled a lot."

"His waiting for you in the car."

"Wasn't *un*usual."

It could mean he'd just arrived from somewhere. "Had he been somewhere before then?"

"No."

"Did anything prompt his coming here or was this a scheduled visit—I mean on Mr. Birchall's schedule?"

"No idea."

He seemed to be sinking toward another coma. I glanced toward Clara, far better at stopping a coma than me.

"Tell us about these surprise visits, Foster," she said. "How often does he do them? Are you always included?"

"He said he liked to keep a finger on the pulse of the stores with these, uh, visits. Sometimes he'd include them in the schedule, especially when he was traveling out of town. Who he took then depended on who was traveling with him. Or if there was a division head he wanted to…" He swallowed. "Uh, wanted to, you know, work with. When he was at headquarters, he'd go if the mood hit him suddenly. That's mostly when he'd bring me."

Sounded like Birchall yanked Utton out of his own schedule whenever he felt like it. Assuming Utton had a schedule.

"Do the visits you've been on with him follow a pattern, a routine? Or would he change up what he did?" Clara asked.

My guess that Utton's head shake was for the idea of Birchall changing up what he did was proved right by his next words.

"Arrives at the store. Finds things wrong. Yells at people. Threatens a few with losing their job—he says it motivates them—then leaves. A lot of time people are crying by then."

Including him? He'd appeared close to nervous tears at times during Birchall's performance.

"Did he always check the back rooms?" I asked.

"Of course. A store can hide any number of failures to adhere to corporate directives behind the service desk counter, in the office, and through the back room." That sounded like a quote.

A candidate for murderer would have to know Birchall had gone in back. Inspecting the back room might have been expected during one of his surprise visits, but could someone predict he'd go alone?

"Did he usually go in back alone?" I asked.

"Usually with the store manager in tow to keep, uh, motivating."

"But not today. Why do you think that was?" Clara asked.

He apparently hadn't thought about it. The bigger question was if he'd thought about anything.

"Uh, he wasn't real pleased it was only the assistant store manager here."

Was that why Birchall didn't call the employees by name, despite the tags giving strong hints? He'd called everyone "you."

Including Utton.

Clara looked down the aisle. I turned and saw the delivery deputy approaching with Jacqueline, his latest charge.

"Have a seat, ma'am," he instructed her. He zeroed in on Foster Utton. "Mr. Utton? Come with me, please."

Utton paled and stood with as little coordination as he'd displayed when he crumpled in the produce section. But having experienced that, the deputy was ready, stepping in with a hand to guide one elbow away from the display of coffee mugs it endangered and helping him to his feet without incident.

As they retreated down the aisle, Jacqueline sat tailor style, her head propped in her hands, her knees supporting her elbows.

"What did they ask you?" Myghavnn demanded. "Was it awful? Did they grill you? Do they know who did it?"

"They don't seem to have any idea." Having answered the last first, she slowly raised her head. Her eyes were wide and dazed. "They think I'm a suspect."

CHAPTER ELEVEN

"YOU'VE BEEN REAL open about not being any fan of the new regime." Yup. Belinda had definitely wanted the assistant manager job. "If they knew the things you said when word came about all those firings, how *personally* you took it all, nobody could blame them for thinking you're a suspect now."

Checking to see if her stinger hit home, Belinda cut a look toward the listening deputy.

He'd heard, though he didn't react.

Jacqueline gave no sign of noticing as she pushed her hair back. "I know I said sharp words. And I stand by them. It makes no sense firing hard-working people when even corporate admits we're understaffed and they're putting out calls to hire. They're getting rid of people making a living so they can hire cheaper. Plus, now there are rumors of even more firings coming. But kill the CEO? Not the solution I had in mind. I thought I'd look for a new job once I had enough months here to look decent on my resume."

Without looking up from his contemplation of a line of measuring cups on the second-to-the-bottom shelf, Petey said, "Not everybody can look for a new job."

Soft and sorrowful, his words dropped a cloud over everyone else. From their expressions and shifting around, their reactions mixed sadness for him—it wouldn't be easy looking for a comparable job at his age—with awkwardness.

Belinda said, "They're not firing people down at your level."

Possibly meant to reassure, but not tactful.

Jacqueline stretched across to rest her hand on his arm momentarily. "You know I'd write you the best recommendation in the world. But it won't do you any good if I'm accused of murder."

"I'm sure it won't come to that." Clara's brisk cheer eased the moment. "Especially since you didn't even know he and Foster Utton were coming, did you, Jacqueline?"

"No." Firm and concise.

"She sure was surprised when I called and said that guy was out front," Petey said.

"But the store manager…?" I didn't want to do more than hint to see how Jacqueline would fill it in, especially if it differed from the three red vests' comments.

"I think he must have known they were coming. He left so suddenly and he seemed … frightened. Truly frightened."

"But he didn't tell you the CEO was coming?" Clara asked.

"No. If he had I—" She shook her head as she broke off. Then she achieved a chuckle. "I probably would have left sick, too."

Not what she'd started to say before she broke off.

Sure would be interesting to know how her original statement of what she'd have done if she'd known the CEO was coming to Haines Tavern would have ended.

No time to wonder long, however, because Clara asked a question I wanted to hear the answer to.

"When *did* you find out the CEO was coming?"

"Like Petey said, when he called from the parking lot as they pulled in. I couldn't believe what I was hearing when he said Rod Birchall was here. I was short with him, when he was trying to give me a heads-up." She looked across at the older man. "Sorry, Petey." He raised one hand in a not-to-worry acknowledgment. "It wasn't until I heard the driver giving Petey a hard time that I realized Petey was telling me the actual truth. The CEO of the Jolly Roger corporation was here. About to walk in the door. I scrambled to get the heads—" She nodded at the three red vests. "—who are in the store today. There wasn't time for more before he came in and—Oh."

We all turned to the front of the aisle to see what prompted her to interrupt herself.

It was the same deputy who'd escorted Petey, this time directing the driver to sit down with "the others" until he was called.

"Called for what? I've told you everything I know."

"Sit down, sir."

The driver sat.

"They'll be with you soon," the deputy said in the same tone doctors' offices' front desk people use when it's going to be hours and hours.

He exchanged a quick look with our guarding deputy, then left, with the driver grumbling under his breath.

No one appeared inclined to reach out to the newcomer or to resume our conversation in his presence.

Except Clara.

"They'll want to talk to all of us who had contact with Mr. Birchall in the last hours of his life. We have to be patient while the sheriff's department does its job."

She sounded so sincere. Yet I knew she was champing at the bit to do the detecting part of their job for them.

I knew because I felt the same way.

"Don't see Utton here waiting to share everything he knows," the driver grumbled.

"He's being questioned by Deputy Hensen right now. Jacqueline was already questioned." Clara's wave directed the driver's attention to the assistant stage manager, who gave a slight nod. "The rest of us are waiting our turn."

The driver grunted acceptance. But his point reminded me one person who should have been here wasn't—the guy in jeans.

No sense pining for who wasn't here, though.

Wishing I were half as disarming as Clara, I went for direct. "Have you driven Mr. Birchall long, Mr. ... uh...?"

"Isaac."

"Mr. Isaac."

"Just Isaac."

"Have you driven for him long?"

"Why?"

"You'd know him better than any of the rest of us. We're all caught up in this from the accident of being here when he died, but we don't know him at all."

"He was in the store an hour talking to you people so you should know him. He was pretty much the same all the time."

"Oh, he wasn't with us the entire time," Clara said. "About half the time was after he'd gone in the back room."

Isaac grunted.

"Do you enjoy driving for Mr. Birchall?"

"Enjoy the paycheck."

Okay, Isaac wasn't going to pour out his impressions and deepest insights into Rod Birchall.

Might as well try for facts.

"What was Mr. Birchall doing earlier today, before coming here?"

"No idea. None of my business until he gets in my car."

He emphasized *none of my business*, indicating it was none of mine what Birchall had been doing.

I summoned up my inner Kit and asked on. "Did you drive him anywhere before here today?"

If he'd made surprise visits to other stores before Utton joined him, he might have had a parade of people wanting him dead.

"No."

"Did you see anyone Rod Birchall knew entering the store?"

"Don't know who all he knew."

Inner Kit turned a corner to irked. "Did you see anyone you've seen before while driving Rod Birchall around or in association with Rod Birchall entering the store here? Or around the store."

Satisfaction glinted his eyes. His lips parted.

But I quickly slid in—as defense against that satisfaction—"In addition to Foster Utton."

Satisfaction gone, he snapped, "No."

As I searched for another question bristling with specificity and caveats, another stir at the front of the aisle saved me from banging my questioning head against the brick wall of his non-answers.

Utton came toward us with his sheriff's department escort.

"Have a seat, sir," the deputy who'd been acting as courier for Hensen said to Utton in what must be department issue verbiage. Then he stepped past us, holding a low-voiced conversation with our guarding deputy.

"Not in handcuffs, huh?" Isaac rumbled.

Utton tried to draw himself up in stiff dignity, but couldn't manage it since he was simultaneously sitting down with an excess of pointy elbows and knees.

"Of course not. I simply told the truth, as each of us must do in these horrible circumstances. To do everything we can to assist the authorities as any good citizen would do."

Ah. Had we just heard the first draft of a public statement?

He'd aimed at dignified reserve, one of the mantles Kit maintained all public figures and many private citizens assumed after a crisis.

Probably a good choice for him. I doubted he could carry off pious dismay or outraged horror, two more of her categories. His natural inclination likely fit screaming meemies—Kit always pointed out people who presented themselves as hysterical with grief yet somehow pointed their faces toward a TV camera. But screaming meemies didn't suit a Jolly Roger executive, especially the presumptive CEO.

It was Kit's voice, ever impatient with such playacting, that came out of my mouth with my next words. "Oh? Did you tell Deputy Hensen you were not outside the door to the back room the entire time?"

"She wasn't, either." His voice climbed toward screaming meemie territory and his finger trembled as he pointed at Jacqueline.

Air sucked in by several floor sitters created an instant shift in the atmosphere, exacerbating the tension, like a headache band caused by barometric pressure changes.

After his break in persona, Utton tried to gather the tatters of his dignified reserve performance back around him. "I was away from the door. For a moment only. I went to the car."

Heads swung to the driver.

With something close to gusto, Isaac said, "Never came out to the car. Haven't seen hide nor hair of him from the moment he scurried inside after the boss until the deputy brought him here right now."

Heads swung back to Utton.

But before he could respond, the delivery deputy broke away from the watchdog deputy and was upon us.

"What's this?" he demanded. "You were away from the door to the back room that the victim went in? You didn't tell Deputy Hensen that."

"It was a small matter. Inconsequential."

Delivery deputy stared at him with the same disbelief I've gotten from law enforcement over my answer to their "Do you know how fast you were going?" question.

Utton cracked under the stare. I never do. But I'm not being disbelieved about murder.

"An oversight." Dignity and reserve frayed toward tatters before our eyes. "Okay, okay. I didn't want to ... All right. I'll say it. I went to the restroom." With a note of defiance, he specified, "To the toilet."

"You should all tell the entire truth in this inquiry. Nothing is inconsequential and you can't afford oversights." He swung his stern look from the group back to Utton. "Did anyone see you in the restroom?"

"No." Back to the whispery voice he'd used with Birchall. Hard to tell if he was reacting to the reprimand or cringing at the idea of anyone seeing him in the restroom.

"No alibi," Isaac said with satisfaction.

Delivery deputy turned the stern look at him, but unlike Utton, it didn't dent Isaac.

Then the delivery deputy's focus shifted to another segment of the group—Clara and me.

"Mrs. Woodrow, Ms. Mackey, Deputy Hensen will talk to you now."

CHAPTER TWELVE

A PHOTOGRAPHER CAREFULLY set up shots of produce.

Not the kind to grace glossy ads.

He was part of the investigative team and taking photos of the doors to the back room and its surroundings, as well as areas Rod Birchall had been.

That put the display of strawberries off limits. To my relief, the deputy escorted us to a mass of carrots against the store's front wall. It could have been Brussels sprouts.

The deputy gestured for us to stay there—the same stop-sign hand command I used with Gracie for "stay"—and went to Hensen.

The deputy spoke in a low voice.

As if we didn't know he was repeating what we'd heard Foster Utton acknowledge about leaving the watch party outside the door Birchall had gone in.

Hensen, hands on hips, watched a technician checking the area around the melons.

Right where Utton had been when he'd crumpled.

Did they think he'd faked it to have an opportunity to slip something into or under the case?

Hensen's attention shifted to sounds of activity behind the doors to the back room, caught in snippets when a coverall-clad technician opened the door slightly and called to the photographer.

Finally, Hensen nodded to the delivery deputy, then joined us. He leaned back so his hips rested against the apple display across from us.

"I've told the other two people who heard it and now I'm telling you both. You are ordered by the North Bend County Sheriff's Department to not tell anyone what that man said about Rod Birchall being hit in the head. There will be serious repercussions if you do. Do you understand?"

I nodded. Clara did more.

"Of course, we won't, what do you take us for? But it's about time you talk to us, Deputy Hensen." She managed to make that scold sound friendly. She truly had a gift. "Because it wasn't only Foster Utton. We saw a bunch of them out in the store."

"A bunch of who?" He'd asked automatically, most of his focus on whatever was going on in his head.

"The suspects, of course."

Did he have a direction to follow investigating? Something gathered from evidence beyond these doors?

Did I regret not going into the back room?

Yes. And no.

Yes, I wanted to know all the evidence.

No, for those three reasons—Hensen, Teague, and an autopsy.

Most great aunts probably take their great nieces and nephews to the zoo, a movie, the park. Kit had taken me to an autopsy. Once.

"Nothing special about seeing the suspects," Hensen said. "Everybody saw each other. They were all in the store. Including you two."

Clara clicked her tongue at him. "We're not suspects." I would not have been surprised if she'd tacked on *You silly*. But she restrained herself, leaving her tone to convey the message. "And everybody—at least Jacqueline, and Foster Utton, and that male customer—saw each other here in the produce section. But *we* saw them out in the *store*."

She'd made a tight circle with her hand when she mentioned the produce section. Now she gestured widely to convey the expansiveness of the rest of the store.

"Who did you see where?"

"And when," Clara added, "might be important, too. First, we saw the guy who said he'd stay with Mr. Birchall's body, but now seems to have disappeared. Unless you found him?"

"I'm asking the questions."

She swung her arm to wave that off. "He was walking—fast—away from the produce section. That wasn't too long after we'd left the others. Us and a couple other customers."

"What other customers?"

"Two women. They weren't together, do you think, Sheila?"

"No. I agree. They weren't together."

"Who were they?" Hensen asked.

"I don't know," Clara and I said in unison. My spirits sank. I'd held out hope she might have known the teacherish woman.

Between the two of us, we described them fairly well, though a lot of our detail relied on what they were wearing. Change their clothes and we were out of luck. Except... "The other woman takes her terrier mix to the dog park. They're often leaving around noon, but the morning side of noon. Send somebody out there a few days and they'll spot her. Look for a dog with a neon green collar. She's the woman with him. Just don't send Deputy Eckles."

"Doesn't know one dog from another," Clara said in deep disapproval.

A muscle beside Hensen's mouth ticked. But that was the limit of his reaction.

"And I think the teacherish woman might have been on her way out when we saw her shortly after we all left the produce section. The dog woman definitely hit the pets aisle, but wasn't there when we were later," I said.

"But back to the guy who said he'd stay with the body," Clara picked up. "Obviously, he went back to the produce section after we saw him walking away from it, or he wouldn't have been there when we found the body."

"We don't know when he returned to the produce section or whether that would have given him enough time to go into the back from another door, kill Birchall, and circle back to the produce section, appearing innocent," I said. "But if he did all that, why call attention to himself by taking off before the sheriff's department arrived?"

"Panic?" Clara asked.

Hensen wasn't drawn into our discussion. "Who else did you see?"

"Isaac—well in front of the guy in jeans, walking the same direction, toward the opposite side of the store from the produce section. Until he turned into an aisle. The seasonal goods or an aisle one side or the other of it," Clara said.

"Isaac?" Hensen asked.

"Mr. Birchall's driver."

"You're on a first-name basis with him?"

"He didn't give his last name when we ques—"

"Talked with him. When we were talking—all of us—about the tragedy." I don't know why I even bothered. Not only had Hensen correctly filled in the end of Clara's word as *questioning*, but watchdog deputy had heard everything.

"Uh-huh," he said.

"Anyway, that's not the point," Clara said earnestly. "The point is if he tells you he was never away from the limo, the way he told us when he said Foster Utton lied when he said he went out to the car— which he did. Lie I mean. Foster Utton did. Because we saw him and he might have been going to the restroom but we couldn't know for sure. But Isaac lied, too, because he was in the store so he *wasn't* always by the car."

Hensen looked a trifle battered, but rallied. "Anyone else?"

"The next one was Foster Utton, also heading away from the produce section, so he *could* have been going to the restroom. Then a gap, because I was telling Sheila a story about my dog, LuLu, and it was at the very end I saw a woman without a cart or anything in her hands."

"Is that significant?" he asked.

"It was to Sheila," Clara said.

Hensen looked at me. I shrugged. "An idle observation, Deputy Hensen. That's all. Anyway, it was Jacqueline, the assistant store manager, we saw next. We were an aisle or two from the far end of the store. We continued down those couple of aisles, then headed back, stopping for dog treats on our way back to the produce section. When we got to produce, Jacqueline was there, along with Foster Utton, and the guy in jeans."

"That's the order of everybody we saw." Clara's eyes brightened.

"We could figure out the timing pretty closely with a re-creation while someone times us."

"We'll see if it comes to that." His tone put it in the same category as pigs doing loop-de-loops in the stratosphere, visibly dashing Clara's glowing hopes. "If you've covered everyone—"

"The woman with the little girl," I blurted out, interrupting Hensen's gear-changing.

Clara frowned. "Right. And we saw them going *away* from this side of the store, so they must have backtracked at some point, because we definitely saw them leave produce earlier. But we didn't see the backtracking."

"We could have missed them because we weren't looking up at the right moment or—"

"Or they were *deliberately* avoiding us," Clara finished with dramatic effect. Then, more pragmatically, "Well, the woman might have been avoiding us. The little girl wouldn't have had any say in it."

"What's this about a woman with a little girl?" Hensen asked.

"Rod Birchall wanted to have his picture taken with the woman's daughter and she decidedly did not want that to happen. They also exchanged words over food labeling. She left before he brought up going in the back room, though."

"What made you think of her, then?" Hensen asked.

Good question. I searched, but couldn't find a logical thread that led to my blurting out about the woman and child.

"I don't know."

Clara clicked her tongue. "I do. Because her reaction to Birchall was so intense. Emotional. She practically vibrated with it. Her voice *did* shake."

Hensen said, "Tell me more about this exchange about… What was it?"

"Food labeling. Things people are allergic to."

We told him.

"…and then it turns out Birchall had a food allergy himself. But Jacqueline must have told you," Clara said.

"You tell me."

She did.

At the end, Hensen nodded, then said abruptly to me, "Why are you so quiet?"

He made it sound like it happened as often as Halley's Comet. I took the high road and ignored that misjustice.

"I was thinking about my saying the woman left before Rod Birchall talked about going in the back room. It is true she left this area. But he was rather loud. If she'd been in the next aisle, she could have heard him."

"You don't know who she was?" He looked at Clara.

She shook her head.

"You didn't see where she went?" That was for both of us.

We shook our heads in unison.

"Okay. Go back to the beginning. When did you arrive at the store?"

We figured the time within fifteen minutes or so, based on when our meeting broke up. But we gave him plenty of detail on the rest, including an impressive amount of verbatim conversation, if I do say so myself.

We fed off each other, correcting, clarifying, and expanding as we went.

Yes, we wanted to investigate, but not by withholding information from the authorities.

"…so you have all the ones who interacted with Rod Birchall sitting in the housewares aisle except for the dog park woman, the teacherish customer, and the woman with the little girl," Clara said. "Oh, yes, and the guy in jeans. I suppose one of the customers who stood around and listened might had been nursing a murderous rage at him, but they hid it quite well if they did. Of the customers, I'd definitely say you should find the guy in jeans and the woman with the little girl. Not trying to tell you your job, but as a witness, that's my take."

"Thank you." He laced that with high levels of sarcasm.

Clara sailed right past it. "But, remember, the woman with the girl is not the only one. All the others we told you about were out and about in the store. As I said, we could narrow the approximate times they must have been away from the others by where we were when we saw them out in the store if—Oh." Her excitement deflated. "Security cameras. This store has security cameras, doesn't it? You'll be able to see everyone and time stamps will tell you exactly when. You don't need us at all."

I leaned forward, looking at Hensen. "Don't despair yet, Clara. We might not be completely obsolete."

"Why? *Oh.* Deputy Hensen?"

He said nothing.

But I was nearly certain she'd have revenge for his sarcasm.

"The Roger definitely has security cameras and not only by the registers," I mused. "And they wouldn't have the old, cruddy ones like businesses in town mostly have. So… A malfunction?" I watched his face. "No. Not a malfunction."

"I'm not saying anything."

Except the way he said it…

"Somebody blocked a camera." My guess didn't change his expression. Darn.

Clara perked up. "Like spray paint over the lens like they do in movies? Is that what you mean, Sheila? Or they put something up in front of it? But wouldn't you see the person as they were going to block it?"

Still no change from Hensen.

"Possibly," I said to Clara. "But, if they saw someone block the camera, I doubt he'd be spending this time with us. He'd be questioning that person."

"Blocked *and* they couldn't see who blocked it?" Clara hypothesized.

We both looked at Hensen. He looked back, blandly indifferent.

"Disabled," I suggested.

"Oh, that's it, Sheila. Someone disabled the cameras. Or one of the cameras. Who—?"

Hensen stood.

"Go on. Both of you. Get out of here."

Defiantly, Clara grabbed the cart. No one objected.

CHAPTER THIRTEEN

DELIVERY DEPUTY ACCOMPANIED us only as far as the housewares aisle.

After exchanging a long-distance nod with a deputy by the cash registers, he instructed us to go directly to the doors and leave. Then he turned into the aisle, aiming for the group.

In the moment of recognition that he was not bringing us back to the group, that we were free to go—or ordered to get out of here, depending on how you looked at it—the faces of those sitting in the aisle declared we'd turned into outsiders.

Next time we talked to them, we'd have to make up ground to reconnect at the level we'd been at when we all shared being herded into the housewares aisle.

I'd leave that to Clara's expertise.

She interrupted my thoughts by saying, "I almost forgot, I have to pay for Ned's orange juice and the rest. Good thing he didn't want ice cream. We'd have soup by now."

As we adjusted our route ever so slightly to include the checkout line, the deputy who'd exchanged nods with delivery deputy frowned, then looked away, tacitly acquiescing to our detour.

He couldn't very well order us to leave without paying.

Clara said in a low voice, "Don't you think it's weird that guy who said he'd stay with the body wasn't there?"

"Beyond weird."

"But for him to leave wouldn't Jacqueline have had to let him out? She *said* she was going to the front to lock the doors."

"If she did, someone—other customers or employees gathered by the doors—probably would have seen."

But there was another possibility.

The front of the store was still locked up, with individual customers being allowed out once the deputies taking statements were satisfied. An unhappy trio by the customer service desk apparently were being held for more conversation.

I didn't recognize any of them.

The woman who'd yelled at Birchall and her daughter were not among either group. Neither was the early forties guy in jeans.

A bored gray-haired cashier operated the one register lane in service. She didn't look any more energized when we unloaded the cart into our separate purchases.

I leaned over and said quietly to Clara, "When we've checked out, let's drive around the back of the store before we leave."

THE FRONT OF the Roger was no Taj Mahal, but the back was your basic modern warehouse un-chic.

Blank brick walls, punctuated by a line of raised garage-type doors, each surrounded by black material. Cushioning? Or a seal for refrigerator trucks?

All the doors were closed and even if they'd been open, it would have been quite a jump to the ground. Maybe the guy in jeans could have done it without injury. Maybe not.

An escape route that might appeal to someone desperate. But the guy in jeans had not appeared desperate.

"Not too exciting," Clara said, clearly sharing my reaction. "Why'd you want to see this? Nobody's back here."

"Now. But a truck could have been there when Birchall was killed."

"The truck driver killed him and then left? Oh, or could someone have gotten away in the back of a truck? Or have been helped by the driver to get away?" She tipped her head. "I bet they keep track of who comes and goes back here. Checking in trucks, checking them out."

"That's good, Clara. I bet you're right. Though it's a long shot." I wrinkled my nose. "Have to admit, it all seems a longer shot than I originally thought."

I told her my wondering about the guy in the jeans and if he could have come out this way.

"Good thinking and there's—"

"Hey. What are you doing here?"

A fierce deputy appeared at Clara's rolled-down window.

As fierce as a twelve-year-old can look.

Seriously, when did law enforcement start employing twelve-year-olds? It's not a sign I'm aging. It's not.

He bent down to extend the fierce look from Clara to me.

"Oh, Officer." Clara fluttered like a length of chiffon caught in a gale. "I got all turned around and my friend here is *so* annoyed with me. I *knew* I was going to cry and of *course* I had to stop because it's *so* dangerous to operate a motor vehicle under emotional distress. Why I saw a documentary that said it's nearly as dangerous as talking on the phone or texting while driving. Of course, if you combine them, that's the *worst*. Really, they should have devices that test your emotions while you're behind the wheel like breathalyzers for people with DUI convictions, which is *awful*, because—"

"Yeah, yeah." He stepped back. "Move along now. You can't stay here."

"*Oh!* Of course. Yes, Officer. Right away, Officer. I'm so sorry, Officer."

"It's okay, ma'am. Just… Go on, now."

"Yes, yes." She raised her window, then fumbled with the keys.

It was a good thing he didn't bend down to look at me again, because controlling my face was beyond me. As she backed away from the building in imitation of an overly cautious driver about to make a turn, he peered in the windshield. I dropped my head, as if in shame over my churlishness driving her to such despair.

"You constantly amaze me, Clara," I said from that position.

"Haven't told you I was in high school plays, huh?" She cranked the wheel with exaggerated motions.

"The star, I'm sure."

"Nah. Character parts."

I laughed. "But you're going the wrong direction."

"A job worth doing is a job worth doing well," she said primly, as she completed the turn toward the end of the building we had yet to see.

"Fine with me. You know, you used to talk a lot more like that when we first met than you do now."

She looked straight ahead. "You intimidated me. Felt more comfortable behind a bit of a part. Besides, there was that business with Gracie and the rescue group."

"We've put that behind us."

"I hope so. Now. But when I was still keeping stuff from you…" Reaching the end of the building, she turned right along its west side. "Ahhhh."

Not only did I appreciate any change of subject from keeping things from each other, but I shared her satisfaction.

There, in the side of the building, was a human-sized door with a human-sized step down to the ground.

Guesstimating the location of the doors separating the produce department from the back room, it appeared to be quite convenient, too.

"Pull over, Clara."

"Be quick before the deputy comes back. I don't know if a second act—"

I exited her SUV, jogged to the door, and tugged on it.

"Locked," I reported two seconds later, back in the vehicle as Clara rolled forward.

But slow enough to give the snail its first victory ever.

"You can go now," I told her.

"Our friend the deputy's watching around the building. If I go any faster, there's no excuse for us not to be farther along. You think that door was locked from the inside?"

"Not necessarily. It probably self-locks when it closes. Too bad we didn't see it from inside."

"After sailing past a dead body," she noted with distaste.

"Picky, picky. It's reasonable to think he waited only a few minutes, then took off through that door for parts unknown."

"Parts unknown for a guy unknown," she grumbled.

I wondered if he'd been as unknown to Jacqueline as the rest of us.

We'd reached the corner to turn along the front of the building, and she embarked on another elaborately cautious turn, stopping completely to lower her window, stick her arm out and wave over the top of the SUV toward the still-watching deputy.

"Curtain call?" I asked.

"An encore in hopes of allaying any final doubts. He didn't take our names. Maybe he won't tell Hensen."

"Don't count on it."

CHAPTER FOURTEEN

WE DISCUSSED THE murder while we picked up a fast-food lunch eaten in the parking lot so we wouldn't be overheard. And continued the topic until Clara pulled in the driveway of my two-story red brick Colonial style house and turned off her SUV's engine.

She'd left her dog, LuLu, here with my Gracie in a sort of playdate.

The overseer of the playdate was Teague O'Donnell, since he brought his dog, Murphy, along while he was working for me and the three dogs were the best of friends.

Yes, the same Teague O'Donnell who was rebuilding the retaining wall in my back yard. Also the ex-cop and ex-detective who thought Clara and I—all civilians, but especially Clara and I—should leave investigating to the sheriff's department.

"You want me to come with to tell Teague what happened?" Clara asked.

Have I mentioned she's my favorite person in the world?

"Yes. Please."

She grinned at me.

After greeting all three dogs, who met us at the gate, we headed down the fenced backyard, which sloped toward a creek at the very back of the property. Previous owners had fenced the upper—and flatter—part of the yard. Across the back, the fence topped a retaining wall. From the retaining wall to the creek was a slope.

North Bend County is snugged within a northern pointing curve of the Ohio River, thus *North Bend.* Pretty wild of those early namers, eh?

Most of the county sits well above the river. Creeks do their best to get down to river level so they can join up with it. They've been working on that long enough to chew down the land along their banks. This makes for a lot of up and down topography.

The founders of Haines Tavern weren't dummies.

They picked a relatively flat area for the original town. One with a spring in the southwest corner of what everyone unblinkingly called Town Square despite its rectangularity.

"Nothing accidental about it," Urban Parham, unofficial Haines Tavern and North Bend County historian, had told me about the square's siting. "The spring served the Haineses' original building on the west side—the post office now—and then the current Tavern on the south side. Better yet, it meant folks congregating at the court-house—the Old Old Courthouse—" That distinguished it from three other courthouses in the same large block. "—had to walk across the square to get spring water. As long as they'd walked that far, a lot went a bit farther to the Tavern and had something worthwhile to drink."

"An early form of geography as marketing?" I'd asked. "Grocery stores do that, putting stuff you buy most in the farthest corner so you'll walk past lots of other stuff and be enticed."

"Indeed. Note the end of the square farthest from the spring was left to the churches. Presumably the holy could stand a longer walk to water."

He bowed his head in gentle appreciation of my chuckle.

Haines Tavern's growth had been slow until the past fifty years. My house, a post-World War II build, was relatively close to the center of town. That meant my yard was also relatively flat, unlike newer subdivisions, such as where Clara and Ned lived.

Still, the slope meant only Teague's head and his shirtless shoulders were visible through the fence as he dug on the downslope side of the wall.

"Maybe we can work the murder into the conversation gradually. Natural-like," Clara said.

I side-eyed her.

"Okay. I guess not. Do you want to start or do you want me to?"

"I'll start. Then you pitch in."

Either spotting us or hearing us, Teague settled a spadeful of soil, then leaned crossed forearms on the top of the end of the handle and said, "Hey. How'd the meeting go?"

"Fine."

The word came out short and not very convincing. But did the man have to have his shirt off? I swear even his elbows had muscles. And he was slightly sweaty. Not enough to bring up associations with being smelly. Just enough to bring up associations with … other things.

As his eyebrows started up, I said in the same tone, "The CEO of the Jolly Roger grocery store chain died here today."

"Not gradual, not natural," Clara murmured.

Teague asked, "Here where?"

"At the Roger."

"The grocery store off the highway?"

"Yeah."

Clara took over, clearly feeling a need for more explanation. "The Roger's on Covert Circle, the road that loops off the highway, down past the dog park. The CEO—his name was Rod Birchall. I guess it's still his name. It's not like you lose your name after you're dead, do you? Anyway, he was here for a surprise visit—inspection—and he was murdered."

Teague straightened away from the shovel handle and turned to looked at her more directly.

"Murdered?" He retraced his turn and looked at me. "And you two *happened* to be there."

"That's right. Pure coincidence. Because for it *not* to be a coincidence we would have had to be involved in the murder." I glared at him until he broke the look. "Which we were not. We were buying orange juice. Ned likes orange juice for breakfast and they were all out. Clara didn't want to deprive him of his orange juice."

"Unbelievable," he muttered.

"Actually, it's not unbelievable at all. Sheila was telling me about a book about oranges and it's not only in the United States that people drink orange juice for breakfast, so Ned's not a rarity. Plus, in other places, people drink it all day and others use oranges for other things, too. Who wrote that book, Sheila?"

"John McPhee."

"John McPhee," Clara told Teague.

He put down the shovel. "Tell me."

"About the book?"

"About the death and *possible* murder."

"Let's get comfortable in the house," Clara proposed. "We'll get lemonade, get out of the sun, and Sheila and I can stow the groceries in her fridge."

And one of us would hope Teague put his shirt back on.

CHAPTER FIFTEEN

"...AND THEN SHEILA told Deputy Hensen the information that could blow open the entire investigation."

"Did she now?"

"She did. But to understand it, first you have to know the back room of the Roger is all connected. It's from one side of the building to the other, though they do have special areas for freezers and chilled areas, plus different unloading areas. We drove around back to look." She huffed slightly. "Didn't get to see much before they shooed us away."

He closed his eyes for significantly longer than a blink. More like a moment of despair.

I had no sympathy for the man. In general, because he was such a stickler about investigating being the sole preserve of the sheriff's department. In particular, because his shirt remained at the worksite.

"You could have left," he said.

"Of course we couldn't leave. We are *witnesses*. It's our *duty* to tell the sheriff's department everything we saw and heard. What they'll listen to, anyway."

At that last sentence, his eyes narrowed. Clara looked back with limpid innocence.

"You know," he said slowly, "most witnesses tell what they observed and then let law enforcement handle the rest."

"Actually, I understand law enforcement can have a very difficult time getting witnesses to cooperate at all. Too many people don't want to get involved," I said.

His face indicated that might be his preference.

Too bad, rose to my lips.

But Clara was undaunted and unirked. "We would never do that. Even if they don't want our help. So I say we solve it without them."

"In fairness, Deputy Hensen did listen to what we said about whom we saw in the store."

"But didn't want to be bothered figuring out the timing, which could be vital especially with all the cameras not working, so time stamps are missing. *And* then he kicked us out."

"An excellent point, Clara. The timing is interesting."

"See," she said in triumph to Teague. "We're already making progress. Even though we gave them a huge advantage by telling Deputy Hensen everything we knew—"

"Not a competition.

"—and that's where the back room being connected from one side of the store to the other comes in. It opens the field of suspects. Sheila pointed it out and—"

"Hensen already knew," I said.

"He did? How do you know?"

"His expression when Jacqueline—"

"That's the assistant store manager, Jacqueline Yancik," Clara reminded Teague.

"—was talking about everybody staying put outside the doors, like that made it a locked room mystery or something. He clearly knew it wasn't."

"Not to mention they *didn't* stay put," Clara told Teague. "They *said* they did, but Sheila and I saw Jacqueline and Foster Utton and the guy in jeans and Isaac the driver out in the store at the time they said they were waiting outside the door. Well, except Isaac. But it's the same difference. They were *not* telling the truth."

"Is that how Sheila blew the case wide open?" Teague asked.

I could practically hear him thinking experienced law enforcement would spot the lies quickly enough without amateur contributions. Maybe. But we'd saved him time.

"No," said Clara, who either didn't hear Teague's thoughts or loftily overlooked them. "That was when she told Hensen about someone else who'd argued with Rod Birchall. A woman. In fact, she was the one who argued the most with him and it was real emotional for her. You could tell. *And* it turns out nobody knew who she was. *And* she had a motive, because she accused Birchall of misusing his power as CEO of Jolly Roger and nearly killing her daughter because he'd changed the Roger's policy on food labeling, so it no longer listed ingredients this mother said could kill her daughter. And *then*, guess what Birchall died of?"

Teague refused to play his part. "Autopsy results couldn't possibly have come back yet, so you can't know what killed him."

"No, but sometimes it's obvious. Like a gun shot. Or a knife wound."

"Sometimes the obvious is wrong."

"Sometimes it's right."

He conceded with a sideways tilt of his head. "What was the obvious cause of death this time, Clara?"

"A food allergy."

This time skepticism triggered a new head tilt. "How can you know?"

"Foster Utton said so—he's the guy we thought was the CEO's assistant until Jacqueline told us he's sort of the heir and he's going to be CEO. Anyway, he said Rod Birchall was allergic to sesame."

"Has that been confirmed?"

Her eyes glinted. "That woman who disappeared knew about it, too." She said to me, "Remember what she said about how he of all people should understand and want the labeling to be complete?"

"I remember."

Triumphant, she faced Teague again. "He was allergic to sesame and guess what was in the snack he ate?"

Teague adjusted his gaze on Clara. He was legally—though not totally, he emphasized—blind in one eye and he did that sometimes, as if trying to dial in focus. Up to this point, I'd noticed him doing it with his carpentry work and me. It was a relief to see him do it to Clara.

"Sesame," she said with more triumph, even though he hadn't

asked her.

"That was on the label?"

"No. That's the entire point. It wasn't on the label."

"Then how do you know——?"

"I looked at the tray and I could see seeds on it. Poppy for sure, probably sesame, too."

"Looked, but didn't taste. And you can't confirm the one he ate had them."

She rolled her eyes. "Hey, you were the one who told Deputy Hensen that Sheila and I have good instincts for this, didn't you?"

"I did." From his tone, Hensen might not receive such confidences in the future.

Wisely, Clara didn't rub it in. "And that guy—Foster Utton, worked with Birchall, so he should know—said Birchall was allergic and that's what probably killed him."

I tried to catch her gaze, but she was carefully avoiding eye contact with me.

"People don't always know as much as they think they do," Teague said. "But even if he's right, it could still be an accident. What would make this murder?"

"We all heard when he swore and a muffled sound, which *might* have been him falling behind the boxes. Nobody went in to help him."

"Depraved indifference," he said.

"Or a reasonable reaction to his behavior," I muttered.

He ignored my comment. "For murder, you'd have to prove someone knew he had the allergy, knew the likely outcome, knew the ingredient he was allergic to was in what he ate, and got him to eat it, which isn't going to work for your theory of murder, since your witnesses—yourselves—say he picked up the food himself."

Something tickled at the back of my mind.

"We can get around that," Clara said. "Can't we, Sheila?"

"Hah." Teague's abbreviated snort doubted it without descending to outright rudeness.

Belatedly, I bolstered her statement. "Sure, we can. And we're going to. In fact, you should get back to work on the retaining wall and we should get started."

There went the last of my time to write, since after the dog park meeting we planned to go directly to our evening yoga class. Which was worse? Failing to write? Or failing to investigate a murder?

"Get started? Is that your way of saying you're going to the dog park to talk to people?" Teague asked, amused for sure, possibly also fatalistic.

"Of course we are." Clara checked her phone for the time. "Not right this second, though. It's been scheduled for five-thirty for more than a week."

"Scheduled?" Sometimes Teague was hard to read. Not this time. He was wondering how our trip to the dog park to get background about the murder could have been scheduled before the murder.

Clara sighed at him. "You didn't read the flyer I gave you, did you?"

He shot a hopeful look at me. I grinned. I wasn't saving him. He was on his own.

"Uh, I haven't had time. Not with Sheila being such a hard task-master."

"Hah. I happen to know she delayed the work on the retaining wall so you could take the job building the Murchisons' entertainment center."

"And I appreciated it. It was a lot more comfortable during that hot spell being in their air-conditioned basement than out digging on the retaining wall. Though it's still plenty warm. So I appreciate this, too." He lifted his lemonade glass. "Heard it's supposed to get even warmer—"

"Enough of the weather report. Did you or did you not read the flyer I gave you?" Clara demanded.

He took his medicine. "Didn't."

"Shame on you."

All three dog's heads came up, looking around warily to Clara's hands-on-hips position, then—with relief—noting it was directed at Teague, not them, they dropped their heads again. They weren't saving him, either.

"It's all about the agility equipment we're getting for the park. That's what the meeting Sheila and I went to this morning with park officials was all about. And now we're going to report to all the dog owners. That's why we chose five-thirty. After people are home from work, but before dinner."

"Oh, yeah." If he'd done undercover work as a cop, I sure hoped he'd been more convincing, because this performance would have gotten him spotted immediately.

Clara clicked her tongue. "You could be a real help, you know. With the agility section, with this meeting, and with the investigating. Your experience—"

"Not me. I need to get back to *my own* work." His cheerfulness took most of the edge off it, while making his point that investigating murder wasn't our work.

Stern boss Mackey said, "Good idea. That wall won't fix itself."

Served him right for going around shirtless.

He left with an unintimidated wave.

CHAPTER SIXTEEN

AS SOON AS Teague was out of earshot, which I doublechecked by getting up to look out the window before a side trip to the fridge for the lemonade pitcher, I said, "Clara, you *do* know the food allergy wasn't what killed Birchall—according to the guy in jeans and Hensen basically confirmed it."

"Sure I do. Someone bashed him in the head. But Hensen told us not to tell anyone. And you almost gave it away. Saw it all over your face."

I suspected Deputy Hensen might make an exception for telling Teague. Hensen knew his background and they'd become rather chummy.

"You could have skipped that without leading Teague to think the cause was the food allergy."

"Hmm. I did, didn't I? At least I let him assume it."

As I added ice to the glasses, I chuffed out a laugh. "What are you up to, Clara?"

"I figured if Teague happens to talk to Ned and says the cause of death was a food allergy, that won't worry him the way a man being bashed over the head would. After all, I could get killed by being bashed over the head, but not from a food allergy. Because I don't have any food allergies. I know it's out of fashion these days, but I don't have a single one."

Fighting a chuckle, I placed her refilled glass in front of her, then took my place with mine. "We don't have a lot of time before the meeting at the dog park. We better get to work."

"And then yoga's right after. We knew it was going to be tight, but with a murder happening… Maybe we should skip yoga tonight."

I shook my head. "Not only do we need the stretching after all the drama and tension, but we might pick up information."

She pointed a pen at me. "And we can stop at the café after. I heard they've changed the dessert menu."

"Definitely need to stop there then. Though we'll have to be careful about what we say and who might be around to overhear us."

"Dessert to go. Now, speaking of eating, our first question has to be who knew about Birchall's food allergy. Was it secret or widely known?"

I tipped my glass at her in salute as she wrote it down. "I'll check. The most likely people to know about a food allergy are people who knew him well."

"The only one in the store was Foster Utton. But why kill him today and that way? There must be ways he could have killed Birchall and not been one of the suspects, much less the main suspect who knew him."

"Agreed. Could there be something making killing Birchall right then necessary?"

"Like Birchall was going to fire him or remove him as heir apparent. That's good. Would the driver have overheard something?"

"We might need a crowbar to get him to talk. While we work on finding one of those, let's pump Petey. We're looking for any hints, any at all."

She made another note.

"For now," I said, "let's start by looking at the sequence of events. Rod Birchall shows up at the Haines Tavern store—"

"With Foster Utton, driven by Isaac."

"—unannounced and—"

"Not entirely unannounced if the manager heard beforehand."

"Right. We need to find out how far ahead he knew and if he told anyone else."

She *mmmed* agreement, making more notes. "It sounded like the manager had barely left when the CEO turned up. And it didn't sound like he told anyone Birchall was coming, though would they admit it if he did? But you're right. We need to check."

"Assuming no one else in the store knew Birchall was coming, the murderer—unless it's Utton—could only have decided to kill Birchall and started looking for opportunities after he arrived. Even Utton couldn't have predicted Birchall would go in the back room alone."

"That makes sense. And that should tell us something about the crime and who committed it, shouldn't it?"

"I'm sure it should. I just don't know exactly what. But it's something to keep in mind."

"There's something else." Clara leaned forward. "I was thinking about how they say poison's a woman's method of murder. Well, I didn't hear somebody say it. I read it."

"Don't say that when you meet Aunt Kit."

"When I meet her? Is she coming to visit you? When? We'll have to have a party. A special book signing. I bet the library would love to have her speak. If you give Amy Kackley the dates, she—"

"Wait, wait. There's no trip planned. I doubt Kit will be here any time soon. She's having too much fun at her new Outer Banks home."

"The cute widower you said she's dating," Clara said wisely.

"Probably. Anyway, I meant a theoretical someday when you meet Kit, don't bring up *they say* about things having to do with murder. A lot of what *they say* is wrong. Don't get her started on the misconceptions about serial killers."

"I won't," she said fervently. "But you didn't let me finish about women using poison. Because after I heard it, I looked up statistics from the FBI. I figured it's good practice if an author wants me to research. More men actually murder by poison than women do, but lots more men are murderers. Only if you go by *percentage*, are women more likely to use poison to murder."

"That's impressive, Clara."

"Thanks. So, shouldn't we look at women more closely in Rod Birchall's murder? The food allergy served as a kind of poison."

"Hmmm. If being bashed in the head was what killed him," I said slowly, "that ordinarily would point more toward a man as the killer.

Or strong, anyway."

"Which pretty much means the guy in jeans, because Foster's not strong."

I heard her, but was following my own line of logic. "Because, a strong murderer would have had the choice of a bunch of things they could have used to kill him in the back room. As rudimentary as knocking his head against the floor enough times."

"Birchall could have cried out if he was being attacked and people could have rushed in."

"They could have rushed in if he'd made noise while reacting to the food allergy, too. *More* noise, if his exclamation was from that." I looked at Clara, and added, "Or not. You're right. If there'd been sounds of a physical attack in the back room, people probably would have rushed back there. But, even if he did make more sounds like he was being sick, would anyone have risked his abuse by going back there? Probably not."

"Almost certainly not," she amended.

Recalling Birchall's behavior and how everyone reacted to him, I agreed.

Tap. Tap. Tap. My pen hit the table.

I felt words rising. Not pausing to review them first, I said, "I think this was a spur of the moment murder. A murder of opportunity. They didn't know he was coming. They didn't have time to select a weapon—the higher percentage of female murderers using poison could figure in if there'd been time for planning. In this the murderer had to use whatever was at hand."

"I see what you're saying." Clara slowly nodded. "There was this huge animosity toward Birchall, then suddenly he's there, and he's acting like a total jerk—"

"Which seemed to be his normal mode."

"—and the murderer's overwhelmed with rage. So, they take the first means that occurs to them. Birchall ate the food voluntarily, but it left him weakened from the allergic reaction, making bashing him in the head a whole lot easier."

Clara continued, "Maybe nobody could have triggered his allergy on purpose because Birchall ate that thing on his own, but someone who knew about his allergy could have stopped him. Or tried. *And* someone who knew him well could have been diabolically clever in pushing his buttons, knowing he'd react by defying logic and good sense to eat something with an incomplete label. Since only Foster and Isaac knew him before today and Isaac wasn't there, it would have to be Foster."

Her excitement immediately ebbed.

"Though diabolically clever doesn't fit him," she concluded.

"You might be on to something. The food allergy could point to someone who knew him at the very least taking advantage of his eating that thing to act. A sort of catalyst."

Was Jacqueline's blankness when Foster Utton mentioned Birchall's food allergy from not knowing he had one? Or … from trying to hide dismay at his bringing it up?

And then there was Utton. Would he view it as clever to be open about the allergy? A facet of an act?

"Even someone who didn't know ahead of time about the allergy, knew about it after the woman with the little girl said it," I said. "Then they could have taken advantage when it happened."

"That makes sense." She chewed on her bottom lip. I waited. It seemed to me her lip-chewing often meant something more was coming. "Foster Utton could be an exception to the spur of the moment crime. Because he knew where they were going and when they'd get here."

"And he knew about Birchall's food allergy. But then why would he bring it up to us and Jacqueline?"

"Guilty conscience? Said it without thinking? Clever ploy to divert suspicion? Figured the woman with the little girl had said enough that if he didn't bring it up someone else would and then he'd look guilty? All of the above?"

"Those are enough possibilities to leave him as a strong contender despite bringing up Birchall's food allergy. But, how would he know ahead of time the snacks would be there and have sesame in them?"

"Something standard they have in all the stores?" She wrote into her note app. "We should ask Jacqueline. But how could he know Birchall would eat it?"

"Clara, that's it—how would *anyone* know he'd eat it?"

"They couldn't. But, if someone knew he had the food allergy, it would let them react faster. Like you said, a catalyst."

Fireworks went off in my head.

Two wrappers.

CHAPTER SEVENTEEN

"**THERE WERE TWO** different wrappers on the floor by his feet. That's what bugged me when Teague talked about Birchall picking up the food himself and nobody being able to know he'd eat it. Because the second wrapper was different from the one from the tray."

"Like someone got the idea from seeing him pop the sample in his mouth and maybe gave him a second dose?"

"Or the second wrapper has nothing to do with it."

She slumped. "I wonder when the sheriff's department will find out if Birchall even ate any sesame."

"Maybe we could find out from—No, no. If that's how it's going to be solved, the sheriff's department will solve it."

"But we have advantages, too. We were actually there. And we can talk to people without them thinking they're being interrogated or going to be arrested any second. We should come up with a list of who to talk to."

"Yes, we should. But first, I was thinking about Rod Birchall usually going in the back room with other people might be significant, too," I said. "Because that could make it a spur of the moment crime for Utton, too."

"Oh. Yes, I see. Because he would have expected Birchall to have a bunch of other people around him and it would only have been when Birchall went in back alone and nobody followed him that Utton saw his chance."

"Exactly."

"Do you think he's that smart?"

"I don't know he's *not* that smart. He's someone we definitely need to talk to—and get other people to talk about."

"Isaac the driver," she said immediately. "I bet he'd tell us anything negative he knows. He didn't seem the least bit fond of Foster. Although, if it wasn't a spur of the moment crime, Isaac would be a prime suspect, too, because he probably knew they were coming here. And he might know about Birchall's food allergy from driving him around a lot."

"He didn't *seem* to have any issues with Birchall, but we should check. Maybe Birchall's assistant—His real assistant. No, wait. Before we start listing folks to talk to, let's take your other brilliant point first, Clara. We were there. And we haven't even compared notes yet."

"But we were together the whole time."

"We could have different interpretations. Let's start at the beginning."

She said, "You spotted the limo in front of the Roger and brought it up because you didn't want to talk about me trying to become an author's assistant."

"What? *No.* How could you think that? You'll be a great author's assistant. And I'm all for you doing whatever you want to do."

"Then why did you change the subject so abruptly."

This is the problem with secrets. They keep jumping up and biting you in your most tender spots.

And causing you to lie to a good friend.

"Because of the limo. It surprised me. Weren't you surprised?"

"Sure, but—"

"And then we pulled into the parking lot and Isaac got all defensive like you were going to plow into that behemoth limo he tends like a baby."

"With my dirty behemoth." Clara grinned, diverted.

"Exactly. So, we got out and…"

Our memories matched with a few minor exceptions, including Clara seeing Birchall's suit jacket on a hanger, while Foster's was scrunched up on his seat.

Our recollections also synced through talking to Petey and joining the group around Birchall.

"You're sure you don't know the woman from the dog park? The one who complained about inferior products pushing out the long-time brands she wants. She comes with a mixed terrier with the neon green collar. They're usually leaving as we arrive."

"That's familiar. I know I've never met her formally." She chuckled. "Though our dogs have with the ritual sniffing routine."

"What about the dignified woman with the white wings in her hair."

"I've never ritually sniffed her," Clara said solemnly. After I tossed a napkin at her, she giggled. "I don't know her, either, but I think she's principal of the elementary school in south Haines Tavern. Or *was*. She might have retired. I'll find out. Millie probably knows."

Millie was a fellow member of Clara's book club and seemed to know everyone.

"What about the guy? The one who stayed with the body?" I asked.

"He was interesting, wasn't he? He didn't say much, but I thought he was truly angry at Birchall. Far more so than any of the others."

"Agreed. But... Did he seem familiar to you?"

She frowned, thinking. "No. I'm sure I'd remember even if I'd seen him around. Why? He seemed familiar to you?"

"Sort of. Not like I knew him, but like something about him reminded me of something else."

"What?"

"I wish I knew. Then it would stop nagging at me. There was one time I heard stuff you didn't. When the guy in jeans said Birchall was dead, Jacqueline made a weird sound, then covered her mouth."

"Weird? Like how?"

I tried to replicate it. Several times. Until I threw up my hands. "Feels like I came in last in an amateur duck-calling contest."

"Try another approach," Clara said. "What emotion did it convey to you?"

I grimaced. "It could have been almost anything. Horror? Fear? Distress? Even amusement. It sounded ... almost like a strangled laugh. But some people do laugh in moments of stress."

"What about her face?"

"Her hands covered too much to even guess, especially with someone I'd just met. That reminds me, did you notice the exchange between the guy in jeans and Jacqueline before she went to close the store doors and wait for the sheriff's department?"

"Didn't hear what they said. I was listening to the dispatcher. First I knew, the guy closed the door with him inside the back room, you on guard duty, and Jacqueline headed off."

"Darn. I would have liked your impression."

"What did they say?"

I repeated the few words as neutrally as I could.

She considered a moment. "It's interesting he said *stay out of this.* Not to stay out of *here.* You'd think the natural reaction would be to tell someone not to come in because of what they'd see. But it sounds more like he was saying it was his business, not hers."

"Possibly. But we jumped ahead. Let's go back to when the customers were arguing with Birchall."

From there, we continued our chronological comparison of notes and impressions through the moment we'd returned to her SUV and could talk freely. Basically in agreement all along.

"Which puts us back where we were."

"Pretty much."

"Okay. Let's write a list of who to talk to. I say we start—"

She broke off because Teague opened the back door and stuck his head and still-bare shoulders in.

"Thought you two were going to be at the dog park by 5:30. I'm stopping for a quick shower at the apartment, then Murph and I will be there, too."

Clara jumped up.

"Oh my gosh, look at the time. We have to leave right now."

On the way to the dog park with LuLu and Gracie, we agreed we needed to work on a list of who to talk to.

But first things first. We needed a strategy for this meeting at the dog park.

CHAPTER EIGHTEEN

TWO TRIPS TO the dog park in a day. Now, *this* was living.

For the dogs, anyway. For us, it was the third trip.

Because of course Clara and I had taken LuLu and Gracie for a good pre-meeting run there, then gone home to change into more suitable attire and returned for our meeting with the parks people.

Priorities.

Clara, Donna, and I stood in a central vestibule area where gates for two large-dog and two small-dog areas opened. Owners gathered close to the gates, while most of the dogs spread throughout the areas, though a few were curious enough to stick around.

Clara who'd already reported basics of our meeting, now said, "We'll start with the king of the hill—that's the slanted board going up, then down—a tunnel, two adjustable jump-over stations, the weave poles, and jumping hoops, one for large dogs and one for small. Oh, a teeter-totter and the raised dog walk."

Berrie interrupted, "How do we schedule our time alone in the agility section so no one can disrupt an ongoing session?"

"We don't," Clara said firmly. "It's first come, first serve. Maximum three dogs in the area at once, but up to that maximum no one is to be turned away—"

"But—"

"And any person can only have two dogs at a time."

I thought of that as the Berrie rule, since she traveled in a cloud of Boston terriers, looking rather like the Peanuts cartoon character Pig Pen and his clouds of dust. Berrie also presented herself as a trainer, giving lessons to dogs and owners. We'd talked extensively with Donna about how to prevent Berrie from monopolizing the area while charging for lessons.

Come to think of it, most of the rules were Berrie rules.

"*What?* That's not fair—"

"It's absolutely fair. It will let more people use the equipment. Also, with fewer dogs in the area and with their people focused on them, the dogs can be off-leash to use the equipment."

"But—"

"Also, no paid lessons are allowed in the agility area."

Berrie squawked an outraged protest.

Clara kept going. "It's not a commercial enterprise. There are facilities available for those charging for lessons. This is for the entire community. An informal, fun area for pets brought by their owners. The other regular rules apply. Pick up after your dog. No aggressive or threatening animals. No incessant barking."

I needed to keep working on the "Quiet" command or others might consider that the Gracie rule.

Berrie opened her mouth.

"Treats," Clara continued quickly, "will be allowed in the agility area for training purposes, but remember not to take them into the general areas."

"Or you'll risk getting licked to death," said an older man named Tony with a well-blended mix of many breeds. "I forgot a couple weeks ago and you'd think I was the Pied Piper of Torrid Avenue Dog Park. Had every dog in the place trying to get into my pocket. Swear a chihuahua went all in, head first."

"But—" Berrie tried again to introduce her desired revisions to the rules.

Clara foiled her by saying loudly to Tony, who wore hearing aids, but often didn't turn them on. "You must have the best treats ever."

"I do. Chicken recipe I make myself."

"Oh, well, chicken," Clara teased him.

"But—" Berrie didn't have a chance. Not against the interest in a new taste treat for dogs.

"Secret is to cook it in bacon grease." A chorus of ohhhs followed. I was almost sure they all came from the humans. Though canine ears perked up at the b-word. "My Jock practically does back flips for it."

I might, too.

Sensing the meeting was breaking up, Clara called out, "The equipment installation is scheduled for two weeks from now and the grand opening is the week after."

Berrie didn't know when to quit. "Wait a minute, wait a minute. We're not done here."

Donna hooked a hand in Clara's arm and drew her into the large dog area. Somehow a number of bodies intervened as Berrie tried to follow.

Almost as if it were choreographed.

Donna caught my eye, jerked her head for me to join Clara. She gave a second head-jerk to someone behind me. I turned. It was Teague. Then Donna returned to the muddle of people by the gates.

As Clara and I walked toward our favorite table, I heard Berrie repeat, "We're not done here. She doesn't get to make the rules."

"As the selected representative of owners using the dog park, they *do* get to make the rules, in conjunction with the parks department, which, among other things didn't want the dogs ever allowed off-leash—"

Now how on earth did she know that?

Wait. This was Donna. Of course she knew.

"—so consider yourself and all of us fortunate we had persuasive representatives. And, yes, we are, indeed, done here, Berrie. Now, see to your dogs. You need to pick up after Major and that young female in the far corner."

"Settled her hash," said Tony, in what was probably supposed to be a mutter to himself. But it was audible to most of those still assembled. Even those of us moving away from the group.

Around a grin, Teague said, "The Chicago Bears could use a few of these folks on the offensive line for pass protection."

"The Cincinnati Bengals," Clara disputed. "That's our home team. That's *your* home team now."

That began a vital conversation about whether a true fan ever changed allegiance no matter how far away.

✧ ✧ ✧ ✧

THE DISPUTE ENDED only when Donna joined us at the table, saying, "Now that the agility area's settled, I'm ready to hear the real news. Ah, another witness just arrived."

We turned to follow the direction of her look and saw Petey entering the small-dog enclosure, wading through the barking froth of Berrie's Terrors behind the erect, happy tail of a beagle mix.

Petey wasn't as successful trying to wade through the human pack around him.

Donna clicked her tongue. "They're all over him to find out what he saw and they don't even know you two are far better witnesses."

"Didn't know Petey came here. Didn't even know he had a dog." I was surprised that, amid the myriad photos of his grandchildren, there'd been none of his dog. Not that a dog is equivalent to a grandchild ... except to a dog person.

"It's his sister's dog. She works a lot. Ever since he came to live with her last year, he brings Banjo regularly."

"I thought he'd lived here forever."

"Grew up around here but he left for a while. Missed his cheerfulness while he was gone."

"Seeing him long-faced at the Roger was a shock. He's always cheerful," Clara said.

Donna clicked her tongue. "Poor soul. It is a triumph of spirit over history. He lived with his daughter somewhere out West, happy as a clam being house grandfather for her kids while she worked in management out there, and he worked part-time with her. Then she lost her job through no fault of her own, fell into a depression, lost her house, lost custody of the kids to her ex, and slid into abusing drugs. Died from an overdose. Petey came back here to share a place with his sister. They seem to be making a go of it with her work and what he picks up at the Roger. If you want to make him happy, ask about his grandkids. Then get comfortable. He must have a million pictures and videos of them."

Murmurs said we'd all experienced that.

"Poor Petey was the first one in Haines Tavern to encounter Rod Birchall," Clara said. "Birchall gave him a hard time out in the parking lot even before starting on the people inside."

"I want to hear all about it," Donna said with gusto. "You were right there when that Jolly Roger executive got it in the neck, weren't you? Right on the scene again. Don't look pained, Teague. These two have a flair."

Teague raised his hands and spread his fingers wide, futilely trying to disavow his expression.

"Not right on the scene," Clara said, "because we had to go get Ned's orange juice and we picked up a few other things, so we left the area right after he'd gone in the back room. And Rod Birchall didn't really get it in the neck. Though the allergic reaction probably closed up his throat."

"But you were there," Donna said.

Teague spoke at the same time. "Allergic reaction." His repetition didn't quite become a question.

I had a sudden suspicion he'd taken time out to communicate with Deputy Hensen.

Teague's former partner up in Illinois used him as a sounding board on cases—I'd heard Teague's side of such phone conversations. Had he started a similar role with Hensen?

"Right before and right after," Clara said to Donna, then turned to Teague, with no sign of the doubts I harbored about his two words. "I told you. Sheila was the one who put Hensen onto it."

"So you did, Clara," he said mildly.

Then he gave me a look. Not the kind I liked getting from him. It was full of ex-detective type questions and potential avenues of inquiry. The worst kind of look for someone with secrets to protect.

Not that I was angling for any other kind of look from Teague O'Donnell.

Though if he happened to give me one all on his own, because he wanted—really, really wanted—to give me a certain kind of look—

"Your insight came as a result of more wisdom from Sam?" he asked me abruptly.

Hah! This time he didn't catch me off guard. I remembered who Sam was almost immediately.

The ex-boyfriend I'd made up with a detective father who became my supposed source for all forensic, investigative, and police procedure knowledge. When it actually came from Great Aunt Kit and the training and research she'd included me in.

Explaining Kit's wealth of knowledge about murders and solving them edged too close to dancing on the head of the pin that I could easily shuffle-ball-change my way right off of and land *splat* into the surrounding hot soup of *Abandon All*. And my role as its supposed author.

"I did learn so much from Sam… and his father," I said with the philosophical nobility of one determined to find growth and meaning in every encounter, every relationship, no matter how painful it might have been at the end.

I allowed myself a small smile. After all, clean living, a change of scenery, and a collie dog to induce daily laughter can do wonders for repairing a broken heart.

Especially a fake one.

Or had I broken up with Sam?

Uh-oh.

"But in this case," I continued, deciding it was wiser to steer away from Sam until I remembered the details of our nonexistent relationship, "it was what those customers said to the CEO of Jolly Roger."

"Yelled at him," Clara amended for Donna's sake. "That reminds me, we wanted to ask you about a woman who brings her dog here. She wasn't happy with Rod Birchall, either. Sheila?"

Her invitation was to give Donna the details, since I'd crossed paths with the woman more than she had.

"Terrier mix. Neon green collar. They're usually leaving about the time we arrive. Dog's friendly. She's a bit more standoffish. She wears a treat bag around her waist, same color as the collar."

That did it. "Oh. Yes. Simba."

"Simba?" Teague repeated.

Amateur.

Clara and I knew Donna named the dog first. If you were patient…

"Aggie Hickmott."

…you got the human's name.

"They've been coming about five years. Let's see… Yes, five years because Berrie'd just taken in her second foster Boston terrier."

Some people might think it's strange to use dog events to pinpoint time, but Clara and I nodded our complete understanding.

"It particularly stands out because after the first one, she's had more and more trouble letting the fosters go to their forever homes. Yes, that's when Aggie started coming with Simba."

"What do you know about her? Aggie, I mean," I quickly added, or I'd hear all about the dog.

"That might connect her to this? Hmm. Not happy with the Roger, I do know that. Had quite the conversation about it a while back. They didn't withdraw a recalled dog food. She wanted to picket. I talked to the manager. The next day it was gone. She still wanted to picket. I encouraged her to put her energy into educating dog owners. So, she had a flyer here at the park and sent information to anyone who emailed her."

"I remember. It was right after Ned and I got LuLu. Scary stuff when the food can be so bad for your dog. It wasn't what we were using, but we did a *lot* more homework after that."

"I wonder if she had any interactions with the Jolly Roger chain," I said. "Especially corporate and the CEO."

"That's good," Clara said admiringly. Even Teague looked impressed. "What about a tall woman, very dignified, dark hair with white above her ears on either side." She gestured, sketching the sweep. "I think she might be or have been principal of the South Haines Tavern Elementary School?"

"Dog?"

"No idea."

"Doesn't sound familiar. Neither one was the yelling customer you mentioned?" At Clara's headshake, Donna added, "Who's that?"

"We don't know. Maybe you would?" Clara raised her brows at Donna hopefully. "Late thirties, probably. Medium height. Slender. Hair streaked to look dark blonde. Chin length, turned under. Well dressed—"

"Very well dressed. Expensive," I inserted.

"—with her daughter, about four years old."

"How do you know the girl was her daughter?" Teague interrupted.

"The girl called her Mommy."

He grunted acceptance of that as a basis for a working hypothesis.

Clara said to Donna, "Sound familiar?"

"No one I can think of right off. What did this customer yell at Birchall?"

Clara recapped that portion of the scene in the produce department. "…and when Sheila told Deputy Hensen about it, how the woman knew about Birchall's food allergy, and we'd seen the woman and her daughter still in the store later…"

"She certainly needs to be a person of interest, don't you think, Teague?" I concluded.

He was spared having to agree when Clara checked the time and said we had to leave right then for yoga.

LuLu and Gracie disagreed it was time to leave the dog park.

Negotiations were protracted, frustrating, and nearly resulted in the death of Teague O'Donnell when he laughed.

CHAPTER NINETEEN

"**Wondered if you** two were going to make it tonight," our yoga instructor said as we entered the Beguiling Way Yoga Studio.

We weren't late. We just weren't as early as usual.

While dropping off our respective and unrepentant dogs, we'd barely had time to grab our yoga clothes.

Other students and their mats already dotted the studio floor. Thankfully, *our* corner—remote and mirrorless to avoid non-yin-like distractions—remained open.

Liz, our instructor, was showing her pregnancy.

We were happy for her and her husband—delighted, in fact, since they'd had difficulty conceiving. This pregnancy was the result of a second round of in vitro fertilization.

But Liz was a reserved person, which made it a touch awkward, because all that about the difficulty conceiving and two rounds of in vitro were things she didn't know we knew.

"Dog park business ran late," Clara said.

Along with her pregnancy, Liz showed skepticism at Clara's explanation. That probably meant the humming Haines Tavern grapevine included our presence at the Roger today when Rod Birchall was killed.

"We better get changed before class," I said with a bright smile.

Clara went first. When I came out of the restroom from changing into leggings and t-shirt, a woman in her eighties named Fern had cornered Clara to pump her about the happenings at the Roger.

Since Fern was our source about Liz's reproductive history, she didn't qualify as a secure repository of secrets. Not to mention everyone in the studio—even the woman obsessed with her daughter's upcoming wedding—had tuned in for any tidbits.

Berrie had not come to class, which she usually did for this evening session. Probably strategizing how to overturn the agility area rules.

"Give me a straight answer. Did you see him get killed? Was it an irate customer? What—?"

I dropped my street clothes in a corner, took Fern's arm, and smiled down at her. "Fern, how nice to see you. How are you? Did you have a good week?"

"Don't interrupt, Sheila. I was asking Clara—"

Liz lowered the lights in the studio and entered through the double doors from the foyer, cuing that class was about to begin.

Using my hold on her arm, I gently turned Fern a bit and encouraged her toward her mat.

She harrumphed, but acquiesced.

Clara collapsed back on her mat in relief.

Which isn't a bad way to start a yin class, where time and gravity stretch crunched up muscles and fascia.

While Liz instructed us to leave the day behind, I invited memories of today's events to come on in. I do some of my best thinking about murder in yin class.

This felt like the first time I'd had a chance to draw a deep breath all day. Certainly, it was the first opportunity to quietly consider what I'd seen and heard at the Roger.

Class wasn't nearly long enough for that sorting job.

But it did appear to mellow Fern's inquisitiveness because she left us alone after class.

As we returned our props to their cubbies and strapped up our rolled mats, I said quietly to Clara, "About going to the café..."

It was our post-class routine to get a dessert there. You know, to celebrate how healthy we'd been by going to yoga.

"Don't say we shouldn't go," Clara pleaded.

"We can go. We'll get takeout and take it somewhere we can talk in private."

"Thank heavens. After this day, I *need* chocolate."

Not bothering to change back to our other clothes, we gathered our belongings and started to the door, saying good night to Liz.

"Wait."

As Clara and I turned to Liz, our gazes met for a second. Neither of us had a clue what this was about.

It became more mysterious when she waited for the door to close behind two other students, leaving the three of us.

Her neutrality didn't alter as she said, "That assistant manager from the Roger takes Eloise's flow class tomorrow evening."

If my outsides matched my insides, my jaw would be on the floor. Clara might have felt the same, because neither of us responded.

"In case you wanted to talk to her in a more informal setting. Like you did… Well, I know you found that killer a while back by talking to people. But—" The corners of her mouth turned up. "—you will need to do a few sun salutations."

We'd done more than a few in the investigation Liz referred to.

"No problem," I said in that mode where you easily agree to something in the future because it feels like the time when you'll need to live up to the agreement will never actually arrive. "And thank you. Thanks a lot."

✧   ✧   ✧   ✧

"IF JACQUELINE WASN'T already at the top of our list of who to talk to, what Liz said puts her there." Clara transferred the spoon she was using to eat ice-cream-topped apple crumble to her left hand and noted Jacqueline's name on her phone's notes app.

No, she hadn't neglected her chocolate craving. She'd eaten a brownie while we walked from the café, past the corner of the Old Main Branch of the North Bend County Library, and found a bench in the otherwise deserted town square … which was rectangular.

I can't describe why, but this fact delighted me and made me certain Haines Tavern was my hometown destiny.

We'd considered going to my house. My unvoiced reluctance was based on the possibility of Teague being there for some aspect of the retaining wall job, as he often and unpredictably was. Clara voted for the square because it was closer, which meant she could eat her apple crumble sooner.

Good thinking.

Even when twilight faded, lights from Historical Haines Tavern across Haines Avenue reached us. Between that and the glow of Clara's phone we had all the light we needed for notes and all the privacy we could want.

Finally, we wrote the list of people to talk to. No surprise, it included the people we'd seen interact with Rod Birchall today.

Clara put aside her biodegradable spoon to check the names, ending with "…and the man in the white shirt who was supposed to stay with Birchall's body, but didn't."

"We'd have to find him before we could talk to him. And to do that, we'd have to figure out who he is." I consoled myself with my last mouthful of flourless chocolate cake.

"We can do that. We can."

"Clara, we have to be realistic. Some things—a lot of things—the sheriff's department is much, much better at than we are. Identifying mystery people is one of those. They have access to the store's cameras. They can probably get video of him, even put out a call to the public if they have to. Plus, probably cameras in the parking lot. If they can read his license plate, then they have him. We can't do any of that."

"Okay, I get it. Play to our strengths. We can do other things, like not interrogating. We'll start with the people who were there and—"

"Actually, I'd like to talk to somebody who wasn't there as soon as we can—the store manager. His name's Kurt Verker, according to those photos on the wall across from the registers. That phone call he got and his reaction might be the start of the day's strange activities."

"I like it." She wrote on her list. "Okay. Kurt Verker, Jacqueline Yancik, the woman from the dog park now that we know her name's Aggie Hickmott, Petey because he might know more about these people, including the woman I think was a principal and we'll see if he or Millie comes through first. When we pin that down, we talk to each of them. Then Gundy Vance."

"Who?"

"Gundy Vance. He owns Shep's Market."

"Shep's Market? The little place in town? The guy who owns the original supermarket in town was at the Roger? *Today*?" My voice kept rising as Clara nodded after each question. "He happened to be on the spot when the CEO of the big rival chain not only was at his closest competitor, but was *murdered*?"

"Uh-huh."

"But, Clara, that makes Gundy Vance a *major* person of interest, at the very least. More like a prime suspect. Why didn't you mention him being there before?"

"Why should I mention him when you saw him, too?"

CHAPTER TWENTY

"ME? I DIDN'T see—"

"Sure you did. You commented on him. The guy without a cart or anything in his hands. The first one. Before Foster Utton. You must remember that."

I did remember a guy in a white oxford shirt and khakis with only a vague impression of his face. "I had no idea he owns Shep's Market."

"Really? He talks to customers all the time."

"I mostly interact with the woman beside the deli counter."

I had a momentary reluctance to say I habitually went straight to the section with prepared meals. We're not talking frozen dinners. They were like those meal delivery deals, only fresh, better made, and I didn't have to cook.

"Judy Vance. She's Gundy's wife. She prepares those meals."

"She's good."

"She is. Great promotion for the market, too. It's helped them a lot. Draws in a lot of customers."

Glad I wasn't alone in going for the meals. "Helped them? Is the store in trouble?"

"Seems to be doing better now, but it was definitely in trouble for quite a while. There was a rumor it was going to be torn down before Gundy and Judy came back. He grew up here, of course. But he'd been living in Charlotte, North Carolina. Was high up in a financial company. That's where he met Judy. She had a catering business. I guess she wasn't real happy about coming here to run a little grocery store. But his dad had a stroke—actually he'd had a couple, but this one was major. He's doing better now. Amazing the things they can do with rehab, especially for somebody who works real hard. And Trent Vance's always worked real hard."

"But the store was in trouble under him?"

"Yeah. He was stuck in his ways and so was the store. It hadn't been updated for ages. Gran said it was still the way she remembered as a girl."

Some might expect a grandmother to prefer that things stay the way she remembered them as a girl. On the other hand, Clara's gran, Trudi, moved to Belize with her boyfriend, so maybe not.

"It's been a real Haines Tavern institution since—Well, I don't know how long. Forever as far as I'm concerned. But I bet Urban could tell you. All I know is the Market's been in the family since it started. My grandmother said Trent—Gundy's dad—never was suited to running the store. That it should have been one of his sisters put in charge, but their father couldn't imagine a woman running the store and he bullied Trent into it. Guess he was something, Trent's dad. Not in a good way."

"What about Gundy? Did he want to take over the market?"

"Probably not his first choice. I mean, he had a career and every-thing, but I get the idea he did it out of loyalty." She considered. "And love. For his dad. I mean, if Trent gave up a lot of what he wanted to do to keep the store going and Gundy let it die, that would be kind of a kick in the pants for his dad."

"For all those years, it had no competition unless you wanted to go to Stringer. Then the Roger came. It was new and shiny—then. And with the Market standing still or going backward, some folks stopped going to Shep's."

"I'm surprised. I mean, I know people shop at the Roger, but it's felt like people hide that as their dirty little secret. I sure was encour-aged to shop at Shep's."

"That's because Gundy Vance has done a good job these past few years playing up Shep's Market as a Haines Tavern institution. Folks shop civic pride unless they really need convenience and then they go to the Roger. Why are you frowning? Didn't that make sense?"

"It makes perfect sense. What I'm wondering is what the owner of Shep's Market is doing at the Roger? Today of all days."

"The very day the Roger CEO was there and got murdered," she nodded wisely. "But, still, how could Gundy know he was going to be there? Plus, Shep's doing okay now and why would he want to kill Birchall today."

All good points.

I frowned. "Remember what Birchall said about the Haines Tavern store? That its numbers weren't as good as they should be? He wasn't happy with Kurt Verker or Jacqueline about that. And then he wasn't happy about something else."

"The stapler?"

"Besides the stapler. Something—Got it. He said Shep's Market runs specials right before the Roger—you mentioned it, too. About Shep's having a deal on the soup last week. And Birchall said—"

"Somebody was leaking the specials early to Shep's Market." Clara bounced up on the bench. "You're right, Sheila. If Gundy has a mole at the Roger, someone feeding him the specials and Birchall found out… *That* could be why Gundy was at the Roger."

"Hold up there, Clara. Let's sort through this. If Gundy has a mole at the Roger, he wouldn't go to the store to meet with the mole. He wouldn't want to expose his source and the source would not want to be associated with him."

"Right, right. I got excited. You're right. But Gundy *was* at the store, so does that mean he doesn't have a source?"

"Not necessarily. He could have a source at the store *and* another reason for being there today. Okay, set that aside for a moment. Because the other hitch is about Birchall finding out. If Birchall knew who the source was, he wouldn't have threatened Jacqueline if she didn't find the leak—traitor. That was his word."

"You're right. He'd have skewered the source on the spot. But that's all the more reason the source would be afraid of being found out. He—or she—had to act right away, so the person took the opportunity right then to get rid of Birchall. Or, if the mole told Gundy Vance, could he have felt he had to get rid of Birchall or be exposed? Except, like you said, he'd be more likely to stay away unless—*Oh.*"

"What?"

"Gundy Vance and Kurt Verker know each other. There was an article about how they were cooperating on a program to get food to people who need it. Say Verker's the mole. He gets the call about Birchall coming and after he leaves the store, he calls Gundy. Then Gundy decides Birchall has to go and—"

Abruptly, she drooped, all the air gushed out of her balloon.

"What?" I asked.

"I hate to think Gundy might be the murderer. It would be pretty rotten for Haines Tavern."

I noticed she didn't include the Roger store manager in that worry.

"I suppose it's moot if we can't catch the person. But—" She perked herself up before I needed to even try, tapping her notes. "—we'll start talking to people tomorrow."

Dessert and natural light gone, our plan for the next day set, we headed out.

Clara would drop me off and pick up her groceries so Ned would have his breakfast orange juice. I would do something I usually enjoyed, but wasn't looking forward to now.

I NEEDED TO call Great Aunt Kit.

If I'd had boots on, I'd be shaking in them.

And this was despite my plan being to be an open book—pun intended—with her.

You'd think I'd be a better liar than I am, considering I'd spent years pretending to be someone I wasn't, namely the author of *Abandon All.* Yes, that *Abandon All.* The holder of the bestseller list throne. The sweeper at the Oscars.

And now I was pretending I'd never pretended to be that person I wasn't.

Before you start jingling handcuffs in anticipation of my confession that I defrauded the actual author of *Abandon All…*

Nope.

Under the guidance of the author, my not-so-sweet, but extremely entertaining great aunt, we were both financially independent.

She'd spent her professional life toiling in traditional publishing's midlist.

Midlist referred to any author whose name you probably haven't heard of who makes the publishers money. In a lot of instances, their steady earnings in often sneered-at genres such as romance, science fiction, historical novels, mysteries, and westerns, support extravagant advances to celebrities you have heard of, who rarely if ever earn out those advances. Now, household name authors do earn out—

What? Earning out? Advances? Sorry. I forget not everyone knows the lingo.

I spent years sharing a New York brownstone with Aunt Kit. Her author cronies came as part of the package. As the supposed author of *Abandon All*, I was allowed to attend their gatherings on the condition that I paid for all the refreshments. No small bill considering their consumption of food and beverages.

It was an education well worth the cost. An education in publishing, surviving, writing, and living.

The lingo was a bonus.

Advances are not gifts from publishers. More like payday loans.

They are *advances against royalties*. That means these loans must be paid back from royalties earned from sales of that book.

No, you *hope* it's from the sales of that book, because if it's not, you have something called combined accounting in your contract, meaning advances on all included books must be earned back before you get royalties.

A strong selling book can be stuck paying back advances on books given lousy covers, books lost in a snowstorm in the Rockies, books miscategorized by the publisher. Or any of thousands of other publishing mishaps. That means you can have a best-selling book and not be earning any money.

Even in the best-case scenario, the bulk of the book's earnings go to the publisher. *All* the author's minority share of goes to the publisher until the advance is paid back. So, again, you can have a best-selling book and not be earning any money.

Oh, yes, and the payout periods can be six months to a year to multiple years after the copies were actually sold.

The glorious tipping point when the book has brought in enough money that the author will begin to receive royalties is called earning out.

It's a great business.

Though not necessarily for authors.

This is why Kit and many friends have chosen indie publishing, which is not for the faint of heart, either.

Why, I hear you asking, would anyone write under these circumstances? Surely whips and chains would be an easier route to masochism.

It's a disease.

And I appear to have caught it.

But I'm not telling Kit. Not yet. Maybe not ever.

No time to let that occupy my thoughts right now, though, or it would be too late to call even my night owl relative.

As tempting as procrastination was, the consequences were not appealing.

CHAPTER TWENTY-ONE

"I'M CALLING YOU before you hear any other way, because—"

"Another murder." Aunt Kit's guesses were legendary. And scary. She didn't wait for my confirmation. "Good heavens. Your mother's right. You're doing something weird out there to attract all these murders."

"I'm not doing anything to attract—"

"This is way past not fair. In all my years—"

"Kit, murders are not doled out on a merit system. Otherwise, we'd have a lot fewer bad people to deal with."

"I don't mean it's not fair to the victims, I mean it's not fair you're on the spot for another one and I'm not. Heck, they wouldn't even let me serve on a jury for an attempted murder case. I would have taken that. Though, with my background and interest, you'd think I get one, maybe mo—

"You've had dozens."

"I mean in real life. I'm coming out there for a visit. Soon." Her dark tone implied there better be a murder for her to solve included in the agenda during her visit or there'd be hell to pay.

"Not that kind of merit system, either. Though if you want to talk about the victim this time…"

"A stinker?" she asked, cheering up.

"A prime stinker." I detailed Rod Birchall's behavior before he'd disappeared into the back room of the grocery store.

"Figures," she said.

"What do you mean? Do you know something about him?"

"Yes. You would, too, if you read more newspapers every day." Kit read three newspapers in print and scanned more for selected topics. She particularly liked business and local papers. "Tell me what you know so I don't waste time covering things you already know."

"He was CEO of the Jolly Roger chain, but not for real long. He was making a lot of changes—none of them popular with employees, especially when he laid off or fired a bunch last week. The assistant manager of the store said he'd come from someplace else, where he'd run a chain that went bankrupt. Idaho, I think."

"The PFFT chain." It sounded like she'd blown raspberries.

"The what?"

"The P-F-F-T chain. An acronym for something or other."

A certain note of satisfaction in her voice alerted me. "Kit, do you have connections with the PFFT chain?"

"No. For one thing you said it's bankrupt. And I didn't have any before it went bankrupt. But I do have connections to the Jolly Roger board."

"You do? That's *great*, Kit. Can you find out about Birchall? And about the guy who's now the acting CEO, Foster Utton. Apparently he was hand-picked by Birchall."

"If you keep me up to date on what you're finding out. In other words, I want in on this murder."

"When have I ever kept you out?" Even if I'd tried, I wouldn't have succeeded. Besides, she was a great resource.

"More. I want more. Deal?"

"Deal."

"Start with the suspects."

"Most of the suspects are local—the assistant store manager, a few customers, a rival store owner. But I'm, especially, curious about Foster Utton. Both Clara and I took him for a low-level assistant."

I described what had happened from the moment I spotted the SUV/limo in front of the Roger.

It took a considerable amount of time because I had to fill her in on North Bend County details as background and because she asked a million questions, with 99.9 percent of them insightful and useful.

"You've wrung me dry," I said at the end. "I'm exhausted."

"First, admit you really called to mine my sources and connections about the CEO and this successor."

"We greatly appreciate you doing that—and I speak for Clara, even though she doesn't know I'm asking you. But it's *not* the primary reason I called. The primary reason is I didn't want to be brow-beaten by you—again—for not contacting you."

She cackled appreciatively. "No promises. Remember, I'm in on this one."

DAY TWO

TUESDAY

CHAPTER TWENTY-TWO

CLARA HAD CLASS this morning for her virtual author assistant course before our regular lunchtime yoga class.

That made this my time to write.

I was not writing.

Murder wasn't the culprit.

Neither was investigating a murder.

The culprit was me. For not prioritizing writing first. For not sticking to it. For being a when-I-have-some-free-time would-be writer. I've been around *real* writers enough to know they got the writing done by writing no matter what. Nothing stood in their way. And here I was letting everything stand in my way.

I was a failure. I'd never be a real writer. I'd never tell the stories in my head.

Slumping forward, with my elbows to either side of the keyboard, I dropped my head to my hands.

After maybe a minute a couple phrases started repeating in my head.

The first was *Woe is me.*

It sure matched my mood. And my posture. But there's something about the phrase that, repeated over and over in my head, sounded silly.

The second was *Nothing stood in their way.*

Not true. Not about Kit. And not about her friends. All sorts of things stood in their way. Parties, sickness, holidays, family gatherings, conferences, computer breakdowns, reader events, visiting friends in crisis, gardening, story problems ... the list was endless. When they included me in their get-togethers—thinking I was a real writer—I'd heard all about those and many more obstacles that got between them and their writing time.

The difference between them and me was they kept going. They didn't clear away all the obstacles—not sure how that could be accomplished without joining the writer's equivalent of a contemplative monastery, where only writing was allowed, but then what would you write about? No, they simply continued on the other side of the obstacle.

That's what I needed to do.

I raised my head.

The cursor blinked at me.

I scrolled back to see what I'd written. My stomach sank.

Never before had I understood Kit's statement that some days the only thing she wanted to write was: And then a bus hit them and they all died.

Trouble was, this romance was set in the backcountry of the Blue Ridge Mountains of North Carolina. How many buses got there? And could they get up enough speed on the narrow winding roads to do the job?

Clearly, I'd have to write with my stomach around my knees.

I put my hands on the keyboard.

I'D BEEN AT it almost two hours when the phone rang.

Rumor has it that when a writer's deeply engrossed s/he will not even hear a phone, much less let it interrupt the flow and concentration.

I answered it.

"Millie came through. Phyllis Ezzard."

I might have been deeper into the writing than I'd thought, because the names meant nothing to me. Heck, I barely recognized

Clara's voice.

"She was a principal, but of a middle school, not the elementary school."

Oh. Right. The woman with the upswept hair.

"I have her email, street address, and phone number. But that for later, because even better, I have an in for us to talk to Foster Utton at the Jolly Roger corporate headquarters. Also through Millie."

"When?"

"We'll leave right from yoga. Not even time to stop at the café after."

That made it serious.

After the call, it made no sense to try to get back to writing.

I could do research in the limited time.

Besides, I had to figure out what clothes I could change into at the yoga studio that would fit in at a corporate headquarters. Good thing yin wouldn't get us sweaty.

✧　✧　✧　✧

YIN DIDN'T GET us sweaty, but Berrie going on and on about the agility area rules had me hot under the collar.

Especially since it cut into my time to expand on the headline I'd given Clara in the drive to class—Birchall's food allergy was widely known. It was in multiple articles written around the time he changed the company's labeling policy to be less complete for items made in-store.

I swear Berrie arrived early to harangue us. Mostly Clara, since I closed my eyes and settled back on my mat with a cloth over my eyes when she started. Clara was too polite for that. Instead, she patiently repeated what she and Donna already told Berrie.

That was fair, since Berrie kept repeating herself.

Fern chimed in, "You know that's the definition of insanity, don't you, Berrie? Doing—or saying—the same thing over and over but expecting a different outcome." Her distinctive blend of country accent and Southern drawl softened the words sufficiently to make their sting a surprise.

Clara splurted a sound beside me.

Berrie sucked in a breath, which delayed any response. By the time she would have spoken, it was too late.

Beyond my eye-covering the lights dimmed and, in the next instant, I heard Liz enter the studio.

✧ ✧ ✧ ✧

WE SHOOK OFF a more relaxed Berrie after class, changed, and headed toward Cincinnati.

In less than twenty minutes, we rounded a curve in the Interstate to see the city's skyline ahead and below us as we descended through what's known as the Cut in the Hill, taking us from the Kentucky heights to bridge level over the Ohio River.

As we went, Clara tried to call Phyllis Ezzard. No answer, and we decided not to leave a message.

I gave Clara the rest of the details I'd learned about Birchall's allergy—to all forms of sesame—and his corporate background.

Even reading between the lines of the Jolly Roger website, which, predictably, presented the sunny side of his career, Rod Birchall had been associated with a high percentage of failures, starting with taking his father's trucking firm through bankruptcy when Rod was a teenager. Two other enterprises closed under his leadership, two were subject to hostile takeovers, three more bankruptcies, including the PFFT chain. Yet Birchall came out of each with an even better job.

"If he'd been captain of the Titanic, it wouldn't have made it out of port," Clara said. "Do you think he was blackmailing people to keep getting jobs?"

"We'll wait to hear what Kit says. So, who's your contact in the executive suite at the Jolly Roger building … and does the building resemble a pirate ship?"

"When I said I had an in, I meant a way into the building."

I groaned. "There'll probably be all sorts of security around the CEO's office, considering what happened. Nobody will let us near Foster Utton."

CHAPTER TWENTY-THREE

I WAS WRONG.

Partly.

Security did swarm around Birchall's office on the top floor, which is where we tried first, upon entering a building that did not in the least resemble a pirate ship, but did resemble a cubist's vision of a part of male anatomy. In other words, it was a boring high rise.

The reception area outside Birchall's office, which had not received the memo about CEO's quarters paring down from lavish to merely plush, sported more than half a dozen men in black hard at work on files. They did not appear to me to be law enforcement. Corporate lawyers? Security?

As if they needed any security around with the firm-jawed assistant behind a bronze nameplate: "Ms. DesJames."

We slid right past the men in black. But there was no sliding past her, even though our footsteps were silent on the uber thick carpeting.

"May I help you?"

"Oh, you must be Ms. DesJames," I said with wide-eyed awe.

"That," she said with no hint of humor, "is what the name plate says. You have no appointment with this office today."

I glanced toward the closed double doors past her sofa-sized desk. "We're looking for a couple of people whom—"

"No one is here whom you can see."

Our dueling *whoms* ended in a draw.

"—we'd like to talk to. Foster Utton and Isaac, the limo driver." Better to plow ahead than try to argue.

"That driver is no longer in our employ." Her intonation on *our* turned it into the royal *we*, with her on the throne. Who'd taken the trouble to fire him so quickly? Couldn't imagine that was one of Foster Utton's first acts.

"Rod Birchall's preference for him was odd," I said. "They seemed to get along well."

"I never underst—"

Her face went rigid as she cut that off. Yup, Ms. DesJames brought down the ax on Isaac. But she'd also had no doubt he and Birchall suited each other.

"Do you know where we'd find him?"

"I have no idea." She thought she had herself back under control, but she'd slipped a bit there, letting her satisfaction leak through. "Nor is it my responsibility to—"

"The other places Mr. Birchall visited yesterday—"

"—know. He was here until leaving for Haines Tavern. Now, if you will please—"

"What about Foster?" Clara asked. "You must know where he is."

At that moment, one side of the double doors to the inner sanctum opened, a man in black appeared and called to one of the men in black where we were, "Black. Come here."

I swear. That's what he said. Would I fib?

Besides, I was too busy craning my neck to see around Man in Black I in the doorway to expend energy on making anything up.

Man in Black 2 responded too quickly for me to get more than an impression of a continuation of the outer office's would-be old-world grandeur overlaid by a probably stupid-expensive modern look. It was as off-putting as Birchall had been.

All satisfaction gone, Ms. DesJames said, "I am not at liberty to divulge such information. You are to leave immediately, before—"

"But—"

Clara tugged my arm. I acquiesced. We weren't making progress with Ms. DesJames.

But as we descended in the elevator to a floor I believed she'd hit at random, Clara said, "I spotted a note with what looked like an office number on her desk. Let's see if it's Foster Utton's."

It was, though it wasn't easy to get to.

Not because of men in black. No one felt it necessary to post security around a cubbyhole with a door under a stairwell. Oliver Twist would have considered the quarters cramped.

Foster Utton resembled a golf umbrella folded to fit in a breast pocket.

His huddled form looked the way I'd felt when I'd sat at the computer this morning. Before my triumph of writing.

We saw that huddled form through the open office door, before Clara breezed in with me on her tail.

Half a second inside and we realized his open-door policy was the result of the stuffiest room I'd ever been in.

Clara didn't let it stop her. She reached across the desk and pressed Utton's forearm while he stared at us, his surprise the only light in his dull face.

"Foster, you poor thing. The day after is always worse than right after a … an event like yesterday's. Somehow the first day you don't take it all in. You don't truly realize all that's happened and the impact it will have on you. Did the sheriff's department keep you there forever yesterday?"

"Yeah." He paused and we both waited for something important to follow. "They fed us."

"Thank heavens for that. But, still, such a difficult day. I suppose the investigators kept Isaac, the driver, too?"

"Yeah." This time nothing more followed.

"We are so hoping to talk to him. For background, you know. Do you have his business number?"

He looked around. No phone numbers jumped up off the desk or walls, so it didn't take long.

"Uh, no. I think… I think the business is his name."

"That's helpful. That's *so* helpful, Foster. Thank you. Do you know his last name?"

"No. Isaac was all Birchall called him."

Better than *you.*

"That's fine, that's fine. We'll talk to him, too."

"Nobody's talking to me," he said. "I mean people didn't used to see me anyway, but it's different today. They're pretending they're not seeing me now even though they do. Afraid I might be the murderer. Or might not be."

Not stupid. Definitely not stupid.

"In the meantime," he continued, "Ms. DesJames said not to talk to anybody except the lawyers and her—"

Ah, she was hedging her bets, making sure she could be the power behind the throne if he survived.

"—and the lawyers said not to talk to law enforcement."

"We're not law enforcement, Foster," Clara said gently. "We were right there with you during those horrible hours."

"Customers. Complaining," he muttered.

He considered *that* the horrible part? Not his boss being murdered and his being a suspect?

"We didn't complain, Foster."

He blinked at her gentle voice. Glanced at me, then hurried his eyes back to Clara. "You didn't, did you?"

"No, we didn't. And I'll tell you something, Foster. I think it's *good* you were there from the start yesterday. You're important—in fact, you're vital—because you can give the definitive account of what happened when you arrived at the store."

I thought Clara's approach was great. Assuming he'd cooperate, easing him into the discussion, not hitting him with questions about the murder right off, and, at the same time, appealing to his vanity by setting him up as the expert.

"I don't know what you mean."

"When the car carrying you and Rod Birchall pulled up in front of the store and stopped," Clara patiently clarified. "Did something happen with a store employee? In the parking lot?"

"The driver put down his window and the employee said CEO or no CEO, the car wasn't going to park there. That throwback driver threatened this poor man, who didn't seem to understand what was happening. We do have a program for hiring the mentally challenged.

Also the old. And he was very old. I got out of the car and explained the CEO was there for a surprise visit and we needed to park in front of the doors.

"He still didn't seem to grasp the situation. The driver threatened to run him over and then nearly did. Almost ran *me* over, because he started moving the car before I was actually seated again."

"And then?"

"Then we went inside. As if the trouble in the parking lot wasn't enough to set Rod off, then that girl said the store manager wasn't there. Nothing more than an assistant manager to meet the CEO and his second in command. Not adequate at all."

He made a scoffing sound, which Clara echoed, though I suspected hers was for his referring to himself as *in command*. Even as a second.

"Then it got even worse with those people complaining. The stores know better—the *experienced* store managers—know better than to let complainers ambush the CEO. I couldn't believe when she actually joined in, taking the part of the complainers against him.

"I knew it was going to be rocky—rockier—after that. And then the woman with the girl ... Nightmare."

"Did you get a photo of him with the girl?"

His mouth dropped open. "I have no idea. I haven't looked."

He made it sound like he'd be committing a solecism of the first order to do such a thing.

"You must have been so very busy. That makes sense. Now would be a good time to check."

Still open-mouthed, he stared at Clara. She smiled back brightly. Then gave him an encouraging nod.

"Well, uh, I suppose..."

"Where's your phone?"

"Right here."

"Great. We can do this right now."

She made it sound reasonable. And her encouraging smile clearly had him wanting to please her. How had this guy gotten so far up the corporate ladder?

He pulled his phone out, turned it on, then fumbled almost as ineptly as he had in trying to take the video.

"May I help?" Clara took the phone from his hands, gently, but firmly. "My husband's phone is like this. Sometimes it's finicky. But if I get it just right… Ah, yes. Here it is."

She clicked a button, then turned the screen, not toward him, but toward the space between her and me.

A dizzying pan of the Jolly Roger produce section came on, like a ship plunging down into the trough of a wave, then climbing so straight up it seemed it would fall over backward. Jumbles of voices even harder to sort than during the original event exacerbated the disorientation.

Clara and I leaned in concert, our instinctive body language trying to keep the whole thing from flipping over.

A slice of dark blue became recognizable as the woman's designer jeans. Then a patterned blur resolved into the girl's safety halter.

The volume faded to nothing, then jumped back loudly, like a finger might have accidently unmuted it.

"*…daughter because it might make the label a line or two longer. You would have killed Lorelei without giving it a second thought.*"

Utton jerked in his chair. "Oh, dear. Not at all what he had in mind. I'm afraid there's nothing usable there."

We both looked at him.

First, because it sounded like he was still worried about not satisfying his dead boss.

Second, because, was he serious? Under what circumstances would he possibly consider using any of that video, no matter what it looked like? But especially not for the cheesy CEO-charming-an-adorable-child footage his former boss had been after.

As it was, no, we agreed with him, there was nothing usable by Rod Birchall's standards.

There was, however, possibly something useful to us.

CHAPTER TWENTY-FOUR

"Can Foster truly be that dense?" Clara said once we were in my car, heading back to Haines Tavern.

"If he's not, he's a great actor. But people can be deadly without being smart or attuned to other people. And, you know, for him to have survived and risen in the corporate atmosphere, he must be somewhat astute."

"Or people wanted him around because he was no threat."

I shot Clara a glance at that glum comment, then returned my attention to the road.

After crossing the Brent Spence Bridge over the Ohio River into Kentucky, we now had to climb through the Cut in the Hill.

These days, the stretch was notorious for accidents when southbound rush hour traffic on I-75 drove into the descending sun or when northbound traffic descended rapidly toward the bridge. It warranted alertness at all times.

The double-decker bridge received more attention and alarm, what with losing chunks of concrete not so long ago and carrying twice as much traffic as it was built to hold. But rumor is local news outlets keep a standing headline ready to slap on the latest incident: "Another Crash Wrecks Commute on Cut in the Hill."

Trying to cheer up Clara, I said, "Wasn't the view from here on a TV show?"

"Opening credits in the *WKRP in Cincinnati* reruns show the skyline and river and Fountain Square."

"I thought Urban told me about another show. An even older

one."

"Oh, right. The view from the Cut in the Hill down to the bridge was on an old TV soap opera called *The Edge of Darkness*, though they didn't call it Cincinnati."

"That's it. That's the one I heard about."

"There've been recent movies shot around here, too." My hopes that I'd cheered her up deflated along with her extended sigh. "Doesn't help us any, though. I had such hopes about this visit."

"Maybe not, but you know, Clara, what you said about Foster Utton not being a threat to anyone was very astute. Utton's very ineptitude might have made him more appealing to those above him on the corporate ladder."

"Thanks, but the Jolly Roger corporate headquarters and Foster Utton were still pretty much dead ends."

"When we get back to my house, we'll start searching for that woman with the bits and pieces we picked up."

"I suppose we can look at the video again in case we missed anything, but it's a long shot."

"Look at it again? But—"

"I sent a copy to my phone while I was helping Foster."

"That's brilliant, Clara. We'll definitely look at the video again."

"Okay. But I'm going to need sustenance. Let's get off at Buttermilk Pike and go to Graeter's for ice cream."

"An ice cream place is on *Buttermilk* Pike?"

"Time for another Cincinnati-Northern Kentucky history lesson, Sheila. Over ice cream."

SHE DELIVERED THE lesson over two generous scoops each. Chocolate chip-toffee for me and salted caramel-chocolate chip for her.

Graeter's was started in the 1870s by Louis Graeter, later joined by his wife Regina, who carried on after his death. The ice cream is still made in something called a French pot and the chocolate chips are actually chips of chocolate.

Clara's story about Buttermilk Pike was almost as good as the ice cream.

"There were lots of dairies in the area and with the wagons carrying the containers over bumpy dirt roads, the milk would start to churn. Voila! Buttermilk Pike."

"I'm going to have to brag to Urban about knowing this. I'm going to get some to take home."

We both did. Clara bought more than me, but only because she added Ned's favorite black cherry-chocolate chip.

At my house, with the containers temporarily stored in the freezer, we settled at the small kitchen table.

"Let's watch the video again, then recap," I suggested.

Nothing new.

"But we did pick up some info," I argued, partly with myself.

"We know her daughter's name is Lorelei," Clara said. "And I remember the woman, Lorelei's mother, saying something about fighting him—*we* fought to get Jolly Roger to improve its labels—like she might be part of a group."

"You're right. And if she's part of a group…" I pulled my laptop in front of me and opened it. "…we might be able to find her."

My first tries bombed. Who knew that many groups advocated better food labels? Or concerned about food allergies. I'd heard about severe allergies to peanuts, but the culprits went way, way beyond peanuts. Wow. Some people were allergic to celery. There were times I'd practically lived on the stuff, trying to get into a certain dress for a certain dance with a certain boy. Ah, youth.

"Try more specific," Clara suggested. "Add Roger—the Jolly Roger."

I raised my index finger, then dropped it to point at her in acknowledgment. "And I'll try a search adding Birchall's name. Since she knew who he was, she might have had dealings with him."

We found multiple groups who'd had dealings with him. None, apparently, pleasant. As my searches pulled up names of specific women, Clara wrote them down. Then we searched for those people. None we found was the woman from the grocery store, though we had no hits for about a third.

Next, we tried names of organizations mentioned.

This took more time as we sorted through their sites for board members, founders, volunteers. Again, not all of them had photos we could find. But all the photos we did find eliminated those women.

Clara leaned back, interlocking her fingers and stretching her arms. "And they say detecting is glamorous."

She'd spoken as the back door opened.

"Who says that? Not anybody who's ever done it." Teague stepped in, eyeing the laptop and array of papers on the table. "Breaker went out again. Get that checked by an electrician, Sheila. Soon."

He strode to the half bath where—oddly—a previous owner had placed the breaker for the outdoor electrical outlets. It had taken us both an age to find it the first time it decided to flip off, but by now it was routine.

Not a routine Teague approved of.

He was back with us in no time, asking, "What are you detecting?"

"Trying to detect," Clara corrected. "Trying to figure out the name of the woman with the little girl Rod Birchall wanted his picture taken with. We told you about her. She was really unhappy with Birchall— the woman, not the girl, although when her mother got upset, she cried. Anyway, things the woman said indicated she might have had a history with him."

As I got up to replenish her coffee and my ice water, Clara told him the searches we'd done.

He added ice to his thermos. "Impressive."

"But we're stuck now and we haven't found her."

"Not finding people is the detective's lot in life. Being stuck isn't. Keep searching. Include anything distinctive about her in your searches. Narrows the field." He opened the back door. "I mean it about the electrician, Sheila. You don't start contacting people and I'll hire one myself and bill you for his services—and mine for finding him."

The door closed behind him and Clara immediately said, "What do you think of what he said?"

"I'll get one, I'll get one. I was going to start calling between the meeting with the parks people and the meeting at the dog park yesterday, but I've been a little busy."

Oddly, I'd had no inclination to give up writing—or not writing—time to call electricians. But Teague didn't need to know that.

"No, no, I meant the other stuff—though you *should* get an electrician if Teague's worried. Ned knows people. I'll ask him. But I meant the other stuff he said about something distinctive."

"We don't know anything distinctive about her. No visible scars. Nice clothes, but how do we add that to a search? She was a woman shopping in the Jolly Roger in Haines Tavern, Kentucky with her daughter, who apparently has food allergies, potentially fatal food allergies and—"

My head jerked up. Clara's eyes sparked. We'd gotten it at the same time.

"Daughter. A daughter named Lorelei."

We got back to work, searching each of the names not yet eliminated in combination with "daughter" and "Lorelei." If that didn't work, we tried "daughter" alone.

One by one by one, we eliminated more. Passing the halfway mark on the list. Then three-quarters. Then—

"Got her. I think." I skimmed an account a second time. "This has *got* to be her. Karen Zalesk." It was the third to the last name.

"Thank heavens. I didn't want to have to start back through all those organizations. Does it mention Lorelei?"

"Not by name, but listen to this. There are a couple paragraphs from a roster of volunteers about what food labels mean to them, explaining why they're volunteering. This part—" I pointed to it on the screen, even though Clara couldn't see it. "—is where Karen Zalesk said her young daughter nearly died from a food allergy."

"That must have been terrifying. Now we know the woman's name, what's next?"

"We see where she lives and pay her a visit."

CHAPTER TWENTY-FIVE

But Karen Zalesk didn't live in Haines Tavern.

Or in Stringer.

Or anywhere in North Bend County that we could find.

We tried the last name without the first name with no better luck. We also searched for Lorelei, with and without Zalesk. No luck there, either.

"Let's expand the search to nearby counties and Cincinnati," Clara said.

"You think someone came from another county, much less across the river from Cincinnati, to shop at the Haines Tavern Jolly Roger?"

"No. But what else are we going to try?"

I started searching.

With the same result—no one by that name.

"What now?"

"Let's try that online neighborhood bulletin board," I said.

The woman wasn't registered. "If we ask if anyone knows her, someone could warn her we're looking for her and she might never be found."

"Right, and if Deputy Eckles found out, he'd have us drawn and quartered."

"Even with Hensen running this investigation, let's not put the idea in Eckles' head."

"Agreed." This time Clara sighed before asking, "So, what now?"

"Give up on this for the moment. And try something else. Like going to the Roger to see if the manager's there."

"We could call—No. Not a good idea considering his history with phone calls. Let's go. Besides, I have something else I want to do at the Roger."

"More orange juice?"

"No. An experiment."

✧ ✧ ✧ ✧

NORMALITY HAD RETURNED to the Haines Tavern Jolly Roger to the extent that Petey greeted us with a smile in the parking lot.

He also, however, shook his head and pursed his lips.

"Rough day, Petey?"

"Not like yesterday."

Clara and I nodded solemnly.

"Trouble," Petey intoned. "Those folks from corporate were trouble from the second they came speeding in here. That's when I let Jacqueline know what was on the doorstep. Car comes barreling straight at me like they'll run me down soon as look at me. I tell them they can't park there and the driver guy starts yelling out his window at me. Nasty. Then that other guy—the string bean that can't hold himself upright—gets out of the car and starts talking to me like I'm a halfwit.

"Didn't care who they inconvenienced, either. Tried to tell them folks couldn't get into the handicapped spots with them there. They didn't care.

"After a while—well, now, some good time after you two went in, a few of the regulars came out, telling me they tried to tell him what was what but he didn't listen. They're not all like that, folks that run companies. The good ones—rare as hen's teeth these days—want to know what customers think. Never him. Anyway, next thing I knew, the deputies were running up on us fast and then they weren't letting anybody in or out."

"Which customers came out and told you about what happened?"

He rattled off names. None were Aggie Hickmott or Phyllis Ezzard. "Said there was a set-to inside, customers telling him off and Mr. Bigshot not paying any attention."

"What about Aggie Hickmott or Phyllis Ezzard? Do you know them? Did you see them leave?"

"Know them. Can't say I saw 'em leaving."

"How about a man in his forties. Dark hair, white shirt, about this tall—" Clara held her hand above her head. Petey started shaking his head. "—wearing jeans. No?"

As Petey shook his head, he must have recognized our disappointment.

"Thing is, I'm not watching the doors all the time. Carts take me to one side or the other and I'm not going to see much of the opposite door, see? As much as I try to pay attention, people do come and go without me spotting them."

"You didn't see anybody in between the customers who told you about others complaining to the CEO and when the deputies arrived?"

He slanted a look up toward me. "Don't want to get anybody in trouble."

"If they didn't do anything wrong, you can't get them in trouble."

"Maybe. Maybe. That driver was out here the whole time."

"What about a woman with a little girl? Really cute little girl, blonde curls, maybe four years old. The woman had on a red top, jeans."

"Got a real nice smile out of the little girl as they went in. A bit of one from her mama—and she seems like a person who could use more smiles."

"What about leaving?"

He shook his head. "That was going in. Mind you, like I said, I'm not paying attention every second a door opens or closes. Got to keep the parking lot cleared of carts, get them wiped down, and back inside for folks to use. Otherwise, I'm not doing my job."

That was reasonable. And disappointing.

Knowing when any of the people left couldn't completely eliminate them, since the murderer could have struck any time from the moment Birchall went in back until Jacqueline spotted him on the floor—a span of at least fifteen minutes, probably closer to twenty. But it might trim the window of opportunity for yet.

Or, better yet, someone might have run out of the building gasping, *What have I done? What have I done?*

That would be a nice little hint.

"Petey, is the manager here today? Or the assistant manager, Jacqueline?"

"She's off today—"

Good thing we knew where to find her later.

"—but Kurt's here. Thing is, he's off on his break. Wouldn't expect him back for another ten minutes anyway. I can tell him when he gets back you want to see him and—"

"No, no. Don't—"

Before I could say more, Clara took my arm as she said to Petey, "We have other things to do inside first. We don't know exactly when we'll finish up. We'll look for him. No need for him to come looking for us until we're ready."

With thanks, we headed inside, with Clara steering me quickly, still with that hold on my arm.

"Why'd you stop me from telling Petey we didn't want him to warn Kurt Verker we want to talk to him?"

"Because then it becomes a matter of loyalty to tell Kurt. But if he thinks Kurt knowing might interfere with *our* convenience, that trumps loyalty to his boss."

"How on earth do you figure that?"

"Because Petey was born and raised in Kentucky and I know Kentucky men. Especially older Kentucky men." She practically tossed her hair as she took a cart and started off.

TORN BETWEEN A desire to laugh and a strong suspicion she was right, I hurried to catch up with her, partway down the frozen vegetable aisle, heading toward the back.

"I take it this is the time to conduct the experiment you mentioned?"

"It is."

"Going to share?"

She looked around. We were alone. "We've been talking lots about time, but we don't know how much time's involved. So we're going to time exactly how long it takes to get from each of the other back room doors to where Birchall was bashed on the head, presumably lying on the floor and vulnerable because of the food allergy reaction."

"Did you bring stopwatches?" I teased.

"Of course not. We'll use our phones.

We did.

But we had to adjust our experiment.

The door from the dairy section into the back was blocked to civilians by police tape. The next door, by the meat department was locked. As was the door between the bakery and the deli.

We timed covering the distances, but on the store side, instead of through the back room.

Clara noted each of our multiple trips.

"This was probably all useless," she grumbled at the end. "We kept needing to go around display cases and people with carts who suddenly stopped in the middle of the aisle."

"The back room path must have obstacles, too. I can't imagine it's a straight shot. Probably crates and freezers and such in the way."

She clicked her tongue. "So doing this was totally useless."

"Not at all. I don't know about you, Clara, but I'm impressed with how little time it took, even when we weren't walking fast. Walk to the door by dairy, walk across the back of the store, hit Birchall on the head, then return the way he or she came. Or come out another door. And if Foster or Jacqueline or the guy in jeans was alone for even a few seconds by the produce door it would take them hardly any time."

"How does that help us?"

"It keeps us from eliminating someone, thinking they didn't have enough time."

She gusted acceptance, mixed with irritation. "I suppose that's a help in a backward sort of way. Let's go see if we can find Kurt Verker now. Maybe that will be more useful."

"First, I have an experiment to try."

✦　✦　✦　✦

MINE WASN'T NEARLY as interesting as Clara's.

It consisted of walking up and down aisles looking at packaging.

"Is this it?" Clara asked for at the four-hundred-and-fifty-seventh time.

"No."

We'd made good time through aisles with laundry detergent, canned soup, pasta, but this snack aisle was slow-going. There were so many similar to—

"*That's* it."

I pointed at the package resembling a power bar in a plastic wrapper with a red ribbon, edged with yellow.

According to the package, it was a sesame snack bar.

Clara and I grinned at each other, then each grabbed a couple.

✦　✦　✦　✦

AS WE TURNED toward the front of the store, we practically ran into Belinda as she stood watching us.

"You, too?"

"Us two, what?" Clara asked.

Belinda jerked her head to the packages. "You and the deputies, getting those sesame snacks."

Clara and I looked at each other, as we realized she'd said "too" not "two," that meant we were behind the sheriff's department, but confirmed we had the right idea and the right wrapper.

"Hope they're good," Clara said with a smile.

Belinda looked uninterested. Yet she didn't move away.

I tried, "That was quite something that happened yesterday, wasn't it?"

She didn't respond.

More direct?

"Belinda, what's the snack in that sample tray by the deli?"

"What do you think?" She shook her head. "You and those deputies."

"Sesame?"

"Duh."

"Is that what's always there?"

"No. Changes all the time.

"Have the deputies been questioning people today?"

"Some. Want to know if we turned off the cameras up and down this aisle and other places. Like Verker wouldn't go ballistic if we did."

"Have they questioned Jacqueline again?"

"No idea. She's off today."

Clara frowned me quiet. "That must be unsettling. This store's so lucky to have you to step up when things go wrong."

"Not that it's appreciated."

"Isn't that the way. The most hard-working person gets over-looked."

"Too busy looking at a young blonde," Belinda grumbled. "Old fool. She's got a live-in boyfriend. Hear her talking to him all the time. *Poor Wade.*" She sneered in a falsetto that didn't sound at all like Jacqueline.

"Wade," Clara repeated in apparent disgust.

Me? I wasn't saying a word after that frown.

"Wade Edwards, something like that." Belinda made it sound like it confirmed all her worst thoughts about Jacqueline. Then she added, "Or Will or Walter or something."

Clara shook her head.

Apparently satisfied, Belinda said, much more cheerfully, "Got work to do."

She passed us and was gone.

"Can I talk yet?" I asked.

"You were going to blow the whole thing. Could tell you were getting fed up with her."

"What whole thing? She'd already confirmed we had the right package. And that Birchall took a sesame snack from the sample tray. That's what matters. And now we know Jacqueline has a boyfriend. That's not exactly shocking. She's a good-looking woman."

"It's a bridge to get Belinda to talk later if we need to and we could ask Jacqueline about it."

"Oh goody."

"You don't like talking about romantic relationships?" she said with great significance.

"I have no idea what you're talking about."

CHAPTER TWENTY-SIX

WE FOUND THE manager in his office.

Better yet, he didn't see us coming, so we got inside and had the door closed, with us in front of it, effectively blocking his escape, before he knew he wanted to escape.

"You can't come in here." Even he appeared to realize that was a futile complaint since we were in there.

The Haines Tavern Jolly Roger store manager was a sway-backed man who resembled a penguin in shape and walk, except he wasn't as colorful. Gray hair, gray face, gray clothes, gray shoes (they might once have been black), made even the black vest a relief. He was half a head shorter than me, which made me wonder if he'd hired Petey to feel tall.

"Mr. Verker, my name's Sheila Mackey."

"And you know me—Clara Woodrow."

"We were both here yesterday during—"

"I wasn't here."

"We know. But we also—"

"I don't know anything. I told the deputies that. Nothing."

"You told the deputies you didn't know *anything?*"

He licked his lips at my emphasis, but still went for bluster. "Yes, because that's the truth. I wasn't here. I don't know anything about the events."

"But you knew he was coming. Someone called and told you Rod Birchall, the CEO of the Jolly Roger chain, was coming here to your store yesterday, didn't they?"

His small eyes tightened to near pinpoints with the playing-possum frozen pose of the fearful.

Yes, I'd shifted from penguin to possum. Penguin was entirely too cute for this guy. Possum suited his coloring. Also his beady eyes and pointy nose.

"I have no idea what you're talking about. No way I could know about a surprise visit. I was taken ill and I went home."

"That's what you told the sheriff's department? Because they can check phone records, you know. Especially if somebody gives them a hint there's a specific reason to check."

His gaze darted from me to Clara, possibly looking for a way out.

He didn't find one.

He shrank into himself, resembling a possum curling up, preparing for the full playing-dead act. Except the protrusion of his belly prevented him from getting very tight.

"We could mention to the deputies our reasons for thinking they should check the phone records—"

"*No.* No." He slumped.

He didn't invite us to ask questions at will, but good as.

"What do you know about Rod Birchall?"

"Nothing. Not a thing. Never met the man."

"You've been with the chain a long, long time."

"He'd only been here a year or so."

"You have a lot of connections and friends and sources," Clara said. "Everybody says how well connected you are. If there's anybody who knows what's going on in the Jolly Roger chain, especially this area and that's including corporate headquarters, with it being just across the river, it's Kurt Verker. That's what everyone says. Why, the one person who'd—"

"He wasn't popular."

Fighting off a grin at Clara wearing him down, I asked, "Less popular than the previous CEO?"

The answer might give us a gauge of whether employee unhappiness centered on Birchall or more general unhappiness with the Jolly Roger chain.

"Oh, yeah. Lot's more unpopular."

It didn't take Freud to notice he'd switched from less popular to more unpopular.

"Why?"

His eyes shifted from me to Clara and back, gauging what we might know and how much he needed to tell.

If this was his demeanor while talking with Deputy Hensen he was probably at the top of the suspect list.

"You heard about all the people let go last week?"

We nodded.

"Tip of the iceberg. It wasn't only the numbers. It was targeted. People about to retire, people with a lot of experience, people providing strong leadership at their stores."

The first two applied to him. I had my doubts about the last one.

"And," Verker continued, "he planned more."

"But he told the media there wouldn't be more," Clara said.

"Yeah, that's what he told them. He was lying. Next round was coming early next month."

"How did that affect morale in this store?"

"How do you think?"

"Who would you say was most upset about it?"

"Jacqueline. She was real outspoken about those firings."

"Who else?"

He paused a moment. "Belinda. She's angry all the time. Gets real wound up about things."

Clara was indignant. "Of all the ungrateful—From what we heard, she was wound up on *your* behalf. She knows you're near retirement and was worried you'd get fired."

Did a possum ever breed with an ostrich? Because that's what Verker resembled—not moving while pretending he didn't see what was right in front of him.

"WE NEED TO keep an eye on Kurt Verker."

"But everybody agrees he wasn't at the store when Birchall was killed," Clara said.

"Everybody agrees he left. But he could have circled back. Petey said he didn't see everyone going in and out and who better to know how to get in and out unseen—not to mention disabling the cameras."

"Good points, he couldn't know Birchall would go in back alone."

"Okay, that's a stumbling block, but he has a motive," I continued. "He admitted barely escaping this recent round of firings, Birchall was targeting people nearing retirement to trim their benefits, and Verker himself said another round's coming."

"You're right. We need to keep him on the list. In the meantime, how about we go to Shep's Market to see if we can talk to Gundy Vance?"

"Perfect."

CHAPTER TWENTY-SEVEN

S**HEP'S** M**ARKET** **WAS** located a block and a half southwest of the yoga studio, with another two blocks to the town square. When Shep's was built in the early 1900s, that was on the outskirts of town.

Now, it reminded me of a Trader Joe's practicality and whimsy, with a touch of Whole Foods pretentiousness. Where the Roger is wide side to side, Shep's is modestly narrow, but deep.

We plunged past the entrance area to get into the store itself.

Automatically, I started toward the back left corner, in the vicinity of the meat and the deli.

On the way there, Clara stopped me with an arm on my sleeve.

She let go to greet the man I now knew as Gundy Vance, the owner of Shep's Market.

"Gundy, how nice to see you." They exchanged a friendly hug. "I was telling Sheila here about the history of Shep's Market. Gundy, this is Sheila Mackey. Sheila, this is Gundy Vance, owner of Shep's."

We exchanged good-to-meet-yous.

"Yes, Shep's been around for generations. I remember when my grandfather was running it and family lore is it was his grandfather who started it, maybe even another generation back. The person you need to talk to is Fern. Do you know—?" At my nod, he continued, "I swear she remembers every time she's walked in the door."

The mention of Fern reminded me that after trying to pump Clara at last night's yoga class, she hadn't seemed as interested at noon today. She must have found another source.

"It's remarkable and admirable to have kept the store running through all these years."

"Thank you. Don't let me hold up your shopping, though," he said. "Ah, no cart?"

Clara made a sound I talked over. "Picking up a few things. All the changes in the business you must have seen. Technology and automation and consolidating."

"It's not easy running a grocery store." He gave a not entirely pleasant chuckle. "Ask the Jolly Roger chain. They're having a tough time of it lately. The big chains had all sorts of advantages over us for a long time with their deals with big food manufacturers. The conglomerates did the advertising and the grocery stores served up the products the ads sent people looking for. But these days, those conglomerates don't need the Jolly Roger and the rest of them. They've got online outlets—their own and others—to drop the food on your doorstep."

"That sounds like it could create a rather dire landscape for a small, local store like this."

But he grinned.

"Stores like Shep's Market all sing *God Bless the Millennials*. They like local. They like small stores. They like individual, not mass produced."

"Oh."

We both looked at Clara after her burble of a syllable.

"Sorry, I was thinking about your ads. It's like you have two kinds. I was telling Sheila about your campaign that emphasizes the tradition of Shep's Market, how it's part of Haines Tavern's history. But you also have the ones that talk about the local producers and how fresh the food is."

He beamed at her. "You are one of the rare North Bend County consumers who straddles the divide, Clara. And very astute. Despite some doubters we took a two-pronged approached and it's worked.

"We give customers of all generations what they can't get at the Roger or online. Local food. Fresh. Not manufactured. And we let the producers set their own prices, so they're not beaten down to making nothing for all their work. We get a little for the selling. And our customers get a good deal.

"Plus, events." He turned to me. "I haven't seen you at any of our classes. Cooking, baking, food prep, wine pairings."

"I do, however, consume your prepared meals. That's what we're here for."

He grinned again. It began to feel like part of his uniform. "That's my wife, Judy. Another major benefit of Shep's Market over Jolly Roger or anywhere else. Come, come, let me walk you there."

He took Clara's arm. I followed along. He interrupted himself frequently to say hello to other shoppers, but still carried on a conversation with Clara. He reminded me of a bonhomous host at a restaurant.

"…and we have a great deal on pork roasts," he said.

"I could use one," Clara said. "Ned's had a rough week with traveling and lots of meetings, but he has Thursday and Friday off, so I'd like to give him a good dinner. He loves pork almost as much as steak and I like to indulge him because—"

"Pork is white meat," I said.

Clara turned an astonished look on me. "Red meat."

I quoted the old ad campaign. "The other white meat."

"It comes from an animal, not a bird."

"You're both right. Anyway, neither of you is wrong." Gundy Vance had our attention. "Traditional culinary view is that it's a white meat. But, since it does come from a mammal, nutrition specialists classify it as red, as does the USDA."

"I don't know if having the U.S. Department of Agriculture on your side makes you more right, but I concede," I said.

"The animal vs. bird argument becomes complicated," Gundy said, "because duck and goose generally have a higher fat content than, say, veal, which comes from an animal yet is often considered white meat."

"Concede," I repeated.

"It's a fascinating topic, especially with white meat being presented as healthier, even than dark meat of, say, chicken or turkey. Yet the war against fat has shown us it's not as straight-forward as people thought. And then butchers call fat white meat, which—"

"Gundy." A woman's voice called him back to the present from his happy contemplation of culinary matters.

He looked around to the small prepared meals kiosk tucked between the meat section and the deli with the same smile. "Judy. My wife and our secret weapon. You know Clara Woodrow, don't you? And this is Shelley—"

"I know Sheila." She made the correction firmly.

"I'm a regular here and now I know I've been enjoying Judy's talent. Thank you."

"You're welcome." She said it without a smile. She didn't smile a lot, though she was pleasant. Her focus stayed on Gundy. What followed sounded automatic. "Can I help you with something today?"

"You can. I'd like the salmon salad, please."

"Oh, me, too," Clara said. "Sounds great."

"But I'm also going to change things up and get a pork roast. Clara, you and Ned come to dinner at my house tomorrow night."

"We will," she said with pleasure. "Teague, too?"

I gave her a don't-push-it look.

She grinned, but said only, "I still want a roast, too, Gundy."

"We'll find you each a perfect one." He moved toward the chest holding the pork roasts, Clara preparing to follow him.

Then, Clara said in her friendliest voice, "But, Gundy, why were you at the Roger yesterday?"

CHAPTER TWENTY-EIGHT

SILENCE FOLLOWING A question like that wasn't unexpected. Add in the impression that time froze, though, and you had a notable reaction.

Gundy shot a look at his wife. Worried? Wary? Not knowing the man, I had no idea.

As far as I could tell, she did not react to the look or to the question.

"Yes, Gundy," Judy Vance said, "tell us why you were at the Roger."

His smile returned, a little rusty. "Checking out the competition, of course. We've turned the corner here at Shep's, but we can't afford to let up now."

Clara's eyes went wide. "Were you trying to find out about upcoming specials the Roger was going to have?"

He laughed—better than the smile. "Like they'd tell me ahead of time, Clara. In fact, they seem to be following *our* specials. Now, let's get a roast for Sheila and one for you and Ned to have later."

Judy watched the retreating pair. Slowly, her gaze shifted from them to me.

"Salmon salads?" she asked coolly.

"Yes, please. Two."

My relief at the normality of her question evaporated with the next one.

"Why are you asking my husband about a murder?"

Where was that advantage Clara said we had of people not thinking we were interrogating them or about to haul them off to jail? I didn't have any of that advantage with this woman.

"We aren't. Only about his being at the Roger yesterday. Lots of people were."

She didn't buy that. "You're asking a lot of questions."

Had she known her husband had been in the Roger yesterday before Clara's question?

I met and held her gaze. "It's hard not to when you were there when a man was murdered."

"It's not a reason to suspect my husband."

"I, uh, I don't suspect anyone specifically." Not to the extent of pointing a finger and shouting, "*J'accuse.*"

She broke the look, sliding the cartons into bags with her usual care, then handing them over, still not smiling.

"Here. As usual, the salmon, salad, and dressing are separate to avoid sogginess. Mix them immediately before eating. The ingredients are listed on the card, also as usual. All the ingredients."

ONE OF THE services Shep's offered was to hold onto purchases, especially the prepared meals, in a cold case. The customer could come back in or have a service deliver it to them. It facilitated customers' impulse buys, when they otherwise would have skipped the purchase because they weren't going home next.

That's what I opted for.

"We have time before yoga to eat our salads," Clara said. "We could stop by your house. In fact, we could go to yours *and* mine, drop everything off."

"Leave yours here, too. C'mon, let's go. We'll eat backward to-night—dessert at the café first, then the salads."

She picked up the message that I had somewhere else I wanted to get to before yoga. She was tactful enough not to ask until we were in the car. "Where are we going?"

"Let's go back and see if Petey's still at the Roger."

"He won't be, not at this time. But I don't mind checking if you tell me why."

"Did you notice when you were asking him about the guy in jeans that he didn't start to shake his head until you indicated his height? And then the head shakes became more vehement, almost relieved when you mentioned jeans."

She frowned. Then her eyebrows popped up. "Oh. Because Gundy was wearing khakis? You think he thought I was describing Gundy?"

"It's a possibility. He never mentioned Vance being at the store. More of his loyalty?"

"Highly possible. He was pretty reluctant to talk about anybody except Foster and Isaac."

"True. Let's see if we can pin him down a bit more."

"Sure. What do you think about what happened in there with the Vances? She was very cool about her husband being at the Roger," Clara said. "Which could be a sign she's certain he's innocent."

"Or she doesn't care whether he's innocent or not. And that could mean a couple things, too. She knows he killed Birchall and she is all for that. Or she doesn't care."

"I've never heard anything about there being trouble in their marriage. Of course, you don't always hear ahead of time. There are always breakups that surprise you, just like there are people who stick together that surprise you."

"All true. The best thing we can probably do now is keep our ears open. We need more information."

"I DON'T BELIEVE it," Clara said after I pulled up next to Petey in the Roger parking lot. As soon as we were out, she said to him, "What are you still doing here at this hour?"

"Double shift. Mother of one of the guys doesn't want her baby where there'd been a murder."

"Petey, was there anyone else you saw coming or going yesterday, say from the time that group of customers came out, telling you about the dispute between other customers and Rod Birchall, to when the deputies arrived."

He rubbed his stubbled chin. "Well, now, not that I recall."

Clara gave me a tiny head shake. I interpreted it as meaning she thought he was holding back. I also took it to mean I was free to try my ignorant-of-Kentucky-men methods.

"Petey, we know Gundy Vance was in the store here yesterday when—"

"During that period," Clara spoke over me.

Another instance of her knowing Kentucky men? I let her ending stand instead of my harsher *the murder was committed*. "We both saw him ourselves."

"Ah. Well, now." He lifted, then lowered his shoulders.

"Why didn't you tell us before?"

"Didn't want to get anybody in trouble. Nonsense to think he could have done anything. Was hardly in there more than five minutes."

Which we knew from our experiments was more than enough time to accomplish the deed. Though spotting Birchall and recognizing the opportunity could expand the time needed.

"When did Gundy Vance come out?"

"Let me think. Not long before the deputies came. Got into two cars and seems to me they were waiting to get on the highway when the lights and sirens started coming over the hill."

He tipped his head in that direction, but neither Clara nor I looked.

"*They?*" we said in unison.

He looked down. "Wasn't anything in it. I don't want to get anybody in trouble."

"About what?"

"His coming out with them, that woman and little girl. He wasn't there when they went in earlier, before that Birchall arrived," he said quickly, as if declaring their innocence.

"You said you didn't see the woman and her daughter leave," Clara accused.

He shook his head. "Said I didn't always see everyone coming or going. A mother like her. Fair dotes on that girl. She wouldn't do anything bad. And she was that upset when she came out. But doing her best to calm that baby girl, with tears streaming from eyes that should only be smilin' blue."

"But you did see them leave? And with Gundy, because you know him, right?"

"I know him right enough. Donates regular to the food bank and brings meals for those who need it. My sister included when she was off work before I came to live with her. And the food he donates is good, not like the garbage from this place. He's a fine man. Fine."

"You saw him leave with the woman and Lorelei?" I asked succinctly and directly.

"Lorelei? Is that the name of the dear little girl?"

"It is. Did you see Gundy leave the store with her and her mother?"

"What if I did? He wouldn't kill anybody, not over business. Even his family's market. I don't want—"

"We know. You don't want to get them in trouble," Clara soothed.

"Do you know who they were? The woman and little girl?"

"First time I've seen them here. Cute little girl."

I was direct. "Would you recognize Gundy Vance's wife?"

"No." His firmness conveyed he did not want to get involved in anything to do with that—which hinted that not only would he recognize Judy Vance, but she wasn't the woman Gundy accompanied out of the store.

The woman with a little girl. Karen Zalesk and Lorelei.

CHAPTER TWENTY-NINE

UNLIKE THE DOGS' feelings about two trips to the dog park in one day, I was not entranced by a second yoga class. Especially not flow. Especially not when we'd been burned a while back by what wasn't even supposed to be a flow class, but inflicted nearly double digit sun salutations on us.

We knew this instructor but hadn't taken classes from her.

Didn't matter. Our reason for attending was Jacqueline taking the class. We exchanged hellos with her, but didn't push now. That would come later.

Also in the class, was a surprise—eighty-something-year-old Fern. At least I'd keep up with her.

✧　✧　✧　✧

I DIDN'T.

I am not talking anymore about that flow class.

Except to say the instructor twice asked if I was okay. Yes, I was breathing heavily, but it might have been the result of flashbacks to another class with more sun salutations than you could shake a stick at, which was followed shortly by murder.

I don't understand the fixation on sun salutations. I held my own with the warriors of various numbers, reverses, triangle, cobra, but those sun salutations—No, I wasn't talking about it.

Fern, of course, was chipper.

And chatty.

Although we kept a close eye on Jacqueline, talking with the instructor, Eloise, we didn't shoo off Fern.

Perhaps Clara, too, was remembering Gundy Vance's recommendation we talk to the older woman.

"You need to come to this class more often," Fern started.

"You're right," Clara said.

I growled—at both of them.

Fern chuckled. "Right there's the proof. What have you two lady detectives been up to today?"

We exchanged a look. By the agreement in that look, I said, "We went into Cincinnati early to talk to Foster Utton—the man who came here with Rod Birchall yesterday. Tried to find the limo driver, too, but he's been fired."

"What did this Foster person tell you?"

"Not a lot. He seems quite out of his depth as the interim CEO."

"When you've been dreaming after something for a long time, reality can bite you in the butt. I'll tell you something interesting in turn. I heard somebody might be staying out at the old Family Place near the river."

For once Clara appeared as lost as I was about something to do with North Bend County.

"That's the *Gundy* old Family Place, not the *Vances'*. Vances've had Shep's Market forever, right back to Shep himself. The old Family Place belonged to the Gundys, only these days, the ones left are part Vance, too. Call it their fishing shack now."

"And there's somebody staying there?" Clara asked.

She sliced a look toward me, asking if I saw how Petey's report of Gundy leaving with a woman and little girl might tie in with somebody staying at Gundy Vance's "old Family Place," and our lack of success finding Karen Zalesk and her daughter.

I did.

"That's what I hear," Fern confirmed.

"A female somebody?"

She tipped her head, less like a coquette than a mischievous squirrel. "Now, why do you ask?"

"There were women customers at the Roger yesterday we'd like to talk to. As witnesses."

She nodded before I finished. "Phyllis Ezzard and Aggie Hickmott. Know about them. They surely aren't staying out at the Gundys' old Family Place."

"There was another customer." I chose my words carefully. "We'd like to talk to her. Get her impressions and recollections."

Her eyes glittering more strongly with mischief, she plowed through my careful words. "You think Gundy Vance has a woman on the side?"

"Now, Fern, don't go starting rumors."

"It's not a rumor if it's true."

"We have no reason to believe it is true, though."

"You might not, but I might."

"What do you know, Fern?"

"Oh. *Know.* That's a strong word. Too strong for my taste. I might have an idea or two." The glitter in her eyes intensified. "Want to know how to get to the Gundy old Family Place on the river?"

We did.

PERFECT TIMING.

Fern had finished giving us the address and a set of directions resembling the path squirrels take through my back yard, including "third tree on the left," when Jacqueline said good-bye to Eloise and started toward the door.

We intercepted her. It almost looked natural.

The vestibule had cleared out, so we had only Fern and Eloise as witnesses when we invited her to a glass of wine and dessert at the café.

She hesitated, then accepted.

More good fortune met us at the café when we spotted a table for four in the corner with none of the seats near it occupied.

After we ordered, Jacqueline said, "I'm sure you've got questions. I hadn't realized you two had been involved in solving a couple murders until people started telling me about it last night and today. But I really shouldn't say anything."

Before Clara or I could respond, Jacqueline added, "Oh. Except thank you. You kept your heads and calmed down the others. I appreciate that. You both were kind to stay yesterday and to talk to the sheriff's department."

If only the sheriff's department felt the same way.

"Amid all the chaos, you were troupers. Thank you."

Clara put one hand over hers on the table. "Of course we wouldn't desert you after what happened. Even before the murder—"

Jacqueline winced at the word.

"—it was pretty appalling the way Rod Birchall acted, the way he treated people. Maybe it wasn't as surprising for you if you knew what was coming, if you'd encountered him before, or—"

"No, I'd never met him before. And we had no warning. I was so shocked, I … I don't know that I handled it well. I was uncomfortable with him from the start and then he irritated me."

She produced a smile, but whatever relaxation Jacqueline had achieved from the yoga class ebbed away, leaving her face rigid. She slid her hand from under Clara's.

Our wines and desserts arrived, fresh strawberries for Jacqueline, chocolate and caramel layers the café called, with great ingenuity, chocolate and caramel layer dessert for Clara and me.

"Though now none of that hardly matters, does it? Considering," Jacqueline said in a low voice as the waiter left us.

"You mean you think the Jolly Roger CEO dying on your watch, so to speak, might be bad for your career?" I asked.

Jacqueline's mouth twisted in acknowledgment. "It sure won't help."

Clara looked indignant. "They can't blame you for that. Not unless—" She stopped herself from tactlessly raising the possibility of Jacqueline being the murderer. "If that hurts your career, you have to fight it. That's not fair."

"I don't think it would do any good to fight it."

"Have you been with the Jolly Roger chain long?" I asked.

"Four years. I started with a store in Indiana, working my way up, all at the one store until four months ago when I was promoted to assistant manager and transferred here. It's been ... different. My manager at the other store was such a dynamo, taught me so much. Truly my mentor. It's been an adjustment coming here and working under a, um, new style."

"And new customers?"

Her first genuine smile appeared. Maybe it was the strawberries. The chocolate and caramel layers dessert made me want to smile, too. And say *Mmmm*. I resisted that temptation, considering our underlying topic.

"The customers have been a true bright spot. Not that the employees aren't hard-working—I'm not saying that. But some are ... wary. And, I guess you could say, worn down. But the customers say hello and they're friendly. Even when there's a complaint, people are generally polite and rather laidback. I think we have Petey to thank."

"Absolutely, you have Petey to thank. He makes everyone feel welcomed and puts them in a good mood." Clara smiled back at her.

"Too bad Petey's charms didn't work on Rod Birchall." I dragged the topic back to yesterday's events. "He seemed incredibly brusque. Had something happened that made him ill-tempered?"

"You mean like being born?" Clara asked.

For a moment, I thought her comment had sent the honesty I'd seen trembling on Jacqueline's lips back into hiding. But Clara, whether from knowledge or instinct, had hit the right note.

"He was like that from the second he walked in," Jacqueline said. "In fact, even before he came in, his driver caused a ruckus with Petey—*Petey*. But from what I've heard, that's how he always was."

I leaned forward.

"Jacqueline, we know that since Birchall was brought in there's a lot of unhappiness among Jolly Roger employees. And never more so than with all those firings last week." This had been widely reported, so I wasn't breaking new ground. "As well as customers, as we heard yesterday."

That last part could have lightened her mood. It didn't.

But she did latch onto the topic of customers, skipping the employees' unhappiness.

"They aren't happy. Can't blame them. But our hands are tied on almost of all of it. We have to tell them to call the customer service line with complaints—but the information never goes up the chain." She grimaced. "Even if it did, would anything change? What does happen is the information's sent back to the individual store and we're told to deal with making the customer happy. We're judged on whether we do or not, even when the complaint is about something the store has no control over."

"Was that what had happened to the customers who confronted Birchall?"

"I couldn't say—"

"The woman with the little girl…"

She shook her head. "I don't know her."

"Did you see her again after the photo-taking fiasco?"

"No." Her eyebrows lifted in surprise, apparently the first she'd heard of the woman being around.

"Or do you know the man in jeans who was supposed to stay with the body."

"I've only been here four months—"

"Aggie Hickmott and Phyllis Ezzard?"

"Yes, we've passed on their issues to corporate, with no success."

"That can't help employee morale."

She looked down and speared another strawberry with her fork.

I pushed a little harder. "How has it been dealing with the employees when there's that lack of support, not to mention the firings."

Another strawberry paid the ultimate price.

"It's been *awful*. They keep changing things. All for the worse. It's like they read every bit of feedback we give them and they do the opposite. Do they think annoying the customers is the way to increase business? Because that's what they're doing. Annoying customers and firing so many of the best workers and then wearing out the rest.

"We're supposed to have a four-person management team, but we have two—two—and the manager's gone most of the time. He's weeks away from retirement and he's terrified if anyone from the company sees him, they'll fire him before his date. I can't really blame him. That sweep of employees last week? They terminated a high percentage of well-salaried butchers and managers near retirement."

"They're kicking them out so they don't have to pay them anything in retirement? That stinks," Clara said.

Jacqueline nodded. "Hourly workers see what happens to management and very few want to get promoted. Which is why we only have two managers at this store. And that's not unusual. Most stores are understaffed—hourly and management."

"If they're that low on managers why don't they hire from outside?"

To my surprise, Clara answered my question. "What I read last night said they can't attract outside hires. Several commenters said outside hires who've previously been in good situations won't stick around."

Jacqueline humphed agreement. "The ones who know better."

"What else did you read last night?" I asked Clara.

"The Jolly Roger chain's supposed to be trying a big turnaround, but it's not going well and the management team led by Birchall is the reason according to several experts. They say they're making exactly the same mistakes that sent a chain in Idaho into bankruptcy—"

"PFFT—P F F T," I said.

"—including downscaling, limiting selection, stocking mostly house brands, cutting employees and service—pretty much what we heard from the customers and Jacqueline yesterday."

The assistant manager added, "Did you notice no upper management jobs were cut? And then, after Birchall ran that chain into the ground, he was rewarded by being put in charge of the Jolly Roger chain."

Something in her voice cut sharper than disgust or even anger.

"That manager who was your mentor at the store in Indiana, she was one of the people fired last week, wasn't she?"

Jacqueline's jaw tightened enough that she needed a moment to get out the word, "Yes."

CHAPTER THIRTY

"How did you know her mentor was fired?" Clara asked as soon as we were in my car.

I held up a finger in a one-minute gesture. "Let's call the delivery service before it closes, get our Shep's groceries to our houses."

"Sure. I'll do that."

When she'd finished, I said, "As for the mentor being fired, pure guess. It seemed to mean too much to Jacqueline for it to *not* be personal. But how did you know all about the corporate turnaround?"

"Research online last night. I was looking for information on Foster Utton before going to see him this morning."

"And you didn't share?"

"Didn't find anything about him. Not a thing. It's like he barely exists. His name's listed in a few places, but no bio or background or anything. But I kept falling over these articles saying how bad the turnaround was going.

"They bought a chain of several stores around Charlotte, North Carolina that had live piano music and short-order grills and wine bars, along with great meat and produce. They were beloved. When the Jolly Roger people took over—in other words, Birchall—everything changed. All the special elements were stripped away practically overnight. Now they're regular Roger stores and sinking fast."

"Sounds dumb. But do you think Birchall was killed because of bad management moves?"

"Doesn't seem likely, does it?"

"No, it doesn't. And with him dying the way he did… Unless it turns out to be an accident after all—"

She shook her head vigorously. "Bashed in the head."

"—it seemed personal."

"I agree. At first I thought maybe Jacqueline, because she was upset with him, but after listening to her and all the stuff about management and employees and demotions and all, that seems more about business. I guess that can be personal, too, but, even as upset as she was about the manager she liked, would she kill the CEO?"

THE SERVICE DELIVERED just after I arrived home.

Putting away the food, I pulled out the ingredients card and left it beside the salad.

As I ate, I considered the card. I'd never looked at them closely before.

If I'd thought about the listing of the ingredients at all, I'd viewed it as a sort of a "nothing up my sleeve" statement.

Or a challenge. *Here are all the things that went into it. If you think you can do as well, go for it.*

Now, I thought about the woman who'd written the card and her husband, who'd been in his rival's store when the CEO was killed.

Had he known Birchall was there? How much coincidence was that if he hadn't known?

But then why go? Despite his bravado in talking about the Roger copying Shep's specials, there'd been worry in his eyes. Fear, even.

If someone was feeding him the specials, could he have been there to meet them? But why the store of all places? And why then? And, finally, why then leave with Karen Zalesk?

Had he gone to meet Karen Zalesk?

A woman with a daughter...

A mother who said the girl had food allergies, potentially fatal food allergies.

I tapped the card against the table. For that little girl and her family a card like this became a lifeline.

DAY THREE

WEDNESDAY

CHAPTER THIRTY-ONE

"**It's supposed to** rain today," Teague announced when I opened my back door to his morning knock.

"Thank you for that weather report."

"Have you found an electrician?"

"Of course not. It's only been—"

"Too long. I found someone. Highly recommended. Including by your friend Urban Parham, the historian. He—"

"How do you know Urban?"

"—says this guy is great on historical houses, which means he should be able to deal with your strange system. He's available now, then not for a long stretch as he's updating several houses for a landlord. I propose he comes today and probably tomorrow. I can be here with him. Show him what I've seen, learn about the system to relay to you. That way you don't have to interrupt your—" He coughed slightly. "—activities, but you'll still have an electrical system I don't wake in a cold sweat worrying will fry you and Gracie."

"You've really been that worried?"

"Close."

I rapidly assessed. No electrician search, a guy vouched for by Urban, getting it done, Teague relieving me of needing to be on hand all day … All I had to do was pay.

"Deal. Thanks. Thanks a lot. In fact," I added impulsively, "I'm cooking dinner for Clara and Ned tonight. Want to join us as a thank you?"

"Thanks. Yes. I'll plan on it."

"Of course I'll pay you for your time."

"Not for dinner you won't."

I laughed in gratitude for his keeping it light and keeping the lines in place. There'd been a time at Clara and Ned's house once—his hand over mine, the warmth and strength—when I wondered... But, no.

"For electrician duty."

THE FOUR OF us—Clara and LuLu, Gracie and me—hit the dog park far earlier than usual.

That was even after I'd been at the house to meet the electrician. He was shockingly young, but touched the woodwork of the house with a respect and fondness. And Gracie liked him.

That left my mind at ease as I moved to the important matters of the day, starting with getting to the dog park early.

Early enough that Aggie Hickmott was not yet there with her dog Simba, when our goal had been to overlap with her.

Early enough to raise Donna's eyebrows, when our goal had been to keep a low profile.

We chatted with Donna and others, not bringing up the murder on Covert Circle and not participating if others did. This appeared to amuse Donna greatly.

As she prepared to leave, she suggested we walk with her and Hattie to the gate.

"Admirable restraint." That murmur appeared to be directed toward Hattie, but since the aging golden was mellow in the extreme, I suspected it was meant for Clara and me. "Surely you have something to ask me."

"As a matter of fact..." Clara asked if she knew anyone in the county named Karen Zalesk.

"I know a number of Karens, but no one with that last name."

Our description didn't help any.

As Donna and Hattie left the gated area for the parking lot, a woman with a terrier mix with a neon green collar and leash approached. Donna looked back at us with a grin. "Good hunting."

I showed further admirable restraint—and good judgment—by keeping quiet and letting Clara make contact with Aggie Hickmott.

"Hi. I *thought* I recognized you at the Roger the other day. What an adorable guy you have there. Simba, right? Isn't it awful how we know the dogs' names and not the humans'?"

Clara clearly didn't think it was awful, but rather the way things should be. Aggie Hickmott appeared to agree.

Contact.

After a few more Clara sentences, drawing me in, and touching on the customer-CEO conflict, Aggie was the one to bring up the subject of his murder.

"Unpleasant man. I don't suppose he deserved to die, though." She didn't sound completely convinced.

"Had you ever met him before?"

"Never."

"Had any correspondence with him?"

"Correspondence? You mean like emailing him or writing a letter?"

"Or a phone call."

"No."

"Oh? That's not—"

Clara talked over me. "We could swear we'd heard you took the lead in a matter involving the Jolly Roger chain…"

"You mean about when they wouldn't recall that dog food?"

That sure deflated my *gotcha* mode. "Yes."

"Mind you, I get Simba's things at Zepke's," she said of a local pet store. "But we can't have dogs getting dangerous food because their owners shop at the Roger. That's why I got on them about not recalling it. Never got to Birchall. Went to see him. Decided it would be better to show up at his office. Closest I got was a shrew outside his door. Has no soul that one. All she could talk about was not leaving dog hair on their furniture. Stayed an extra hour after it was clear he wasn't coming in, just to get her goat."

"Then you gave up?"

"Heck, no, I didn't give up. I got a call from a reporter from Channel 8—you know the one," she said to Clara. "The little one with the long dark hair who's interviewed you?"

"Bianca Abernathy? She's a sweetheart, isn't she?"

"More important, she has a dog," Aggie said. "She turned up the heat under Birchall and he folded."

"As he should have. In fact, they should have withdrawn that food without any heat," Clara said. "Were you at the Roger to check over the dog food or pick up a few things?"

"I keep my eye on the pet aisle whenever I'm there." She shifted her weight. "Wish I could find a few things when I went there. Half the time I come away without half of what I wanted."

"I know what you mean. It's crazy a store that big seems to have half as much as Shep's."

The woman's expression simultaneously closed off and sharpened. Her shoulders rose. Either she was trying to keep her ears warm or she was defensive.

An awfully strong reaction to Clara's casual comment about grocery inventories.

"I prefer Shep's, of course, but sometimes you can't avoid going to the Roger." Clara was feeling her way.

"Nobody can. *Nobody.*"

A light went on in Clara's eyes. She'd just comprehended something in Haines Tavern-speak that remained a foreign language to me. One no translation app had tackled.

"That's so true. And there's nothing to be done about it and no reason to feel odd about it. Especially not when ... well, when *everyone* comes into the Roger."

"They do, don't they." She and Clara had created a rapport.

"Though," Clara said delicately, "it can still be a surprise when…"

"Beyond a surprise."

"I *know.*" Clara's warm agreement was actually for the woman agreeing with *her,* but I detected Aggie's shoulders easing slightly, though still in earmuff territory. "I nearly hid behind my cart when I saw… Which makes no sense. I mean being embarrassed about being at the Roger when… Well, I wasn't the only one."

"I reacted the exact same way. I ducked out of his sight when he went past. It's instinct to not have him see you, even though he's there, too."

Him?

I realized Clara had been careful not to specify gender—or anything else. Smart.

And now, as I reviewed what had been said, the mists parted.

Aggie Hickmott had seen Gundy Vance.

"I imagine he knows that woman," Aggie said.

What woman trembled on Clara's lips. I was sure, because it trembled on my lips, too.

Our lips did not succumb, however.

"I'm sure you're right," Clara assured her.

Aggie's shoulders dropped toward a more comfortable position. "Friend of the family, no doubt. Wife probably sent him."

"That would be just like her, wouldn't it?"

"Exactly." She expelled a long breath. "And that woman sure was upset after what happened with Birchall and her daughter."

Ding. Ding. Ding.

CHAPTER THIRTY-TWO

NOT ONLY HAD Aggie seen Gundy in the Roger around the time of Rod Birchall's murder, but she confirmed he'd been with our former mystery woman, Karen Zalesk. Well, still partial mystery woman.

And with a different slant from Petey's sighting.

"I mean, she was angry with Birchall," Aggie said, "but she was practically beside herself when Gundy came around that floor case in front of the cheese—you know, where they have pre-packaged seafood and such."

I did know, as I was sure Clara did. It was in front of the door to the back room by the dairy products.

"My, my, my." Clara sounded as if she belonged on a veranda, fanning herself. "She was angry at him? Gundy?"

"She was so angry about Birchall I doubt there was room for much of anything else." She slid a look toward Clara, then away. "The little girl clearly knew him."

"As you said, a friend of the family."

"Of course, of course. That must be it. You could say he was protective, too, sort of bundling them all toward the door at double speed." She paused a moment. Her vacant stare made me guess she was thinking back to what she'd seen and heard. "Must know each other quite well, the way he scolded and she snapped back at him."

She blinked back to us and—unfortunately—an apparent awareness of all she'd said.

I rushed in with, "How did you discover the Jolly Roger CEO was in our store in the first place?"

The *our* was a nice touch, I thought.

She started with the obligatory justification.

"I'd gone in to pick up a few things, only because I was driving past and I had a full schedule. Shep's is my regular store. I'm barely in to an aisle and I heard him. Hard not to. He was braying at the new assistant store manager. Birchall wanted the manager, which proves he was an idiot, because anyone more useless than Kurt Verker I've yet to meet. As if any further proof were needed about Birchall's stupidity."

I'll admit, my first thought was the teacherly woman—and my great aunt—would be pleased at her correct use of the conditional "were" in that last sentence.

Secondarily, I agreed with the sense of what she'd said.

Rod Birchall hadn't exhibited a high level of logic in his dispute with her. Low cunning maybe, but not high logic.

"Then," Aggie continued, "he piled on more proof every time he opened his mouth."

She repeated all of the conversation we'd already heard because we'd been there. No, I didn't point that out. Clara's tact might be rubbing off on me.

Abruptly, as if she realized she'd said too much, or possibly spotting rain-threatening clouds overhead, she said, "Gotta go. Way past time to get Simba home. We popped in for a short visit."

Simba looked up at her with a clear message of *Don't blame it on me.*

CLARA AND I collected our dogs, made easier because this was a lull between waves of dogs—possibly a protracted lull considering the thickening and spreading clouds—and they wouldn't be missing anything by leaving.

"She should tell Deputy Hensen about Gundy Vance and Karen Zalesk," I said.

"You sound like Teague now," Clara protested.

"This is serious, Clara. A man with a strong motive—perhaps the strongest motive—was not only in the store at the right time for Birchall's murder but with the woman who'd had the most acrimonious confrontation with Birchall, *and* Vance hustled her out of the building."

"Hensen's had the chance to talk to the same people we have."

"We didn't tell him we'd seen Gundy in the store—I didn't even know we had. And Petey left out Gundy being there when he first talked to us, much less about seeing him with Karen Zalesk and Lorelei—even if he doesn't know their names. What if he hasn't told Hensen? That's important information. It pushes finding her higher up our priority list."

"It does," she agreed eagerly. "We can drop the dogs off and take Fern's directions and—"

"Not now. Yes, to dropping the dogs off, but then we have an appointment."

"We do?"

"After what Ms. DesJames and Foster said yesterday, I Googled car and hire and Isaac in Cincinnati and there he was. We're going for a drive today."

"That's great. But I'm not sure he'll consider it exactly an appointment."

We both chuckled. I stopped first.

"Back to telling Hensen. Between what Petey said—though he downplayed the woman being upset—and what Aggie said, it changes the complexion of Gundy coming out with them."

"When you put it like that…"

"That's how *she* put it."

"Not exactly. Besides, Hensen could have asked her the same things I did and heard the same thing."

"He couldn't have asked the same way. That was masterly."

Clara turned to me, beaming. "I know why you said masterly and not masterful. Because masterly is about mastering a skill, but masterful is about dominating, often another person. I looked that up recently."

"You are amazing, Clara. And not only for doing all this work toward being an author assistant. You can get anyone to tell you the truth."

"Like you?"

"Far better than me. I ask them what I want to know, but you get them to voluntarily tell you what you want to know."

"I mean like I could even get you to tell me the truth?"

My breath stopped. I was about to become an experiment in how long before a human popped from holding her breath.

Or be scared to death by the prospect of the truth.

Damn secrets.

Pretending to examine raindrops hitting the windshield, I produced a chuckle, as if she'd been kidding. Actually not a bad one. Was I getting good at this?

"I'm not forgetting about telling Hensen." I pretended not to hear her sigh following my words. "In fairness, he can't ask these questions the way you did or in a laidback atmosphere like this."

"Laidback? Not so sure," she said dryly, as two owners in the small-dog area fussed at each other over whose dog had done what in a slight and long-over scuffle, while the dogs trotted over to the same blade of grass for a thorough side-by-side sniff.

"You know what I mean. Not a whiff of officialdom. And if he tried your wide-eyed best-buddy routine, he'd probably get slapped with sanctions."

She chuckled. "Tell you what, if we don't have it solved by Monday, we'll tell him."

Great. A deadline.

Considering I'd reacted to my self-imposed writing deadlines by blowing them off to solve a murder, I could hardly wait to see what I found to counter that deadline.

CHAPTER THIRTY-THREE

"YOU TWO? WHAT the hell do you want?"

Isaac's greeting ruined the effect of his standing by the driver's side passenger door, politely holding it open with an umbrella overhead.

Clara went around to the far side, so I went to the open door. "We hired a car and driver—your car and you—that's what we want."

"To go where?"

"Nowhere. To stay here and talk."

"You're going to pay me to sit and talk?"

"Your regular rate."

"With maybe a tip," Clara said, "Since you've got it set up so I've got a grownup seat, instead of that little one facing the back."

THE PROMISE OF pay—and possible tip—relaxed Isaac.

He insisted on sitting in the driver's seat, but with the divider down and him slewed around to face us, it was a good setup.

"Birchall wasn't all bad. Get him where he wanted to go when he wanted to be there without him ever noticing the trip and he was okay. Got real pissed when traffic screwed things up. Not the only one I drive like that. Whatever he said bounced off as long as his check didn't bounce. And it never did. Otherwise, the job's mostly waiting around, being ready to go the second he wanted, and making sure morons don't mess up my car."

Without success, we tried different approaches to get some insight to Birchall's time since becoming CEO of the Jolly Roger chain, his relationship with the board, any threats or enemies.

As he had in the housewares aisle, Isaac maintained he was the hear-no-evil monkey. His evil-seeing was reserved for other drivers.

That he'd have happily expounded on. Since we were paying, though, I cut off the rant.

"Let's start at the beginning of Monday. Had you driven Rod Birchall earlier in the day, before driving him here to Haines Tavern?"

"Sure. Drove him to the corporate building like I did every day unless he was flying somewhere or was out of town."

"Anywhere else that morning?"

"Nope. Got called to have the car at the rear entrance, got there early, Birchall was about a minute late. He called to Utton while I was reconfiguring the car so Utton faced backward. Then Birchall reamed him out for being late." Isaac grinned appreciatively at this petty tactic.

Or perhaps it was at both tactics—the reconfiguration and the late call. Unless…

"Was someone else supposed to accompany Birchall on the surprise visit to the Haines Tavern store?"

"No. Ms. Des-Bitch said it was going to be Utton when she gave me the day's rundown."

Birchall's late call to Utton had been a little entertainment for a bully.

"You arrive at Haines Tavern. What happens next?"

"Pipsqueak in the parking lot mouths off from the start about not caring if he was the CEO, he wasn't parking in front of the door. That lame-ass Utton tries to make peace. Gets nowhere, as always." I believed we might have stumbled on the reason Isaac was not driving for the acting Jolly Roger CEO. "So, I get out and tell the pipsqueak we we're parking there, if I have to run his scrawny ass over." He and Birchall sounded like they'd been soul brothers.

"Then what?"

"What do you mean, *then what?* I wait. Like always. Set up cones so no idiot drivers could scratch her up. Or those carts—God, those carts ought to be outlawed. Then I check the inside. Use the vacuum, pick up after them. Outside, wipe marks so she glows. Then wait and wait more."

"And went in the store. When?" His lips had parted to deny it. I added the question in hopes of avoiding the no-I-didn't yes-you-did back and forth waste of time.

It worked.

"Hell if I know. Needed to use the can. Went in, did that, came back and waited more."

Yet we'd seen him in the store.

"Turns out, I could've been waiting forever. First I knew was the cops showing up. Though didn't know what for. Didn't know a thing until one of those cops grabbed me and said they had questions. Wasn't sharing any answers with me. Hitting me with questions, over and over. All sorts of questions I didn't have the answers to. I don't know what the hell went on in there. Can't tell them what I don't know."

"Of course you can't." Clara's reflected indignation calmed him. She was going to be so good with authors. Scary good. "They had you right there as a one-of-a-kind resource and instead they were asking you about mundane things. What they should have been asking you about was how Birchall and Utton got along? Because that's something you—and only you—would know."

"Not great." His smile wasn't pleasant. "Was going to get worse."

"Oh? Did you hear Rod Birchall say something?"

"Me? I don't hear anything. *Ever.*" Then he contradicted himself. "All I know is he said something to pasty-face about a vote next week and he practically fell out of the car. Thought he was going to cry."

"Was Utton the one who fired you?"

"No way. That bi—" He cut that off, but the sentiment was clear. No love lost there. "Thinks she runs the whole place. She'll make Utton's life a living hell." That pleased him.

"Why don't you like Foster Utton? Has he ever done anything to you?"

"Him? No way. But he's ... sneaky. Birchall was six kinds of an SOB, but you knew right where you were with him. Utton, he tries to be all nice and polite. Makes me nervous."

I wondered what Isaac's tips were like when he treated people trying to be nice and polite with suspicion.

In Birchall, he'd had a boss who truly suited him.

Guess there's a match for everybody.

CLARA VOLUNTEERED TO drive, which left me reading Fern's idiosyncratic directions. The rain had stopped, but the light still wasn't great. And there wasn't a distance or a point of the compass in the entire string of turns.

That didn't seem to bother Clara, as we left the relative safety of the highway for sadistic amusement park rides masquerading as roads.

"I've got something to tell you, Sheila." She negotiated a ninety-degree turn in the road to avoid an old barn. "I've wanted to but we've been so busy… I'm so excited. I got this great opportunity. The woman teaching the authors assistant course has a regular assistant who helps her with all the tasks for the teacher's authors and the regular assistant will be taking maternity leave and she's asked me—*me*—to fill in for those months. Instead of trying to find my own clients at the very start, I'll keep learning from her and her assistant, and I'll get paid while I'm doing it. And then I'll know how to handle things with clients myself later."

She slanted me a look.

"You mean when you have your own business?" I asked.

"Yeah. But more. When I work for you."

"Work for me?" My ribs suddenly felt as if they couldn't contain my heart. Had she somehow learned of my *Abandon All* connection? Was she thinking…?

What *was* she thinking?

"Of course. When you finish your novel and start selling it and become a world-renowned and best-selling author."

For the last two parts, been there, done that, didn't want to go back. The first two steps seemed impossible at the moment.

"*Me?*" I got out.

"Sure. I happened to see something on your computer the other day. It was good, Sheila."

This secret. Not the other ones.

Despite the relief, I felt the heat signifying color rising from my chest to my forehead.

"It's not. It's really, really not. Just notes. Barely. I'm sort of playing around with it for now. It might not—probably won't—go anyplace."

"I know it will. And by then, I'll be good at this VA stuff—author assistant—and I can help you get your name out there, build your brand, establish a readership."

Those sounded like phrases from her course.

I wondered if they had segments on keeping the author you were assisting out of the spotlight, keeping their brand unknown, leaving their name alone?

Not likely.

"That sounds great," I lied. "But first you have to finish your course. And—though it's far less likely to matter—I need to finish a book. Or write *something* someone would want to read."

"I want to read whatever else you've written. That little bit I read? I really liked those characters. Not that I'm pushing you to let me read it. Not until you're ready." She touched my arm. "And don't worry, Sheila. I won't tell anyone you're writing a book. Your secret's safe with me."

That secret.

But what about all the others?

✧　✧　✧　✧

"CAN THIS BE it?" I asked. "It looks awfully overgrown. Doesn't look like anybody's been here for ages."

"Then this is probably it. Some of these old families like to keep a real low profile. They also like to keep things original. Except… Yeah, there are power lines going in. I'm turning in."

I was glad we were in her SUV, not my sedan. My closer-to-the-ground vehicle probably would have bottomed out on the ridge between the ruts on this less-than-a-road.

"I don't know, Clara… I can't believe anybody's living back here."

"You lived in New York City too long. Gotta get back to your country roots."

"All my roots are suburban. If there weren't street lights and ice cream trucks roaming the streets, it wasn't civilization."

"High time you expanded your horizons, then."

But I noticed she had her hands tight on the wheel as the ruts jerked the SUV one way then the other.

I drew in a breath to re-voice my doubt, but she spoke first. "We're definitely getting closer to the river. I can smell it."

I sniffed in air. I smelled air conditioning—and was grateful for it. There was a faint whiff of wet vegetation, but since the tangled leaves of the trees, bushes, and vines all glistened from the earlier rain, that didn't say river to me.

"Ah," Clara said as we rounded a curve. "Here we are."

If this was the Gundy old Family Place, I was surprised any of them had survived long enough to procreate and pass this or anything else down to their progeny.

I wasn't expecting a palace, but this log structure looked like the second of the Three Little Pigs' efforts—after the wolf huffed and puffed.

"Clara…" Had Fern sent us on a wild goose chase—or to a death-trap—on purpose?

"And, look. Two vehicles."

Both solid, new, and well-cared-for despite recent mud, they were the most promising things I'd seen.

We got out and picked our way past puddles—the way Clara did it looked like skipping—and reached a front porch. It sloped from side to side. The good thing was it was about six inches off the ground, so there wouldn't be far to fall when—not if—it collapsed.

The door was out of square, but so was the doorframe, so they matched.

Knocking on it was like knocking on the highest grit sandpaper imaginable. After two knocks, I yanked back my hand to see if my knuckles were bleeding.

They weren't. Which seemed unjust, considering how they felt.

The door opened about a foot, enough to recognize the little girl with the curls from the day of the murder at the Roger.

Forget the Three Little Pigs. We'd fallen down the hole with Alice, into Wonderland.

CHAPTER THIRTY-FOUR

WE GAPED AT her.

"Nobody comes to this door," she told us with disapproval. She held a package of colored pens.

An adult-sized shadow appeared from out of the gloom behind her.

Gundy Vance.

"Lorelei. What are you—?"

He stopped dead for an instant when he recognized us.

Then slowly came the rest of the way forward, into the relative light of the doorway.

Relative, because the trees overhead and the dense vegetation all around left the door in the equivalent of twilight.

He put his hand on the girl's head, his wide palm flattening the wild curls slightly, the gesture familiar, fond, and proprietary. All those were fine with the girl. She leaned back against him.

"What the hell are you doing here?" a third voice asked. No big surprise it was the mystery woman from the Roger. Karen Zalesk, mother of Lorelei.

"Fern sent us," I blurted out.

"*Fern* did?"

"Yes," Clara said firmly. "And gave us the directions."

"Has she lost her mind?" the woman demanded. "I know she's getting old, but I thought—"

"She still has all her faculties." Gundy shifted his stare from us to the top of the little girl's head. "Okay. Come in."

His yanking at the old door left an ungenerous slice to enter. We made do.

The woman had disappeared into the dimness, the girl followed, leaving Gundy to escort us through a room, along a hallway, then a wider one.

Like some weird time travel where you walked from one century to the next, going from the cabin front, to a solid brick structure of the 1800s, then a sort of bridge to a couple rooms that had been modern in the mid-twentieth century, then up stairs to burst into a great room of glass, rock, gleaming kitchen surfaces, and views down and across the river that outshone the kitchen.

This building had grown in layers, like a tree.

Irresistibly drawn, I went past where Lorelei colored on papers strewn across a coffee table to the windows. Eventually, I turned with a gesture encompassing all of the building as I said, "This is … amazing."

"Amazing," Clara echoed.

The only way anyone could see the modern additions was to be on the property or from a drone. The way it was nestled into the trees and curve of the earth, it would be mostly blocked from view, even on the river.

Our obvious appreciation visibly softened the expressions of both adults.

"The first Gundys to come here built down at river level. They soon learned to respect its power—lost livestock and children to the Ohio."

Interesting the order he put them in.

"Josiah and Anna Gundy moved their house up here, hauling up the original logs. That started a family history of never starting fresh, never starting over, never wiping the slate clean."

That left a pause that vibrated with echoes of previous arguments and accusations.

There seemed to be messages going between the man and woman at a rapid rate. The pause from my end—and I suspect from Clara's—was trying to sort out what we'd walked into.

"You've discovered the deep dark family secret," Gundy said.

My breath hitched.

"Our family fishing shack isn't a shack."

Clara flicked me a look. *Our?*

"Not anymore, anyway," Gundy continued. "It's been added onto over the years as you can see, but it's always been kept a secret."

"How on earth do you keep renovations like this a secret?"

"Family's done the work. Most recently cousins who live across the country, but still have strong enough family feelings to keep the secret. Permits and such—" He dismissed those with a wave. "—we're grandfathered in. Actually about five-time great-grandfathered in."

"Oh, for heaven's sake." The woman spoke for the first time. "Quit talking about the house. They think I'm your bit on the side, kept out here at the family place. Suppose they think Lorelei is yours, too." She turned to us—or on us. She had enough anger in most of what she said that it was hard to tell the difference. "I'm his sister, not his floozy. And Lorelei is his niece. Nothing more."

"Karen Vance." Clara's voice held recognition of the name.

"Yes. Now, Karen—"

"Zalesk," Clara and I said along with her.

She gave us a quick look, but continued, "Legally. Not for much longer."

The girl glanced up at her mother at the anger and venom in those words.

"You've got quite the place here." I addressed Gundy Vance. Yes, I wanted information. I also wanted to redirect the conversation away from what appeared to cause the little girl distress. "I thought you were a struggling market owner, scrambling to survive against the titan Jolly Roger chain?"

"I am—the market owner, struggling, and scrambling. Also surviving. This—" His gesture encompassed both the layers of the past we'd walked through and the up-to-date impressiveness around us. "—is not mine. Or my sister's. It belongs to the family, especially to the parts of it not yet born. Her children's children. That's how it's always been for the Vances."

"Actually, the Gundys," Karen said, echoing Fern. "Our last name comes from a descendant of Josiah and Anna Gundy, who eventually married a Vance. So much for male lineage."

Her brother grimaced slightly, more with the air of intolerantly tolerating a long-running dispute. "My sister is going through a difficult divorce. It's coloring her world view."

"Forget difficult. They're all difficult. This is cut-throat, acrimonious warfare."

"Karen." His single word was a warning.

Without a word, Lorelei picked up the top paper and the package of colored pens, went into a room, and closed the door behind her.

"There's no sense trying to shield her. Cut-throat, acrimonious warfare is hard for any child to miss, much less one as intelligent as Lorelei. Of course, that's on his part only. I'm a sweetheart. A font of reason and courtesy." Karen pinched the bridge of her nose. "I want this to be over. So Lorelei and I can go on with our lives. So we can have lives."

"Anyway," Gundy pursued with that uniform smile, "I said for you to come in so we could explain, so you won't tell anyone she's staying here."

"You're hiding from your husband?" Clara's gaze shifted in the direction the little girl had gone. "If you don't have custody—"

Karen crossed her arms. "I do. I can show you the papers if you want. Or give you my lawyer's number. You can check with her."

"Then why all the hiding out and secrecy?"

"Because I don't want to be asked a whole lot of questions," she snapped.

"Cut it out. Let me talk," Gundy ordered.

She raised one hand, flicking away his words. "More male certitude. Go ahead. Talk. Talk."

"I imagine you're here more about Monday than my sister's matrimonial issues. She saw Birchall at the Roger. She was shocked and angry and upset when that jackass bulled his way into trying to get a photo with Lorelei. Of all the people in the world—her."

"Because of her allergies or because she's a member of the Vance family?" I asked.

"Both." Another snap from Karen. It didn't feel personal, though.

Maybe, like Isaac with Birchall, it was a style of communication that didn't bother me.

"We nearly lost her—Lorelei—when she was barely two because her father gave her a small piece of a wrap from a store in a chain Birchall ran. We all knew about her allergy from an early reaction and everyone was careful because we all love that little girl—" He shot his sister a look. She returned it, sneering. In the throes of divorce was she sowing doubts about the father's love for his daughter because of an accident? "—but all the ingredients weren't on the label and it was in the bread as oil, so not obvious at all…"

Both their faces shadowed with memories.

"We're fortunate, very fortunate Lorelei received excellent medical care as quickly as she did," Gundy said. "No thanks to Birchall trying to pad his pocket."

Would Petey think differently about Gundy's possible guilt if he knew the family held Birchall responsible for nearly killing Lorelei?

"This was at a store in the P-F-F-T chain?"

Gundy's face closed in caution, but Karen didn't seem to recognize our knowledge was wider than she might have expected.

"Yeah. We asked and asked them to improve the labeling. Instead, they've gone backward on it, thanks to Birchall. And then the Jolly Roger chain *rewards* him and brings him here. To *my* hometown. So when I walk in to grab colored pens—which Shep's doesn't even *carry*—" She flung that at her brother as an apparent sharp point in some unfinished dispute. "—there he is, the chinless wonder, strutting around like king of the dunghill. And then he had the nerve to try to put *his* hands on *my* daughter. To have her in a photo with *him*. I should have killed him right then. I—"

"*Karen.*"

That broke her rant. But didn't make her repent.

"If they think I meant I went and killed him later, they're too stupid to bother about." She stomped into the kitchen and poured herself something from a pitcher on the counter. It was clear, but I wasn't prepared to swear it was water.

"Anyway," Gundy said with a fair shot at wry humor, "that's why I went to the Roger. To get Karen and Lorelei out of there. To calm them down."

"Who saw you there?"

"Apparently you did."

"Start at the beginning."

He frowned. Unclear if it was from annoyance or concentration. "The driver of that ostentatious overcompensation for something or other parked in front looked at me when I walked past. I can't say whether he saw me or not. Petey, the guy getting the carts—I see him around, know him to wave to. A customer I didn't recognize. Might have been somebody from Stringer." He made it sound as foreign as Mars. "Avoided a couple I did recognize. Didn't see you two, or I would have avoided you, too."

His mouth twisted sideways. Then he shrugged.

"That's all I remember."

Thinking of one of Birchall's complaints about the Haines Tavern store, I asked, "What about the specials?"

"What about them?"

Paydirt.

From relaxed and easy, his voice had gone tight this time the topic came up.

"Birchall said you've been having specials just before they run the same thing as the Roger. He seemed to think you were finding out what the Roger had scheduled and jumping in before them."

"Maybe they're copying us."

"That would have been a lot more believable if you didn't say *maybe*," his sister said.

"Shut up, Karen."

"Are you receiving information about the Roger's planned specials ahead of time?"

"No."

None of us believed Gundy.

I proved my part of that by saying, "Is it someone in the Haines

Tavern store who's giving you the information ahead of time?

"I told you, I'm not receiving any information."

"Nobody believes you."

"Shut up, Karen." This time his tone sounded like his sister's.

I tried a few more questions, but we'd reached an impasse.

Clara started the micromovements that indicated we were leaving.

"There are stairs up the outside, easier for getting to your car," Gundy said.

"And then you don't have to use that Addams Family door."

He rolled his eyes at his sister, but said nothing as he showed us the door to the stairway. Surprisingly, Karen drifted along with.

Abruptly, she said, "How did you know my married name?"

"Research."

Her eyes narrowed.

"Using only public resources." That forestalled the threat I saw brewing.

Gundy slid in, "Thank you for not telling anyone Karen's staying here."

"We haven't agreed not to tell anyone. If we're asked by law enforcement, we'll tell them. And we would like that lawyer's number. To be sure."

Karen's mouth twisted. "To be sure you don't get in trouble?"

"Yes," I said calmly to her mocking. "And to be sure Lorelei is where she's supposed to be."

I CALLED THE lawyer as soon as my phone had cell reception, which was about halfway back to Haines Tavern.

The lawyer took our call, saying Karen Zalesk had already called, giving her permission to talk to us. The lawyer's voice gave no hint of what I suspected had have been a fraught conversation. Maybe she was used to this client by now. Maybe she experienced that in a lot of clients.

The lawyer confirmed Karen Zalesk had custody and was doing nothing illegal. "She's giving herself and her soon-to-be ex-husband the space they need."

When I hung up, I repeated all to Clara.

"The space they need not to kill each other? How can people who produced such an adorable little girl want to tear each other apart?"

"Figure that out and you can put a whole lot of divorce lawyers out of business."

CHAPTER THIRTY-FIVE

WE STOPPED FOR sandwiches at a little place Clara knew, specializing in local, fresh fare.

It was delicious and surprisingly fast service. Which was a good thing, because as soon as we sat down, Clara checked her phone and excitedly announced, "Phyllis Ezzard has invited us to come by. Any time this afternoon."

✧　✧　✧　✧

PHYLLIS EZZARD'S HOUSE on the south side of town was as neat and precise and dignified as the woman.

This area was a mix of grand houses that had once been palaces of forbidden pleasures and working-class homes. Now each kind also represented a mix of decrepit and restored. The Ezzard home had the rare air of never having been allowed to deteriorate.

Over cool drinks and lemon cookies, we settled in a tiny sunroom at the back.

"I understand from Millie that you are interested in my memories and impressions of Monday's unpleasantness at the Jolly Roger grocery store. I consider myself fortunate to have left the premises before that even deeper level of unpleasantness was enacted."

That matched our view of her going toward the exit as we left the produce section.

That didn't mean she couldn't have come back in.

"You are fortunate." Clara's mournful head-shake said she shuddered at the memory of not being equally fortunate... As if she could have been driven away by anything short of a direct law enforcement order.

She continued, without any sign butter ever considered melting in her mouth, "You must have been in the store when Rod Birchall arrived?"

"I was."

Without further prompting, she gave a succinct account of Birchall's arrival. It contributed a few details without differing from Aggie Hickmott's or Jacqueline's.

It struck me that most of the differing details were a matter of angle. As if she might have been deeper into the store when Birchall and Utton arrived.

I asked, "How about before Rod Birchall arrived? Did you notice anything then?"

Her expression lightened without any overt change in her features, like one of those overcast days when, without any visible parting of the clouds, the sunlight abruptly becomes strong enough to cast a sharper shadow.

"I did witness the manager's exit from the store. An exit accomplished in great haste and with the woman in the red vest who later formed part of Rod Birchall's entourage—"

She paused slightly, checking if we'd understood whom she meant.

Assured by Clara's murmur of "not the girl," she resumed.

"—running after him and calling out questions about where he was going and what was the matter."

Interesting. The way Jacqueline had told it, *she'd* heard the manager receive the call and his immediate reaction.

From Aggie's account, Jacqueline must have heard about it from Belinda and appropriated it as her own experience. Unconsciously? Or deliberately?

"That woman in the red vest, was the only one following him?"

"The only one to follow him out of the store, yes. However, Petey intercepted him, also expressing concern. The manager brushed him off. Literally, he pushed away Petey's hands as he continued his path to a line of vehicles well away from the store. He said he felt unwell and needed to leave for home immediately, which was more response than I heard him give the woman in the red vest. The manager's explanation was not credible.

"The woman in the red vest, by this time, had stopped. Soon, she returned to the store, her posture thoroughly dejected.

"I had parked a good distance from the doors as well, as is my habit to increase the number of steps I walk each day. The result was that, as I walked toward the store, I heard the manager's next exchange quite clearly. It was with the young assistant manager—"

"Jacqueline."

"—and her young man."

"Her young man?" Clara repeated.

"I know it sounds old-fashioned, but the appellation is more apt when he is not a boy and friendship did not appear to be the emotion involved when I inadvertently saw them in the front seat of a truck when I parked my vehicle nearby. They were—" She paused again, searching for an apt appellation. "—*entwined.*"

Ah. That might explain Jacqueline appropriating Belinda's observations. To hide she'd been out on a no-doubt unauthorized break, in a truck with a man.

"The manager's flight and the calls after him appeared to disrupt their interlude and the assistant manager, Jacqueline, stumbled out of the truck, restoring her disarranged clothing to order."

"Did she talk to the manager?" Clara asked.

"She attempted to, but he rushed past her as well, not answering her questions. He did shout back as he entered his car, *You're in charge.* The young woman said something quickly to her young man, then ran into the store. I proceeded at my usual pace."

Wow. Quite the going-ons in the Roger parking lot before we got there.

"The young man, do you know who he is?" I asked.

"I do not."

That seemed to be the end of that.

Until she added, "However, you would recognize him. He was the only man who spoke up to Mr. Birchall."

Clara and I stared at her for an extra beat.

"The guy in jeans? With the white shirt? The one who said *bull*? You're certain *that's* Jacqueline's boyfriend—young man?"

"Yes."

CLARA AND I left without either of us giving way to the impulse to wrap Phyllis Ezzard in a hug and twirl her around the room.

I called the Roger as soon as we were in the SUV, with rain starting to fall again.

Jacqueline never breathed a word, in all her open and heartfelt discussion after yoga, she omitted the boyfriend in the truck … along with the canoodling. Time for another talk with the assistant store manager.

"Is Jacqueline Yancik there, please."

The young male voice on the other end—Josh of the red vest?—said, "She's not here."

"When do you expect her?"

"No idea. She's at the sheriff's department."

Clara had heard my two standard questions, could guess at the first answer, but had to wait for me to relay the second.

"Darn. You think they've arrested her as the murderer?"

"Probably not yet. But they might. We have to keep going anyway. And after what Phyllis said, talking to Jacqueline has to be our top priority."

"You're right. I'll put out the call to let folks know we'd love to know when she's back at the Roger."

"And in the meantime, I need to get home and start dinner."

"Don't worry, I'll help."

CHAPTER THIRTY-SIX

I PUT CLARA and Teague, who'd stayed to update me on the electrician's progress, to work cutting up ingredients for the sweet potato and apple casserole that would accompany the pork roast for tonight's dinner. The electrician had left for the day, but was returning tomorrow.

Of course, the conversation centered on Rod Birchall's murder.

I went back and forth to the dining room, setting things up there.

"Hensen will solve it," Teague said. "He's good. He's got lots of resources to find out lots of things from lots of sources. He's got forensics. You said the store has security cameras—"

"Disabled," Clara said. "Doesn't help him."

"And might help us. I was thinking about that. The good thing from our point of view is someone messing with the security camera over the door between meat and dairy indicates it was someone familiar with the store, the way an employee would be. They had to know where the cameras are, where the controls are, and how to use them."

"Assuming you interpreted Deputy Hensen's silences correctly," Teague said.

"You've never found someone *not* saying something to be informative?"

He looked at me with enough meaning that I was fighting the urge to squirm even before he spoke. "Oh, I've found the things some people don't say very informative."

And then he held the look. Forcing me to return it while my brain screamed *Look innocent!* at my facial muscles.

If I'd had any question of whether he knew I was withholding information, it was answered now.

That wasn't great, but as long as he didn't know *what* information I was withholding, I should be okay. There's a big gap between knowing someone has a generic secret and knowing what the secret is. Right?

At last, he gave a small nod, as if confirming something in his own head—*My innocence?* I hoped with unrealistic optimism—then released the look.

After a couple breaths of mentally mopping my brow, I decided I had one more task in the dining room. Those salt and pepper shakers really needed straightening.

Instead, I snapped to attention at his next words, which were not directed at me.

"What is it, Clara?"

From Teague's face, I zoomed to hers.

She did not look happy. In fact, she looked almost… guilty.

"Clara?"

She sighed. "What you said about the good thing being that knowing how to turn off cameras would narrow it to people who work at the Roger? Um, it's not so narrow." She picked at something on her sleeve. Something invisible. "For instance, knowing where the controls are? The monitors are on a couple desks in the office. Each control's labeled with where the camera's located. And the instructions are posted right beside the monitors. It's simple to disable a camera. Just a few clicks."

"How do you know all this?" Teague asked.

"Everybody knows about the monitors being in the office. Didn't you, Sheila?" She read my answer in my face. "Well, most everybody. Especially if you have to stand and wait to get rainchecks, because they're forever running out of stock on sale items and you stand there forever, they fill out enough paperwork to get a mortgage and then you lose the raincheck or they still don't have the item when the raincheck's about to run out so you have to get another one and eventually you lose it anyway, so it was a big waste, spending all that time in line, watching people go in and out of the office door and sometimes they don't even bother to close it, so you see things. But I guess you don't get rainchecks," she concluded.

"I might have to after this."

I got the casserole dish out and started preparing it. I'd made this recipe with my mother as a teenager and felt secure enough to listen at the same time.

"So, you've seen the monitors and the set-up, but how do you know it takes a few clicks to disable a specific camera, Clara?" Teague asked.

"Oh." Her cheeks grew pink. "I was in the store one night, quite late, when they have very few customers and a lot of people stocking, you know? There were three boys in the office laughing—giggling really—and no one at the desk, so I went to the open office door and over their shoulders I saw they had one of the cameras pointed at a girl's backside as she bent over to stock lower shelves."

Her pink cheeks were indignation, not embarrassment.

"I reached over their shoulders and turned it off—that's how easy the instructions were. I read them in that instant of stepping forward. I didn't even say anything, looked at them and they scattered like rabbits."

"Good for you, Clara."

She grinned back at me, then sobered. "But it does mean the field of possible suspects is still wide open."

"You know, I don't think that's a handicap for us. Not the part about there being more suspects, but the whole aspect of forensic evidence and that sort of thing. If forensics is going to solve this, the sheriff's department is going to figure it out before we do, no matter what. So, we should leave that to them."

"Thank you." Teague's emphasis added the subtext *That's what I've been saying all along* without saying the words. This time.

"But," I continued with my own emphasis, reaching for the pan and rack I'd use for the roast, "as we've seen in other circumstances, forensics isn't always the best or fastest answer. Talking with people informally can get us to the answer."

"It can also get you into dangerous situations."

"We're careful," Clara assured him.

"I've seen how careful you two are." His tone might best be described as sardonic.

"Sometimes things happen," Clara conceded.

"But we got the answers," I pointed out.

"How about focusing less on answers and more on staying alive."

"No worries for you," I said cheerily, pulling off foil to line the pan. Since moving into my own house, I've become a big believer in prevention to cut cleaning tasks. "If I die, the estate would still need to employ you to finish fixing up this place so it could be sold. Your employment prospects here would continue, in addition to substitute teaching."

"Is that what you're worried about, Teague?"

Clara has a habit of saying—or asking—what other people are thinking. A lot of times I appreciated it. Sometimes I didn't.

Like now.

"Among other things," he said. "Like the way you two speculate. Speculation can take you in wild directions."

As much as I appreciated his redirecting the conversation, I wasn't going to agree with him. "Everything's speculation until you confirm it. Speculation is the same thing as a lead."

I gathered ingredients for coating the roast.

"If you have evidence—"

I interrupted him. "Once you confirm it, it's evidence. Before that it's a lead. You can call it speculation. We call it something to look into. And so would you if we were with the sheriff's department."

I took the pork roast out of the packaging, turned it over and discovered a thick pad of fat. "For Pete's sake. They hid all the fat on the bottom," I grumbled. "I thought better of Shep's."

"My former partner—Harris—" Teague amended the identification since we both knew who Harris was and Clara was practically best buds with him. "—worked as a butcher in college and calls it white meat, since you pay the same price per pound for it as the meat."

His chuckle fizzled as he looked from Clara to me.

"*Now* what is it?" he asked.

Without taking her gaze off me, Clara said, "Sheila's figured out something."

I heard them, but it seemed from a distance.

"What?" he asked.

Clara said, "I'm not exactly sure, but Gundy said something similar yesterday about white meat and fat."

"Why would that be significant?"

At the same time Teague spoke, I said, "Maybe. Maybe I've figured it out. *Oh.*"

I swung around holding the knife I'd used to remove the packaging, upright and outstretched. "A knife. That's it. A knife. I think I *do* have it figure out."

They both slid backed on their chairs.

"Be careful with that thing." Teague reached for it, but I drew it back to me.

"Birchall wasn't stabbed." Clara's objection overlooked any potential personal danger and focused on the crime. Had to love the woman's single-mindedness.

"No, he wasn't. But the guy in jeans wasn't a customer. He wasn't just Jacqueline's boyfriend, either. He's—"

"What?" Teague asked.

"Later," Clara promised. "Let her finish."

"—a *butcher.*"

"The guy in jeans is a butcher," Clara repeated. Not questioning, but in wide-eyed excitement.

"And Belinda said Jacqueline had *personal reasons* for being upset about the firings last week. Like her live-in boyfriend being one those fired?"

"Wait a minute, wait a minute," Teague said. "How you get to the guy in jeans being a butcher—possibly a butcher, based on what leap of logic is beyond me. But, okay, say he is a butcher, how do you get to that assistant store manager—"

"Jacqueline," Clara supplied.

"Jacqueline living with him, with this supposed butcher?"

"Belinda said—"

"You said her name is Jacqueline."

"Belinda is one of the red vests. She told us Jacqueline has a boy-friend named … Edwards. I think it was Wade Edwards, though she didn't seem real sure. She also—earlier, when we were all on the floor in housewares—said Jacqueline took last week's firings personally."

"Thin," he grumbled. "Go back to the butcher part. What makes you think he's a butcher?"

"The knife's part of it. That's what was familiar about the slightly weird way he held his hand. It wasn't a fist or a tennis grip. It was a butcher's grip. There was a shop in Manhattan—" Oops. Not so close to my previous life. "Anyway, that's what made me envision him in a white coat. I thought maybe he was in something medical, but it was the *butcher*'s white coats, not lab coats."

"You lost me," Clara said.

"When he talked to Rod Birchall, the guy in jeans—God, I wish we knew his name—held his arm, his hand a weird way. Not fisted. Not a tennis grip. But it seemed familiar. It was. It was exactly the way Shep's butcher did when he cut that rib roast for you last month, Clara."

She squinted at my knife-holding arm. My form wasn't great, but I hoped it got the point across.

"They use the machines so much, but…" Her gaze jerked from my knife-holding arm to my face. "You're right. You're absolutely right. I never would have thought of that. And the guy in jeans *did* hold his hand kind of weird, but I barely remembered it, much less figured out he's a butcher and living with Jacqueline from it."

"That's conjecture, not a fact," Teague objected. "You can't go jumping to conclusions. You've gone from the way he held his hand to connecting him with a white coat and the guy who cut Clara's meat. And now you've put him at the top of your suspect list—"

"We didn't say that."

"Well, he is kind of at the top of the list now," Clara said.

"Yeah, fine. But we hadn't *said* it. Besides, Teague, it's all indica-tive. It all hangs together. And—"

"Or hangs apart—"

"—there's the other part. *White meat.*"

That stopped him. "What about white meat?"

"He used that term, too, the way you said Harris did. And it seemed strange at the time. Most people use white meat to refer to chicken or turkey. But what he said didn't fit with that usage. He said something about how the Roger's pre-packaging meat meant Birchall was selling customers mostly white meat and it sounded like an accusation. But if the package held chicken or turkey, so what? A customer could see what they were getting, they weren't being cheated. *But* if he meant it the way Harris learned as a butcher—as fat—then he was saying Birchall's program put more fat in the packages, where customers couldn't see it until they got it home and started to cook it—" I gestured to the pork roast. "—which is underhanded, if not outright cheating the consumer. Making white meat a term—"

"A butcher would use," Clara finished happily. "Wonderful, Sheila. That's absolutely wonderful."

Teague rubbed his chin. "Even *if*—and it's a big if—the guy's a butcher, what evidence do you have he's connected with the assistant store manager—besides the gossip of Belinda."

"That's easy." Clara looked a question at me.

"Be my guest. I'll work on the marinade."

So, while I retrieved olive oil, a multi-herb rub my brother had shared, and a bit of sesame ginger dressing, Clara told him how our mystery man had interacted with Jacqueline.

"A couple words? A touch? A few looks? And he backed off when she asked him to? That's all you've got."

"It's plenty when you know how to read people." Clara ruined her assumed condescension with her next breath. "Plus, we saw and heard each of those, absorbing all the subtext in real time. Trust us, there was something going on between those two." Her eyes widened. "You do trust us, don't you, Teague?"

I laughed. "You play dirty, Clara. One of the things I love about you."

Her eyes wide with innocence, she said, "And then there's what Phyllis Ezzard told us about them being entwined in a truck in the parking lot."

After her brief explanation, Teague gave a mock disgusted, "Sheesh. You could have started with that."

"We were waiting until dinner to tell you and Ned together."

Clara's phone rang. She went into the dining room to answer.

Teague was silent a moment, slicing an apple. "You need a hell of a lot more than these little pieces to accuse someone of a crime, Sheila. Any crime. Much less murder."

I turned with the bowl holding the whisked marinade. That sounded like something even deeper than the professional standards he adhered to, even though it was his former profession now.

Dropping any flippancy, I said, "We aren't accusing him. We do suspect him. Along with several other people. We'll keep looking for evidence."

He rubbed his forehead again.

"While you're doing that, could you please remember that, if you're right, this guy knows how to use a knife?" Then the line of his mouth eased slightly. "And Gracie might be able to get Timmy out of the well or bark at intruders, but don't count on her disarming a knife-wielding murderer."

Of course I didn't count on her doing that.

Because I'd be standing between her and the knife-wielding murderer to protect her.

Clara came back into the kitchen. "We've got to go, Sheila."

CHAPTER THIRTY-SEVEN

BEFORE WE LEFT, I covered the roast with marinade, put it in a high heat oven with strict instructions to Teague to turn it way down in twenty minutes. Then check on it while it was cooking.

"If it's close to temperature and we're not back, turn it lower, but not off."

When I started to go over the instructions for the casserole a second time, he said, "Yeah, yeah, I've got it. Why won't you tell me where you're going?"

I shrugged. "It's all Clara's show. I don't know either."

Clara honked from the driveway and I left.

"WHERE ARE WE going?" I asked from the passenger seat.

"Jacqueline's back on duty at the Roger. Millie texted me. After what Phyllis said, I thought we should get to her as soon as possible."

"Great. But why wouldn't you tell Teague?"

"He was being such a killjoy. I didn't want him saying we needed an armed escort to go to the Roger."

WE SPOTTED JACQUELINE walking into the office and followed her.

She gave us a weak welcoming smile.

After hellos, I said, "Tell us about the security cameras at the Roger, Jacqueline."

"God, you, too?" I'd thought it would ease us into the real questions, but not by her reaction. "The deputies were on and on about them. Was it normal to have several cameras pointed toward the produce section? Well, no, because that would be stupid—we want to cover the most territory with them, not the least. And was it normal to have a bunch of cameras pointed at those doors to the back room? No, one. And was it normal to have cameras disabled from the front to the back of the store? No, the whole idea of the cameras is to not have blank spots. And how hard is it to operate the cameras or disable them? Not very hard for someone who's ever worked the system or anything similar, which is about anybody who's ever worked in a store of any kind, ever."

Clara winced, but Jacqueline didn't notice, having turned toward the computer on the desk.

"Sorry. Sorry," the assistant store manager said. "I didn't mean to explode, but it's so frustrating to be asked these questions over and over from forty different angles, the same questions and the same answers."

As long as we weren't easing into this, I changed tactics. Gently swinging the door closed to limit being overheard, I went for direct.

"We know he's a butcher."

She spun around, then, belatedly tried for the wide-eyed innocent look. In another few years it would look ridiculous on her. Right now it simply didn't work.

"Who is?" she tried.

"The guy in jeans who was one of the people confronting Rod Birchall. And when he did, you tried to smooth it over and then he backed off, like he didn't want to upset you. The guy who said he'd stay with the body, then didn't."

She shook her head, adding a shrug to emphasize her supposed confusion. "I don't know who—"

"C'mon, you can't possibly pretend you don't remember him. Not when he found the Jolly Roger CEO dead in the back room of your store."

She latched onto that. "That's probably what drove everything else out of my mind."

"You remembered us," Clara said quietly.

Jacqueline blinked twice rapidly.

"You do know him, don't you?"

"No. I told you, I've only been here a few months. Even if he's a regular customer, I might not know him. And he could have been in the store for the first time for all I know. Customers come and go."

"But he wasn't a customer. He's a butcher."

She paused, chewing on the corner of her thumbnail for a telling instant. "Of course he was a customer. I haven't been here long, but I know all the employees."

"You know all the butchers who work here?"

"Yes." She said it fast and firm.

"Of course there are fewer to remember after the firings last week."

"I would have recognized him if he'd ever worked here," she said doggedly.

"So he worked as a butcher at another store."

She said nothing.

"He was one of the butchers let go in the recent layoffs and firings, wasn't he? That explains his anger at Birchall."

Nothing.

Clara contributed, "If he was let go and you knew how angry he was at Birchall, how he blamed the CEO, that explains your trying to get him to leave. Didn't work, but you probably knew it wouldn't end well."

"Definitely didn't end well," I agreed. "Not for Rod Birchall and possibly not for your butcher friend."

Her silence had become rigid.

"Which store in Indiana did you work in before coming here?"

She flashed a look up—not at us, but possibly at the heavens asking for help. Then her gaze dropped to the floor again, and she remained silent except for the faintest grinding as she worked on the corner of her thumbnail.

"We'll find the manager of that store and ask—"

"You can't, because she's gone. Best store manager they ever had and they cut her. Birchall shows up at the store for a surprise visit there and the next day she's fired."

And then he'd come to Jacqueline's store.

She had to be thinking she would be the next to go. But would that be a motive? Would anyone think that was the way to keep a job?

On the other hand, with him dying, nobody got fired, so...

Clara pursued our previous tack. "The manager wouldn't be the only one at your old store who'd know the guy. A butcher involved with the fast-rising young woman who went off to be assistant manager at another store. There'll be plenty to fill in the gaps."

"I suppose Belinda will remember which store Jacqueline was at before," I said to Clara.

"I bet she will," she agreed. "Or one of those two younger ones— Myghavnn and Josh. If worse came to worst, we could call stores one by one, asking if they know of Jacqueline Yancik. But I bet our friend Foster Utton could find out in a snap of his fingers. Do you want to call him at corporate or should I and ask—?"

"All right, all right. Don't. Having my name all over—even more than it is now..." She raised her chin. "It's not like we did anything wrong."

"You are living together?"

"Yeah. But I didn't supervise him. I was never head of his department. I didn't have any say in his schedule or reviews or anything. That's when people get in trouble. We decided to keep our seeing each other quiet ... just to keep it ours, you know? To not have everybody in the store knowing and talking about us and gnawing over our relationship."

She expelled a breath through her teeth.

"It was fun, especially at first. Romantic. We moved in together. Figured word would get out then and it did. But it was okay. The store manager knew we weren't doing anything wrong. She said it was all fine, as long as it didn't interfere with our work. It never did. He worked hard. We both did. We were saving to get married, get a house in an area with good schools, have a family.

"He's a good man. He's having a hard time right now, but he's truly a good man. It's hard on anybody to have his job pulled out from under him like that. You don't understand."

"What's his name, Jacqueline?" Clara asked.

"Ward. Ward Ebersole."

"Where is he now?"

"I… I don't know."

"You better tell the sheriff's department what you do know. Better yet, get him to turn himself in."

"He won't tell me where he is."

"So, you're in communication with him."

"Not really. He left his cell phone at our place and I truly don't know where he is. Before I got home that night, he'd packed up a few things and was gone. His note said he loved me, not to worry, and he'd be in touch. I *am* worried. I know he didn't do this. But if they know that was him here when Birchall was killed, what are they supposed to think?"

As tears slid between Jacqueline's closed eyelids, Clara put an arm around her shoulders.

"Has he been in touch?"

"I heard him pick up messages from our house phone twice. He's left me a few messages. Only saying he's okay, not to worry, and he l-loves me."

"Next time he calls, tell him we need to talk to him."

CHAPTER THIRTY-EIGHT

"HE MIGHT CALL us," Clara said.

"Nope. Not going to happen. Even if Jacqueline catches one of his calls and is her most persuasive, it won't happen. Not when it sounds as if he's trying to avoid her."

"Any ideas?"

"Of how to find him? Especially fast? No. But I have another idea."

Sitting in Clara's SUV in the Roger parking lot, I called my great aunt.

After introducing Clara and Kit over the phone, I said, "We're stymied on Ward Ebersole, he's the third person who waited outside the doors Birchall went in. The guy in jeans, remember?"

Of course she remembered.

I explained about "white meat" and a knife grip pointing us toward his being a butcher.

"We got Jacqueline to confirm he's her boyfriend—they live together. But she says he left his phone at their place and she swears up and down she doesn't know where he is, gets only occasional messages."

"I believe her," Clara inserted.

"I'm inclined to believe her, too," I admitted. "But we need to find him and talk to him, if for no other reason than to eliminate the possibility he has something vital to tell us. Which means the faster the better. We could try real estate records to see if there's a place he might be staying, or dig into family, or start contacting hotels and short-term rentals—"

"All slow, when you want fast. Tell me about him."

"I've already told you everything that involved him at the murder scene."

"Not that. Tell me about *him*. Everything you know."

I did, with fill-ins from Clara.

At the end, I was surprised we'd known anything. I'd have said he was a blank slate.

I was not surprised Kit was silent, digesting all we'd said.

I started wondering if Phyllis Ezzard might agree to hypnosis for the license plate of his truck. Or Petey? Maybe former co-workers would know more about Ward Ebersole.

"The two most important things," Kit declared at last. "He's picking up messages through the landline he shares with Jacqueline. And—"

"Of *course*," I breathed. That was our communication pathway. "But—"

"—he's recently unemployed."

Kit's second *important thing*, drew a blank.

"What do people do who are unemployed?" she asked, impatient with the silence.

"File for unemployment," Clara said eagerly. "I bet he's filed for unemployment."

"Excellent, Clara. His income stream has been cut. He'll want that unemployment."

CLARA USED A voice from one of her high school plays. Someone both officious and not overly bright.

"This message is for Ward Ebersole. You failed to include all the necessary information on your unemployment insurance application. I understand your situation, it's the only reason I'm calling after hours from my personal phone. You have an appointment for tomorrow at 1:45 p.m. Ask for Ms. Henschalt. Otherwise we won't be able to help you this month. Be sure to bring your latest pay stub."

"That part about the pay stub was a nice touch," I said when she'd clicked off.

"I thought so, too. Hope he accepts the excuse for the phone number being from Kentucky. Now what?"

"Dinner."

✧ ✧ ✧ ✧

CLARA DROPPED ME off, having obtained my pledge to say nothing of this to Teague until we could tell him together. I gladly agreed.

When he tried to pump me, I shooed him out, saying the cook needed solo time.

True.

I also wanted mulling time.

Good thing they could be accomplished simultaneously.

Much of what I mulled was recalling moments when it seemed Jacqueline had tried to keep Ward Ebersole from interacting with Birchall.

Phyllis's observations filled in one of Jacqueline's broken-off statements, providing the answer to what she would have done if she'd known the Jolly Roger CEO was coming to the Haines Tavern store Monday. She would have made sure Ward was as far away as she could get him.

I liked having gaps like that filled in.

On the other hand, it didn't point more toward either of them being the murderer. All it did was say she'd worried about a confrontation.

Well, maybe a smidge more, because if she hadn't thought her honey was capable of *something*—if not murder—she wouldn't have worried.

On the other *other* hand, was this kind of murder his style?

I stood by what I'd said to Clara about the use of poison in this murder, yet it still didn't quite fit the guy in jeans—Ward Ebersole.

I clicked my tongue.

Right. *Didn't fit him.* Like I knew the guy.

Bottom line? Jacqueline would have avoided having her significant other interact with Birchall if she could have. Beyond that, I was speculating, as Teague would tell me in a heartbeat. Heck, he'd call my saying Jacqueline would have kept the two men apart speculation.

But on that point I was confident.

✧ ✧ ✧ ✧

BEFORE DINNER AND amidst mulling, I called Kit.

Time might have been tight if she had a lot to tell me. But all she had said was she was out to dinner—judging from the voice in the background, with the widower—and would talk to me later.

Much later.

CHAPTER THIRTY-NINE

CLARA ENTERED MY house with dessert and a request.

As I put the key lime pie she'd brought in the fridge, she asked if I'd take LuLu to the park the next day. She needed to be able to talk on her computer during her class and LuLu tended to join in on such conversations with barking.

"I'd keep her outside with me," Ned said, "but top of my agenda tomorrow is dealing with poison ivy."

"We do not want LuLu in poison ivy," Clara added. "Plus, if you take her while I have class, we can start our day's detecting sooner, Sheila."

"Sure thing," I said over Teague's groan.

The pork roast was a great success. As were the roasted sweet potato and apple casserole, green salad, and blue cheese drop biscuits, still warm from the oven.

Ned marveled that his orange juice landed us as witnesses, asked questions, and listened avidly to our answers about what had happened at the Jolly Roger and what had followed so far.

"I'm with Sheila that it was a spur of the moment murder," Clara said. "Someone might not have thought it through. So, we shouldn't be too strict about motive."

I grimaced. "Spur of the moment, but seems like it should have someone with passion behind it, like—"

"The mother of that little girl," Ned said.

"Exactly. She blamed him for Lorelei nearly dying. That's motive. Especially with what she said about the labeling."

As we went over the suspects, we edged close to the cause of death a couple times, but Clara adroitly steered us away each time *bashed on the head* neared.

When we reached today's events, Teague said, "You don't have any proof this guy's a butcher. Or that he and the assistant manager are involved."

We tried not to be too triumphant as we updated both men on our latest talk with Jacqueline.

Teague willingly acknowledged we'd turned speculation into leads, if not fully evidence in his view.

"Murdering someone over his cutting jobs, doesn't that seem extreme?" Ned asked. "Unless they knew for sure the next CEO wouldn't cut jobs."

Clara and I looked at each other.

She voiced what we were both thinking. "He'll cut the jobs. He'll go with inertia."

"And I can't imagine anyone who was there would think otherwise, undercutting that as a motive," I said.

Even Teague joined in the chuckles about Phyllis's delicacy over what Jacqueline and her significant other had been doing in the truck.

"She wouldn't have been as careful if she'd spent her teaching career at the high school level, right, Sheila?"

My backstory for Haines Tavern was I'd been a high school English teacher in New York when an inheritance let me quit and move here.

I knew the story inside and out, but Teague's question caught me unprepared and he knew it, even as he covered my silence. "What goes on in high school parking lots goes way past entangled. Some stuff there shocks me despite the years as a cop. Must have been the same for you."

"I'm very good at looking away. Besides, it wasn't part of my duties."

"You didn't have to do patrol duty? That school of yours must have been fat with staff."

"Not bad, but of course we all did some. I was spared the parking lot."

His raised eyebrows were more a demand than a question.

"Cafeteria." It was the only place I could remember teachers patrolling in high school. I'm sure they were other places, but I was a pretty good kid and didn't run afoul of them.

"Whoa. I'd rather have parking lot than cafeteria."

"But only occasionally," I backtracked as fast as I could. "Mostly the halls."

He shook his head. "Still, that means the bathrooms. No fun there, either. Easier to strap on the weapon again and rejoin the force." He gave a mock shudder.

"But you can't shoot a gun," Clara protested.

"Sure I can."

"But your eye, your medical retirement?"

"Oh, that."

"Yeah, that." I spotted the glint in his eyes—one of them might be legally blind, but it was an equal mischief-glinter. "Now you're going to say you can shoot, you just can't hit things?"

The glint intensified. "Good line, but I wasn't going to say that. I'm still a good enough shot."

"But you said your eyesight was the reason for your medical retirement," Clara said.

"True. I didn't say it was right or reasonable." No eye-glinting now. "Other departments' regs would have let me qualify. As long as I could meet the standard it was okay with them. But not my department."

"Then why not move?"

"I did. Like you did." He shifted his head, giving me the full force of his good eye.

"I meant move to a different department. Near where you were before or even here."

"Ready for a new life. Again, like you." He rocked one shoulder forward, then back. Staring at me, challenging. "Working with kids, which was the best—and worst—part of law enforcement. Only, now, I can try to get them a step or two before they're in real trouble. Sort of pre-emptive community policing."

"But the way you feel about law enforcement—"

Ned interrupted his wife to ask, "What about the store manager as a suspect? What's his name?"

"Kurt Verker," I said. "He's a possibility, because he could have come back to the store and certainly nobody knows the camera system and the rest of the store better than he does. But other factors argue against him."

"Like what?"

"Like he ran away when he heard the Jolly Roger CEO was coming to his store. He ran away from Belinda. He ran away when Jacqueline tried to find out what was going on. And he tried to run away when we asked him questions." I concluded, "Running away does seem to be his modus operandi."

Later, while everyone pitched in with cleanup, I heard Ned say quietly to Clara, "You shouldn't ask Teague so many nosy questions."

"That's what we do," she said complacently. "Besides, we care about him."

He moaned. "Let up on him some, okay?"

She kissed him on the cheek. "Yes, dear."

He grinned and pretended to flick her with a dish towel.

✧   ✧   ✧   ✧

WITH CLEAN-UP DONE and the others gone, I checked my phone as I took my last swallow of wine.

Kit had left a message only a few minutes earlier, saying to call her.

"I thought I wouldn't hear from you until morning, because your date wouldn't be over until then," I teased her.

"They do things early here and the retirees do them even earlier."

"So he's gone home and—"

"No, he hasn't. But he goes to sleep early. Gives me writing time after and then he has private time in the morning."

I swallowed a bit of surprise and something else. Perhaps protectiveness. I'd been there to vet the men she'd let into her life over the previous decade. Now, she was on her own.

And I'd mention that to her when I wanted my head handed to

me.

"That works out well," I said.

"It does. You should find your own system that works out well."

"Kit—"

"No, don't bother giving me any hogwash you give your mother. You don't want to talk about it, you're not going to talk about it. Despite all the wisdom at your disposal."

"Did you know the FBI has stats on methods used for murder and breaks it down by gender?"

Sure it was an obvious change of subject. Subtlety doesn't work with Kit.

"Of course. The Supplementary Homicide report. You know about that."

"I don't think so. Not until Clara mentioned it."

"I could have sworn it was covered in one of the day-long programs we did with the FBI." A click of her tongue dismissed that as unimportant. "So, Clara found it, did she?"

"Yes, she was checking on the common wisdom that poison is a woman's murder weapon."

"Good for her. We need more of that kind of thinking."

"Especially among author assistants?" I asked dryly.

"Absolutely. We need them to keep their authors on their toes. I need to meet your Clara."

"Yes, you do. Also her husband, Ned, and Donna from the dog park, and several of my neighbors and most of all, Gracie."

"Gracie first. But aren't you forgetting someone?" Before I could say no I wasn't forgetting anyone, she said, "Teague O'Donnell. I need to meet him, too."

"He doesn't talk much about his days as a detective, so he wouldn't be a good source for you." And, oddly, after all the years of watching Kit in action pumping people for background material, I didn't want her doing that to Teague.

"I've got a good many law enforcement sources already. Maybe I want to meet him for something else."

I said nothing.

She sighed.

Some people sigh in resignation or to not express an emotion. Not Kit. Her sighs are as good as a paragraph and she's not resigned to anything.

"All right, Sheila, now that you've heard about my sex life and you won't talk about yours, ready for what we didn't have time to talk about in your earlier call? You tell me yours and I'll tell you mine."

"Yours?"

"Want to hear what I found out about Rod Birchall and the Jolly Roger board?"

"Yes."

DAY FOUR

THURSDAY

CHAPTER FORTY

CLARA ANSWERED THE door in a rush.

"*Just* finished class. It ran long. Thank you for taking LuLu, especially so early. You can let the dogs out in the back yard. Ned's there. Poison ivy's sprayed and the area's closed off. Now he's trimming the regular ivy."

"He's working hard."

"Says he's making up for the neglect during the hottest days and he wanted to beat the rain that's supposed to come in later. Anything at the dog park?"

"Bear's over his diarrhea." Bear was a Newfoundland. Enough said.

"Very good news, but not what I meant."

"Nothing on the murder, but I talked to Kit again last night."

"Oh, good. Want iced tea while you tell me?"

"A FACTION OF the board isn't as blind to Birchall's faults as it might appear," Kit had told me last night. "Trouble is, others either were loyal to him or forced to be loyal."

"Corporate skullduggery?" I'd asked.

"All the time. Too bad none of them were around when he was killed. You'd have prime suspects. Anyway, he outmaneuvered the group trying to maneuver him out by getting Foster Utton named successor."

"He selected Utton as his successor to be sure the board would think twice about dumping him?"

"That's it. Birchall had enough votes to secure his position—for now, anyway. Word was Utton would've been out before the end of the day after next week."

"As long as he was Birchall's heir that's his most obvious motive, but if he knew he wouldn't be heir much longer that makes the motive urgent."

"Unless he's stupid, he knows," Kit had said. "From what I hear, the jury's out on whether or not he's stupid."

"Clara said maybe he'd gone up the corporate ladder because he didn't threaten the people above him. In other words, he was safe."

"Exactly. And that's why Birchall named him successor. He knew the board wouldn't want Utton as CEO, so it became a kind of job security."

"But not life insurance."

"Definitely not life insurance. Also not long-term job security for Utton. They're searching for a replacement at a record-setting pace for this sort of thing."

"THAT'S INTERESTING," CLARA said at the end of my recitation of my conversation with Kit.

"Utton knowing about that could explain what Isaac overheard and gives him a motive. He sees Birchall eat the snack—"

"How did he know it had sesame in it?"

"He didn't. But it gives him the idea to go find a snack he knows includes sesame. Then he goes back and waits for his opportunity when both Jacqueline and the guy in jeans were gone—"

"If they were both gone at the same time. We've got to find that guy to ask."

"—or he uses another door directly to the back room after getting that sesame snack off the shelves, kills Birchall, circles back around and returns to wait with the other two or one if—"

"*Clara! Sheila!*" Ned shouted from the backyard.

We barely took time to exchange a glance before we were out on their back deck and pelting down a story's worth of steps to their ground level patio.

That's how urgent his shout was.

We were propelled by that and an ominous lack of barking.

CHAPTER FORTY-ONE

GRACIE AND LULU had gotten out of the fence enclosing Clara and Ned's yard.

This was bad.

The depth of the bad started with neither dog being street-smart. The rest of the bad rested with geography, the founders of Haines Tavern, and modern real estate.

Since earlier arrivals staked claim to the flatter land and since there are a whole lot of creeks in North Bend County, that left subdivision builders with high ground between creeks and low land along creeks.

Their solution was to level off the ridge of the high ground, run a street along the center of the leveled area, then build houses on either side. The lots had flat or flat-ish front yards, then houses that were two stories in front and three stories in back, and back yards that could serve as ski jumps.

Ski jumps landing in a creek.

If Gracie and LuLu had escaped out the front, we would have had neatly mown lawns to chase them across. Heck, we could have carried parasols and played a game or two of croquet as we went along.

They didn't.

All this flashed through my mind as we ran to Ned.

"I don't remember how long it's been since I noticed them. I saw kids by our back gate." Their yard, like most of the others I could see, had grass on the first part of their back slope, enclosed by a fence with double gates allowing egress to the steepest part of their yard close to the creek. "But I didn't check if they'd opened it. I should have checked. After the last time when LuLu nearly got out, I should have—"

Calm, certain, Clara said, "They must have gone down to the creek. C'mon, let's go."

I felt neither calm nor certain, but we all hurried to the double gates. One gate was opened about a foot. Plenty of space for one or the other of our dogs to lead the other through the gap and into the wild.

Because wild was what awaited us past the gate.

Tangled bushes, clumps of weeds—was that poison ivy?—fallen tree limbs and sharply angled trees seeking sun amid heavy competition.

Despite my instinct to take the lead, good sense said to leave it to them. They had to be more familiar with the area than I was. Ned went first, taking the brunt of the prickly branches on his spread-wide arms. Plenty remained, though. One caught Clara's hair and forehead. Ned pivoted back to her.

"Keep going, keep going." She put her fingers to her temple, came back with blood, wiped her hand on her pants and took her own advice.

A thorn branch snagged my top. I yanked it free, ignored the ripping sound and followed them.

I caught glimpses through the underbrush of the creek bed, half dry, the other half murky with sluggish water following an irregular path.

And then I wasn't behind them anymore, I was shooting forward.

The sharper descent, my slick sandals, and underlying moisture had turned this slip and slide into a demolition derby.

Windmilling my arms to try to stay upright, I slipped and slid into shallow water framed by mud on either side. I encountered both sides, because my downhill speed carried me through the water, through the other line of mud and partway into their back neighbor's wild creek-side fringe. The momentum kept my upper body going, while my feet stayed put in the mud. I went down like a felled tree.

"*Sheila*. Stay still. You're hurt. We'll get help—"

"No." That would take too much time. I tried to pop up convincingly. It was more of a stagger. "I'm okay. Which direction?"

Ned finished hauling me up as we all looked up and down the creek. No dogs, no pawprints, no helpful tufts of fur caught by a branch to show us the way.

"We split up," Ned said. "Cover more territory. I'll go that way." He nodded toward the right. "You guys go the other way."

We stumbled along past first one yard, another, and a third. I stumbled. Clara did fine. We called their names over and over. Alternating. In case Gracie associated being called by me and LuLu by Clara with being in trouble, maybe being called by the other would encourage them to come.

No dice.

The charms of the creek likely kept them fully enthralled.

I was torn.

If they wandered up through a yard on the opposite side of the creek from Clara and Ned's house they'd be in an entirely different neighborhood, where no one would recognize LuLu and possibly contact Clara or Ned.

But the creek led to dangers I tried not to focus on as we kept going.

"Over here." A shout echoed from our left.

We crashed along the creek. My feet slid into the creek—twice. I kept going, dripping water and mud from the sides of my sandals.

Two more yards down and on the opposite side of the creek, a white-haired man stood with a hose, watering tomato plants in a raised bed.

But no dogs in sight.

"You're looking for two dogs?" he called.

"Yes. A Great Pyrenees mix and a collie," Clara said.

He looked blank.

"One mostly white, one mostly brown," I said.

"They were pretty dirty, but probably, yeah."

"How long ago?"

"A few minutes. Maybe five. Tried whistling to them. They were having too much fun. Headed that way."

A flip of the hose indicated away from Clara and Ned's house.

"Thank you, thank you."

I started forward, but Clara held up. "I have to let Ned know. Damn. I don't have my phone. I left it on the table."

"I have mine."

She grimaced. "Ned doesn't have his. He never does in the yard. Maybe… Ned! *Ned!* They went this way." She got no answer. "You go ahead. I'll catch up."

While she retraced our steps, I continued on, pulling out my phone while I also looked for any sign of our dogs.

Teague answered cheerfully after three rings.

"Gracie and LuLu are lost. I don't know when I'll be there."

"Lost? Where? When?" Totally different tone. The cop on duty.

"They got out of Clara and Ned's yard. We don't know how long ago. Can't be more than fifteen minutes. Looks like they got down to the creek and they're headed toward the highway," I said grimly.

"I'll be right there."

"Teague—"

He'd hung up.

That let me hear Ned's answering call to Clara behind me. That meant she'd be starting back toward me.

I resumed my soggy, sloppy, slow progress in the direction the tomato-waterer had indicated.

Clara caught up with me. "Ned's coming, too. Oh, God, if something's happened to them… It will break his heart if LuLu's hurt, but if Gracie is, he'll never forgive himself. Never."

"We're not going to think that way. Clara, these shoes are slowing me down. You go ahead since you can move faster."

She did. Soon she had nearly two yards' worth of a lead on me. I heard her calling the dogs' names, along with "Good girl" and "Come." I knew "Come" wouldn't work and had little hope for "Good girl." They were surely having too much fun.

Ned caught up with me, panting and red-faced. He slowed to my pace. "I'm so sorry, Sheila. I can't believe—"

"We'll find them." I had to interrupt him. I couldn't bear to hear the dire possibilities lurking in those somber tones.

"Lulu! Gracie!"

Clara's call was different, though we couldn't see her around a clot of trees forcing a bend in the creek. "She's spotted them," I told him.

Driven by two spurs—hope and a sound I now identified as vehicles on the highway, I picked up my pace as much as I could against the dragging-me-down sandals. I'd ditch the darned things if I thought I could move faster barefoot. But I'd be hobbled in a half dozen strides on these rocks.

I cleared the trees and could see ahead.

To the rear ends of two mud-soaked dogs, their tails high and happy.

And to the highway, with cars and pickups and big trucks whizzing along.

It was raised the height of a house above the creek, but access to it was provided by a sloped embankment that would be all too apparent to adventuring dogs.

Their alternative would be to go under the highway through a concrete tube.

I thought of the agility equipment coming soon. If they were already used to those tunnels, they'd more likely accept that safer path now. But they weren't used to it.

I pushed for more speed, almost even with Clara and Ned now.

"Gracie! Gracie!" I shouted. I swear her ears flickered around like furry radar dishes.

But she didn't slow and she didn't look back. LuLu had her head down, sniffing, letting Gracie take the lead. If Gracie went through the tunnel, LuLu would, too.

"Go through the pipe," I muttered. "Go through the pipe."

"Maybe if we flank them, we can guide them into the pipe," Clara said.

"We can try, but from this far back…"

"We'll try. Ned, you go up that way." She pointed left. "I'll go up this other side. Sheila, you stay in the middle."

After only a few feet of following his diagonal path, Ned called, "Somebody's pulling over. On the highway."

My brain went six ways at once. A dog snatcher. The dog catcher. A good Samaritan. A ghoul prepared to take pot shots at "strays."

I could see only part of one tire, offering no reassurance.

Ned, Clara, and I surged forward.

Gracie's head came up, her attention caught by a change in activity—not ours, but on the highway shoulder above her.

And then, as if my earlier thoughts conjured the actions, she started up the embankment.

"No. No. *No!*" I shouted.

Not even an ear flicker. She disappeared around a clump of bushes, then Lulu, trotting after her.

Gasping and slipping, I desperately tried to go faster. To defy the equation putting me, Ned, Clara, all there too late. The equation of dogs and a highway.

My phone rang. Teague. Panting, I jabbed at it with a shaking finger, still moving.

"Teague—"

His voice interrupted, clear and certain. "Got 'em."

CHAPTER FORTY-TWO

I HEARD THE solid *thunk* of his truck door closing in stereo—on his phone and ahead of me up the embankment.

Ned made it up to the highway first, then leaned over to help Clara.

Teague came around the back of his truck and reached down to me. We clasped wrists and my abused feet barely touched the surface as he hauled me up.

"You look like hell." He gazed down at me. "Trying out for a season of *Survivor*?"

I continued the motion his hauling started by stepping into him and hugging him. "Thank you."

He held on, his breath stirring my hair as he teased, "For the compliment?"

"For Gracie and LuLu."

He felt solid and reliable and oh, so good.

He felt like somebody I was lying to.

My arms dropped from around him. His didn't release me.

"How did you do it?" I asked as I stepped back.

"I held onto Murph's leash, opened the back door, let him bark, and they came straight for us. Jumped right into the back seat of the truck like flowing water. Only hitch was getting the door closed without catching any of the wagging tails."

That explained the smear of mud across his noise and one cheek. I raised a hand to rub it away, then dropped it.

Instead, I said, "You've got mud on your face."

"You've got mud everywhere."

He was right.

Also one of my feet was bleeding. Clara's face and both of Ned's arms had oozing scratches.

"C'mon, everybody get in the truck and we'll get the two escapees back and get you all cleaned up."

Saying, "This is all my fault because I let them get out," Ned insisted on sitting in back with the three dogs, two of them even muddier than we were and all of them vying to sit in his lap.

Clara pushed me into the front seat of the truck cab ahead of her, then nudged me over until I was flush against Teague's side.

I gave her a dirty look, but she pretended to be busy fastening her seat belt.

She had to ease up pushing against me to let me fasten mine, but as soon as it was clicked, I was shoved back to his side. His warm, solid, muscled side.

Teague glanced at me, but said nothing, as he returned his attention to driving. Specifically doing a spritely U-turn to head to Clara and Ned's.

✧ ✧ ✧ ✧

WE HOSED DOWN as best we could outside, Clara, Ned, me, Gracie and LuLu. Even Teague and Murphy needed a little cleanup.

I left Gracie, with her leash hooked to the railings of the deck, so she'd dry out.

All the dogs were secured that way, in a taking no chances precaution of the closing the barn door after the horse is out variety.

Especially since Gracie and LuLu were now happily exhausted. I borrowed old towels and rugs to protect my car from my soggy clothes. At home, they went right in the washer and I went right in the shower.

Clean hair, clean body, clean clothes did wonders. Bandages on my foot protected the scrapes that had been bleeding, adding a challenge to finding shoes. But I overcame that and headed back to Clara and Ned's.

Going around back, I found Teague sitting on the deck with the three snoozing dogs. He had his legs stretched out, crossed at the ankle and the glass of ice water balanced on his flat abdomen.

He looked—

"Where are Clara and Ned?" I asked instead of finishing my thought.

"Inside. Showering."

Just then, giggling came through to us from inside, accompanied by a deeper chuckle.

Our gazes, connected during the mundane earlier exchange, caught. And held.

He grinned slightly, both appreciating their pleasure and acknowledging the awkwardness of overhearing it.

Did it also acknowledge an awareness between…?

The reminder on my phone went off. Saved by a ringtone.

I shouted, "Clara, we have to leave or we'll be late for our appointment. Our appointment in Indianapolis."

"Oh. Yes," came her muted voice. "Okay. I'll be right there. We can't be late for that!"

CHAPTER FORTY-THREE

"**THERE HE IS,**" I said.

We'd driven to Indianapolis in good time, allowing us to pick up a fast food lunch consumed while staking out the unemployment office near where two interstates connected on the east side.

The downside of the set-up was a central circle divided the parking. If he parked far to one side or the other, we could have a hard time intercepting him before he reached the doors. We did not want to have to talk to him after he'd been inside and discovered he did not have an appointment or a problem with his application.

We parked as close as we could to the center then watched carefully.

Fortunately, Ward Ebersole also parked close to the center, a few rows away from the doors. As he walked toward the entrance, we hopped out, separated as we'd agreed, with me getting behind him.

When he was boxed in between cars, Clara, from in front of him, said, "Ward Ebersole, right?"

Immediately, he spun around. And found me behind him.

"You," he said in surely unintentional mimicry of Rod Birchall.

"We want to talk to you. We know you're Ward Ebersole. We know you were a butcher with Jolly Roger and were among those fired last week. We know you were there in the Haines Tavern store when Birchall was murdered. We know you and Jacqueline live together. All that and more will go to law enforcement if we don't stop transmission in a few minutes."

I glanced up at the building. He turned his head, looking in the direction I'd looked.

If he saw someone in a window, he had far better vision than I did, but all he had to do was wonder if someone was watching us.

"What happened when you went in the back room after we all saw Birchall on the floor?" I asked.

"What do you think happened? I made sure he was dead." Facing me again, he smiled grimly at his own turn of phrase. "Then I got the hell out of there."

"Why?"

He said nothing.

"Did you kill him?"

"Then?" he asked dryly.

"Then or at any time."

"No comment."

"Okay, let's back up. While Foster Utton was away from the produce section and it was just you and Jacqueline, did either of you go into the back room?"

He didn't ask who Foster was, so presumably he'd been following coverage on TV or in the newspaper, which had all run the Jolly Roger corporate website photo of the acting CEO. The newspaper had far more complete information than the TV coverage, but both were well behind us.

"No."

"While Jacqueline was away, did either you or Foster go into the back room?"

There was a pause, then an almost reluctant, "No."

He'd seen a possible way out, a future for his romance with Jacqueline that didn't include one of them in prison for life. He hadn't taken it.

"Did you know Foster Utton before Monday at the Haines Tavern store?"

"No."

"Did you see anyone go into the back room by any door after Rod Birchall did?"

A flicker of his eyelids made me wonder if the idea of someone going in another door was new to him.

"No." More reluctance.

"Did you hear anything from that back room after the rest of us left?"

"No."

"Did anyone say anything that might shed any light on Birchall's death?"

"No."

"If Jacqueline killed him—?"

"She didn't." Without meaning to, he'd answered my question, which would have been if he would lie to protect her ... this one answered with a rare *yes*.

"What do you think you're accomplishing by disappearing like this, much less this clam routine? If you truly believe in her innocence, you should be down at the North Bend County Sheriff's Department, unburdening your soul of every last detail. As it is, you're muddying the waters and making Jacqueline a strong suspect. Unless you know she murdered Birchall and—"

"There's another explanation."

"Yeah. That you killed him. Did you?"

The muscle beside his eye ticked. "I'm not saying if I did or I didn't."

"If you did, they'll probably get you with forensics. Eventually. Sometimes takes years and years. Even decades. In the meantime, are you *trying* to make her look guilty?"

"She didn't kill him."

"That's sure not what your actions say. Your actions say she did it and you know it and you're trying to cover for her."

"We're done here."

"Not quite. We want your phone number."

"Are you kidding?"

"No. We're trying to figure out this mess. If neither you nor Jacqueline committed the crime, everything we do will move the case closer to being solved and proving your innocence. You should want to help us."

"No way."

I eyed him. "Look, we have a witness who saw you and Jacqueline together in the parking lot before Birchall arrived, not to mention all the people at your old store and in your lives who would testify you're involved. Another whole bunch of people saw you in the Haines Tavern store at the time Birchall was there. Then there's you and Jacqueline being feet away from where Birchall lay dead with a set of swinging doors between you. You're tied to this. Jacqueline's tied to this. All that can go to law enforcement and they'll take it from there. Is that what you want?

"At least we're looking beyond the obvious of you and Jacqueline as the prime suspects."

I thought I heard his teeth gnashing. "Leave a message the way you did this time. That's all you get."

Not letting on that it was better than I'd expected, I growled. "Check your messages. Frequently."

I backed up, opening the aisle for him to exit. He glanced toward the building, recognized he didn't have an appointment to keep and walked past me, saying, "You two are nuts."

"Are not," Clara said, mostly to us, since he was out of earshot for her quiet words.

I turned her toward my car and we started walking. "Why didn't you say anything, Clara?"

"Because you were doing so well with honest, forthright, and blunt, which you do so well."

I wasn't touching honest and forthright with a ten-foot pole—or my history with *Abandon All*. "Surprised you'd think blunt would work," I muttered.

"Oh, Kentucky men often need blunt."

"Uh, Clara. I think he's from Indiana."

"That explains a lot."

CHAPTER FORTY-FOUR

WE CALLED KAREN Zalesk on the way back to North Bend County.

She agreed we could stop by to talk … after we dangled the hint that we wanted to talk about food allergies and labeling.

She wasted no time on chit-chat when we arrived, finding her alone at the old Family Place. Heck, she barely invited us to come in when we knocked on the door we'd left by on our first visit.

The only sign of Lorelei was the sound of a children's movie from another room.

We received a precise and extensive rundown of discoveries in food allergies and wrongdoing in food labeling. She did know her stuff.

"The laws have loopholes," Karen said. "Some of the companies slip through them. Since Birchall arrived, the Jolly Roger chain drove Mack Trucks through them.

"First of all, they don't have to list every ingredient. Only certain foods are considered major allergens and those are the only ones required to be listed in the United States."

"Even if they know something can kill people?"

Clara's indignation fed Karen. "Wait, it gets worse. Most countries have their own lists of which ones have to be listed, so there's no standardization. You have to know which allergens have to be listed in which country to be sure the one that can kill your child isn't lurking. And then there are the exceptions, which has included 'fresh food.' Labels for foods prepared on-site don't have to include allergens—if there are labels at all. When Birchall—"

The outside door opened and Judy and Gundy Vance walked in.

"—realized that, suddenly all sorts of things were labeled as 'fresh.' Then he sat back smugly and essentially said catch me if you can. Well, I guess he was caught."

As understandable as her anger was, her satisfaction at Birchall's death was unsettling.

"He deserved everything he got and mo—"

"Karen—"

She spun on her brother. "I didn't tell you they were coming so you could try to shut me up."

"Of course you did," Judy Vance said calmly. "You wouldn't have called Gundy if you hadn't wanted him to save you from yourself. Again."

"Hadn't you better put all your energies into saving your husband, Judy? Especially from that cute, young assistant manager at the Roger. I understood a lot when I got a look at her."

Judy's face went tight and angry, but she held it in, saying coolly. "For someone who values correct information, you are wildly misinformed. Again."

"I know enough to—"

"Cut it out. Both of you," Gundy ordered, though it was clear he meant it only for Karen. "It's clear they didn't come to talk to you about food allergies and labeling."

"We did, actually," I said. "Though we'd also like to know where Karen went and what she did Monday from the time she took Lorelei away from Birchall in the produce section and leaving the store."

Before Gundy could stop her, she said, "I raged and tried to disguise the fact of my rage from my distressed daughter by pretending to study the shelves of our family business' rival. One side of the store to the other, as if my observations would ever be given any weight—"

"God," Gundy breathed.

"—until he finally arrived. The anointed one, handing out aid. The *boy*. The reason I would never be considered worthy of being the caretaker of precious Shep's, the family legacy."

"This again? You could have come home. You could have taken over Shep's Market when Dad had the bad stroke."

"Me? He never wanted me in charge. Never believed I was worthy. Dad said as much that last Christmas I was here." She turned to me. "He said he'd never expected me to graduate from college and he was quite surprised I was doing as well as I was in the working world. I was vice president of a marketing company."

Gundy tried. "He was proud of you. That's what he was saying."

"He'd expected me to get married and start popping out kids and I wasn't meeting his expectations. Overachieving messed with his expectations. Meanwhile, Gundy got the family name—and business—while I got a leftover."

"You got a family name, too."

"Some dead cousin's name to make her mother—her rich mother—happy. Except it didn't. She cried every time she saw me, so I soon learned to run away whenever I saw her.

"And a fat lot of good it did me being named for a dead girl. Her mother left all her money to build baseball fields for kids because that's what her Karen liked. A real tomboy or a—"

"Really, Karen," Judy said, still cool. "Will you please think before you speak? It might help in your divorce proceedings as well as in a murder inquiry."

✧　✧　✧　✧

JUDY WALKED US to the car.

"You'll have to excuse my sister-in-law. She is going through a very difficult time. Almost losing Lorelei and the divorce. She's always had a sharp edge. Now she is her own worst enemy."

✧　✧　✧　✧

"JUDY WAS RIGHT, Karen Zalesk is her own worst enemy," Clara said. "I don't know that I believed a word of what she said about walking around the store after her confrontation with Birchall.

"The only thing that stops me from thinking she's a top suspect is what she would have done with Lorelei while committing murder. Leave her out in the store? No way. Take her with? Again, no way.

Take her in the back room but a little way off and risk the girl seeing or hearing her commit murder? That doesn't work either."

"Judy Vance might be right about Karen, but she is also worried. Possibly angry, too. Did you see her face after Karen's comment about Jacqueline…? Do you think Judy thinks Gundy is having an affair?"

Clara did her lip chewing. "I suppose it's possible, but I didn't get a jealousy vibe off her. Maybe the anger is what she's feeling for her sister-in-law? Thinking Karen drew Vance into a mess and now her temper is digging them both in deeper?"

"Possible. Definitely possible. Karen was the most demonstrably upset of any of them Monday. But does that mean she was more likely to kill Birchall because she was angry? Or less likely to kill him and pull it off, because she was upset?"

"Let's go back to Jacqueline. Revenge for Birchall's firing her mentor and her boyfriend as her motive? That seems like a stretch," Clara said.

I told her my thoughts about Jacqueline possibly fearing for her own job adding a potential layer to her motive.

Then I added, "Like we said before, a spur of the moment murder. She's angry about her mentor and Ward. Birchall suddenly shows up and then she's also worried about her job. He's there, there's an opportunity. She takes it."

"What about Ward? He was angry, too," Clara said. "He could have lied about Birchall being dead. Say Birchall was sick, incapacitated, but not dead. Ward Ebersole waits until he's back there with the supposed body and that's when he hits Birchall in the head. That's when he commits murder. And then he walks out the side door. Petey missed seeing him or he waited until Petey was looking in the other direction. In a minute, he could be in his truck and gone."

"That's good."

"Then why do you sound depressed?"

"Because we have plausible scenarios for all of them, the ones we just talked about and Foster Utton and Kurt Verker while nothing points more to one than the other."

Clara patted my shoulder.

"It's been a long day with The Great Dog Pursuit taking a lot out of us. Not to mention, we could use more salve on our nicks and cuts. Let's make an early night of it and start fresh tomorrow."

I DREAMT ABOUT the dogs running away and our pursuit.

But as if from the perspective of a drone. Looking down, seeing the pattern of the creek, with the houses on one side of it not connected to those on the other side. Close when looking down, yet distant if judged by roads and borders.

And then the highway, with the culvert carrying the creek underneath.

And the fear.

Though that was mine. Not the drone's and not the dogs'. They padded on below my drone view, noses to the ground, tails high, prepared to make any sacrifice for this moment of supreme satisfaction.

I woke abruptly from the dream. Unsure for a breath where I was, where I'd been. Both came back quickly. Yet leaving a sense of incompleteness.

Which made no sense. I was not a drone. I had no need to know the pattern of Clara's neighborhood. I had no cause for fear. Not anymore. The dogs were back. Safe.

And dreams would not help catch a murderer.

Or would they?

I rolled over to find out.

DAY FIVE

FRIDAY

CHAPTER FORTY-FIVE

IF DREAMS WERE going to help, they sure weren't serving up the aid on a silver platter.

Nothing cleared up with the additional sleep.

And, Clara kindly pointed out, as we sat on aging lawn chairs outside my back door, I still looked tired. We'd returned from the dog park with all three dogs, who now lolled in the shade. Teague continued work on the retaining wall.

Clara and I had rehashed what we knew, agreed it eliminated no one. Now we were tossing around ideas of how to organize what we knew in order to figure out what to do next.

"How about if we look at who's told lies and what those lies are," I suggested.

"Told lies? Jacqueline Yancik. Ward Ebersole. Foster Utton. Gundy Vance. Even Isaac. Oh, and Kurt Verker. In other words, everybody. Maybe except Karen Zalesk. On the other hand, if there were camera footage, maybe we'd know she lied, too."

"Then we go deeper than the outright lies, examining the small, seemingly inconsequential inconsistencies…"

I was saying that when my conscious mind went on hiatus while another part of my brain assembled, rearranged, and collated small, seemingly inconsequential inconsistencies.

Until Clara asked a question that snapped me back to the here and now.

"Why are you looking at Teague like you've never seen him before?"

"It's not Teague." I barely even saw him. *Barely*. I had to think *that* word.

"Of course it is. Teague O'Donnell. Right there in your back yard. Shirtless. Which I must say is not hard to look at and—"

"It's not Teague, it's what he did to catch the dogs yesterday."

"You mean the murderer's run away?"

"Sort of. It's also that pieces that seem very far away from each other if you take the normal routes can actually be quite close together if you get a bird's-eye view. Also, we're *chasing* the murderer, which sends him—or her—farther away from where things started. We need to stop and think about the lever we can use to have the murderer come to us. Like Teague did."

"You mean use a lure like Murphy."

I turned to her slowly. "That's right, Clara. That's exactly right. A lever *and* a lure."

"Okay." She dragged it out to seven syllables.

"Don't you see? We use what the murderer handed us."

CLARA DIDN'T SEE. Not until much later.

But she went along with me in gathering everybody at the Roger. Not only went along, but tossed around more than her share of fibs.

That let me confirm a large part of what Teague would surely call speculation, but Clara called brilliant.

Her faith in me was touching.

Also nerve-wracking.

What if I was wrong? Sure, I'd be embarrassed. Worse, I'd disappoint Clara.

And Hensen…?

He'd have my liver for garters.

So why gather everybody together to witness my potential humiliation?

Because the audience was crucial. Especially since this was going to be one of those interactive events where the audience's participation would make or break the play.

✧ ✧ ✧ ✧

A DIFFERENT FOSTER Utton from the one we'd seen Tuesday in his closet-sized office, strode into the Haines Tavern Jolly Roger store, almost hitting the slow automatic doors.

His suit matched Birchall's, his hair had been styled, his posture was straighter, his confidence higher. I suspected the king-making hand of Ms. DesJames.

Or was this the real Foster Utton?

"You're out of uniform," he scolded Myghavnn as she walked past.

"No, I'm not."

"You're supposed to wear black slacks. Those are tights. Cheap tights."

"Not according to the label from the store where I bought them. According to that, they're dress pants."

"You've been cheated. Return them and get your money back."

"Can't. They're from the Jolly Roger superstore in Stringer and the policy—your policy—is no returns after ten days or without the price tag attached."

She snapped her gum and walked off ahead of him.

Inside the suit, under the haircut, he deflated halfway back to Tuesday's Foster Utton.

Clara stepped forward and gently guided him to the gathering in the back room.

No, not through the doors from produce, but the next set of doors over.

Several people already waited there on a horseshoe of folding chairs, courtesy of Jacqueline.

Courtesy might be misleading. That was one of the fibs. We'd told her if she didn't cooperate we'd tell Deputy Hensen everything we knew about Ward Ebersole.

We'd already told him a fair amount. Not quite everything. Our fibs with Hensen were fibs of omission.

Then we told Ward Ebersole that if he didn't come to this meeting, deputies were going to arrest Jacqueline.

We also fibbed to Gundy Vance, Karen Zalesk, and Kurt Verker.

We invited Phyllis, Aggie, Petey, the three red vests, and Judy Vance, saying we might need information from them and they'd find out what happened. Sure hoped *that* wasn't a fib.

Clara and I stood at the open end of the horseshoe.

The doors opened to our last guest. "Oh, hell." Isaac had arrived. "This isn't a job, is it?"

Yup, if we didn't pull this off, we'd have a bunch of irked people.

Including a murderer.

CHAPTER FORTY-SIX

"YOU'VE ALL HEARD of means, motive, and opportunity—"

"Nah," Josh said.

I gave him a sharp look, but needn't have bothered. He met Phyllis Ezzard's gaze and clamped his mouth closed.

"The means in this case started with Birchall being immobilized by his allergic reaction to sesame—first by the snack he took from the tray without a warning labeling on it—"

Karen Zalesk made a sound.

"—then reinforced with a pre-packaged sesame snack when Birchall couldn't defend himself."

"That's why you and the deputies were interested in those snack packages," Belinda muttered.

Her mention of deputies sifted a new dusting of solemnity over the gathering.

"The cameras for the snack aisle were disabled, which also covered the route to the back room doors by dairy, then across the back room to Birchall, weakened and on the floor. The sesame might have killed him on its own, but the murderer didn't wait to see. It was easy to dispose of Birchall at that point. Anyone could do it. Also, anyone could have disabled the cameras easily and quickly. Looking at means eliminates no one."

I looked around the group, then drew in a breath.

"Next, there's a big gap in everyone's alibis called opportunity. Anyone who was in the store had time—the short amount of time needed—to go to the office, click off the appropriate cameras, grab the

sesame snack, come into this back room, walk to where Birchall was—"
I gestured in that direction. "—kill him, then return to wherever their
alibi resumes. And those who weren't known to be in the store had
even more time."

"What about the ones right on the spot," Karen asked. "Three of
them, weren't there?"

"Yes. Jacqueline Yancik, the assistant store manager. Foster Utton,
now CEO of Jolly Roger. And Ward Ebersole here. Not all of you
might know him by name yet."

"Sheila and I kept calling you the guy in jeans. It's nice to have
your name."

He did not return Clara's friendly smile.

"Who is he?" Karen asked.

Ward stared them all down. "I'm a butcher, formerly employed by
the Jolly Roger chain."

Belinda popped up, excited by discovery. "Jacqueline's boyfriend.
The famous boyfriend. And he was one of the ones right outside the
doors where Birchall got murdered."

"He didn't do anything. There wasn't time—"

I interrupted Jacqueline. "There was plenty time for each of you
when you were out in the store and if two of you were gone at the
same time, the one left..."

"Jacqueline and I were both gone for a while," Ward said.

"That's not what you said yesterday."

Before Ward could respond, Foster spluttered into speech.

"You're saying—You're saying, I—?"

"We're saying you had means and opportunity," I said, "without
Ward Ebersole lying about your being alone by the doors yesterday."

Ward didn't rise to that challenge.

I continued, "That leaves motive. That's what separates out people
who had means and opportunity, but not motive—" I gestured toward
the red vests and other witnesses. "—from the rest of you. But first,
let's address something else."

Did I imagine a stir of impatience emanating from behind the
boxes strategically stacked on one side?

"That something is that after Rod Birchall was found, Ward Ebersole said he was going to stay with the body, but, instead, disappeared. What happened back there, Ward?"

"I closed of that part of the back room like I told Jacqueline I'd do, then I left."

"We know. Why?"

"Didn't want to get involved."

"You mean you didn't want to get Jacqueline even more involved than she already is. You hoped to deflect attention from her? Or did you hope authorities would *think* you were trying to deflect attention from her, setting up doubt about your guilt?"

"She's not involved."

"Yes, she is," Kurt Verker intruded. "She has a better motive than anybody else."

That got everyone's attention.

"She's been leaking advance information to Vance about our specials."

CHAPTER FORTY-SEVEN

"You're fired," Foster Utton said to Jacqueline.

No one paid him any attention. Ms. DesJames still had a steep climb to transform him … assuming he wasn't on trial for murder.

Judy Vance gave her husband an I-told-you-it-was-a-bad-idea glare, but said nothing.

Ah. She'd known and hadn't approved. That, not suspicion of an affair, explained her anger.

"I knew it, I knew it," Belinda crowed.

"Well, well, well, you have more gumption than I thought," Karen said to her brother.

"Shut up, Karen."

"I will not shut—"

Jacqueline succeeded quieting Karen where Gundy had not. "I'm not sorry I did it. This chain's been pulling dirty tricks on Shep's Market and others like it for years, trying to drive them out of business, sometimes succeeding. I'd watched it happen in Indiana until an ethical manager took over. When I came here, I couldn't watch it anymore without doing something. I believe in small stores."

Kurt Verker sneered. "You took money for it. It's not about belief."

"Yes, I need the income." Her effort not to look at Ward made her eyes twitch. "But I do believe."

It was what I'd suspected, but something wasn't quite right…

With everybody else turned toward Jacqueline, I kept watching Kurt.

Why would he attack Jacqueline this way? I still believe his MO was running away. Was this some version of running away? But if so, how? What could he be running away from by attacking her?

"Oh." Got it. "*You* were the original leak."

Kurt's head snapped around to me so fast that his front-heavy body almost toppled out of the chair. Belinda steadied him with a hand on his arm, then withdrew it immediately.

"How do you—? What? What are you talking about? I have no idea what you mean." Not only had he given himself away with the physical reaction and his first words, but his other words lacked conviction. "I don't even know the man."

"Yes, you do. You were in a program together to use unsold food to help the homeless," Clara said. "It was in the newspaper. I read about it."

Verker gawked.

Gundy cleared his throat. "Very good, Clara. That is how we met. And how it started."

"Motive," I said, "for Jacqueline Yancik, Gundy Vance, and Kurt Verker."

"Not me, not me. She took money—"

Gundy cut across Verker's protests. "You took money, too. You just didn't hold up your end of the bargain well. More from incompetence, I believe, than any loyalty to Jolly Roger."

Does a possum's face turn red? Because his did. "You're lashing out because you got caught, Vance."

"If I'm caught, you're caught, too. I have recordings of our conversations."

"Th—that's not legal."

Gundy laughed. "Good luck pleading that to the Jolly Roger chain. They won't care."

"You're fired," Foster said to Verker.

That reminded me.

"Foster, did Birchall order changes in the labeling that give less information to those who might be allergic to ingredients?"

"Um…"

"Making the type small, changing the rules about what needs to be listed…"

"Um, yeah. He did."

"Are you going to undo it?" demanded Karen.

"Me?"

"Yes, you, you weak-kneed—"

I talked over Karen. "And that's the second motive for Gundy Vance, who was spotted near dairy section doors to the back room. The cameras on those doors were disabled. But motive…" I raised one finger. "First motive, the protection of his ongoing source of information on the specials, to keep Shep's Market on the upswing." Another finger. "Second, Birchall's role in the labeling issues, which nearly cost the life of Gundy's niece, Lorelei. Though that motive can be seen as stronger for the girl's mother."

Forestalling another eruption from Karen, I quickly continued.

"More motives. Foster Utton, as we know now, was the heir to the CEO job, so there's one level of motive. Plus, Birchall planned to remove him from his position next week, so that made it urgent."

"You're—"

"You can't fire me. I don't work for Jolly Roger," I said. "And then there's Verker's phone call."

"I didn't—"

"You did, too," Belinda said harshly. "I heard the whole thing. I tried to ask how I could help you. I would have done anyth…"

This time I talked over to cover her vulnerability. Even possums can be an object of love.

"Jacqueline told us about Kurt Verker running out of his office after a phone call, saying he was taken ill. But she wasn't there because she and Ward were in his truck in the parking lot, canoodling."

"Canoe—what?" Myghavnn asked.

Phyllis Ezzard's mouth twitched in appreciation.

"Verker ran off, hoping avoiding Birchall might save his job long enough for him to retire, as well as hiding his being the original leak."

"What about her? What about her?" he possum-squeaked, pointing at Jacqueline.

Ward half rose from his chair.

"Don't be stupid," I snapped at him. "We all know Jacqueline has motive—her role as the leak and you. And your motives were protecting her and rage at Birchall for being fired."

He'd sat even before Hensen stepped out from behind the boxes, drawing gasps.

Hensen zeroed in on Clara and me, but clearly not from concern for our physical safety. "What are you two doing? So far you've accused everybody here."

"Not everybody," Clara said to his second sentence.

"Figuring it out," I said to his first.

"I thought you called us all here because you already figured it out," Gundy grumbled. "Or I wouldn't have come."

"Yes, you would have," Clara said. "You were as curious as everybody else and as worried. Now all of you be quiet and let Sheila think this through."

I heard all that, but most of my attention was elsewhere.

"Things that don't fit," I started.

"Like Petey saying he didn't know Karen, but that's not so," Clara said encouragingly.

"Actually, Petey *didn't* say he didn't know Karen and Lorelei. He said it was the first time he'd seen them at the Roger. That could be true. And his telling us Isaac never went inside, when we know he did, because you and I saw him—that could have been a mistake because Petey was actually in the store himself. That explains why he didn't see some people leaving, too.

"But set that aside for a moment." I spoke quickly. I'd heard an indrawn breath as of someone preparing to speak, probably to dispute. Not yet. There was more to pile on to reach the tipping point. "Let's go back to when Birchall arrived.

"Jacqueline said Petey called and told her the CEO was at the store as the limo arrived. Isaac and Foster said Petey was complaining about them parking—*CEO or no CEO*—the instant Isaac got out of the car."

"That's right, he did. Before I said who was in my car."

Neither Clara nor I acknowledged the driver's contribution as I asked the question, "How did Petey know it was the CEO?"

She pulled her bottom lip in and set her top teeth on it. "Recognized him? Newspaper or the internet or a corporate newsletter?"

"Why hide that? Plus, Petey said he'd never seen Rod Birchall before."

"Kurt Verker told him as he ran out of the store?" Clara suggested.

"I didn't know," Verker said. "I keep telling you, I got sick and—"

I talked over the interruption no one believed. "Why would Verker hide it from everyone inside the store, make up an unlikely excuse about why he was leaving, then blab to Petey in the parking lot? They aren't close friends or anything."

"But then…"

I slowly nodded. "Exactly. Petey *did* recognize Rod Birchall as the CEO. Recognized him from one quick glance. But he chose to lie about it. Why?"

CHAPTER FORTY-EIGHT

CLARA'S TIMING WAS impeccable. "There's no reason he shouldn't recognize the company's CEO, so the fact he lied about it must be significant."

"Entirely significant. Think of why Petey moved back here—his daughter's sad death. Of Petey showing photos of his grandkids against backdrops of mountains. Of Petey lying about recognizing the CEO, who'd been brought in from that bankrupt chain in—"

"Idaho. And that's where Petey moved from."

"And where his grandkids still are."

"The chain Rod Birchall ran that went bankrupt, that was in Idaho, wasn't it?"

"It was."

"You think Petey and Birchall knew each other from there?"

"Or maybe only Petey knew *of* Birchall, while Birchall had no knowledge of Petey. Petey's daughter, the mother of those grandchildren he's so proud of, Donna told us about her sad downward spiral— losing her house, losing her kids, getting into drugs, and dying. And it all started with being let go from her job through no fault of her own. That's what Donna said. *Through no fault of her own.* What if—?"

"His daughter managed a store in the chain Birchall ran there? Donna said Petey worked part-time with his daughter out West and what could be more natural than for him to look for the same kind of job here."

I nodded at Clara. "And one day, in walks the man behind her losing her job, starting her downward spiral—Rod Birchall."

"The man responsible for my girl losing everything, including her babies, and her life. He deserved to die," Petey said quietly.

He stood and looked around.

"I did it. And I don't want to get anybody else in trouble."

CHAPTER FORTY-NINE

Hensen told Teague, who told us, that they confirmed when Petey went inside the Roger from a camera on the neighboring bank building.

"But he confessed," Clara said. "Why do they want evidence when he already confessed?"

"In case he unconfesses, which happens, especially when lawyers get involved," Teague said.

"Petey won't," Clara said.

"No, he won't," I agreed. "That's part of Petey. Like his not wanting to get other people in trouble. Especially not for what he did. That was the one lever we had. Getting everybody together and having him see other people were in trouble, were suspected … I figured he wouldn't let that happen."

"A leap," Teague said.

"A hope," I countered. "There were things Petey didn't tell us, but the only thing he told us that wasn't true was that Isaac stayed by his limo the whole time and that was a mistake. Petey assumed Isaac was there.

"Petey never said he saw Gundy Vance going *in* the store, because Petey wasn't there to see him go in after Karen called him. That's why he missed Phyllis Ezzard and Aggie Hickmott leaving, too. And why he thought Isaac never left his spot.

"Because Petey was inside. First, looking at the cameras, watching Birchall on them, leaving those produce cameras all pointing at the doors to the back room. And then disabling all the cameras on his path past the sesame snacks to the back room doors by dairy."

Clara said, "He didn't want to say who he'd seen because he truly didn't want to get them in trouble. Didn't want to cast suspicion on people for the crime he committed," Clara said.

"Or, he didn't want to risk pinning down his timeline too tight and having it reveal he hadn't been outside the entire time."

Teague's comment drew a look of reproach from Clara.

"The way he'd talked about Karen and Lorelei. Almost poetic," she said. "He had to be thinking of his daughter and grandchildren. Grandchildren he might never see again because the father has custody now."

Also, because Petey was likely to be in prison for a long time, if not the rest of his life.

No, I didn't say that. I wasn't inviting Clara's reproach the way Teague had.

DURING OUR PHONE conversation that night, I cried a little when I told Kit about Petey's daughter and grandchildren. But not about his being arrested for murder.

It was like we'd told him. He couldn't get anybody in trouble if they hadn't done anything wrong.

CLARA HAD NEARLY finished her course in being an author's assistant. She already was working as the instructor's assistant.

School was back in session, though Teague hadn't yet been called to substitute teach.

I'd put aside the romance novel set in the Blue Ridge Mountains I'd been trying to write. I hope to—no, I *will*—get back to it. But I heard a snippet of dialogue in my head while walking Gracie the other evening and I've been following its lead.

The scary thing is it might lead me so deep into the woods I'll never get out. Or it will be like the yellow brick road in Oz and expose me to trees that throw apples, flying monkeys, poppy fields—a nap does sound good—and lead to a charlatan who isn't entirely wicked and a witch who is, but eventually home, having made a trio of great friends.

I'm betting lost in the woods.

But I won't know unless I try it.

What is the snippet of dialogue project about? I'm not sure. It starts with a character coming to a writer and asking her to take him back. I know, I know, characters talking to their writer. Strange. And it's getting stranger as I write.

The agility area opened on a glorious, sunny day. Hot, but not stifling.

It was happy chaos, made even better because Berrie brought only two of her younger Boston terriers.

Adding to the pleasure for Clara, Teague, and me was the news Kit had delivered the night before that the Jolly Roger board had voted in safeguards against mass firings, along with a fund to help previously fired employees and their dependent children.

I suspected Petey would consider that worth his freedom, which was admirable, and worth Birchall's life, which wasn't.

Late in the afternoon, I was sitting on a picnic table in the agility area, chin in hands.

"What's wrong, Sheila?" Clara plopped next to me.

"I had a thought. A question, really."

"What?"

"Do you think training our dogs to jump over things, to crawl through things, to walk over things might not be the best idea?"

"What do you mean? It's agility training. They love it. And it's so good for them. The physical and mental exercise."

"Yeah, they love it—"

With a few exceptions. I was remembering the mixed reviews of the weave poles from our three.

Gracie took the weave poles precisely, but at a pace that would have had Queen Victoria in her final days ordering her to get a move on, for heaven's sake.

Murphy started into the line at a nice clip, then slowed significantly. He appeared to instinctively understand the goal, but wanted to think about it.

LuLu started in after Murphy, following him around the first two poles, then coming head to butt with him when he didn't move fast enough for her.

He continued at his own pace.

She peeled off to the center of the arena, looking for something more fun.

Clara went after her to try again with lots of praise and cajoling.

We tried having LuLu follow Gracie's stately progression. LuLu knocked into poles, then took the side exit to run around to the finish and bark at Gracie.

We tried having her follow Murphy again—with more lead time to avoid tailgating. He still didn't move fast enough for her.

We tried one of us on each side to encourage her to stay there. She found Dodge the Humans a great game and would have endorsed it for the agility curriculum in a heartbeat.

"—and it is good for them," I added. "But is the behavior they're learning going to be good for *us?*"

"Oh, but it's only here they'll do these things," Clara said.

"You think LuLu is going to recognize the difference between the hurdles here at the dog park and the chairs you put in the doorway to keep her out of the kitchen when you leave meat out defrosting?"

She frowned a moment, then it cleared. "I'll have to plan ahead more so it can defrost in the fridge."

THE NEXT DAY, Teague arrived at my house to settle up.

"The retaining wall repair is complete, holding up your yard against gravity for another good long stretch, job site's spick and span."

"Excellent. And the electricity's fixed—a major bonus. Here's your check. Next, I was thinking about built-ins in—"

"No."

"No? You haven't even heard what I'm thinking about."

"I don't care." He reached out, letting the ends of my hair curl around his finger.

My senses reacted. My brain and mouth muddled along in confusion. "But—"

"I'm taking you out on a date—a real date, not something casual with Clara and Ned—and that's not going to happen with you as my employer. Assuming you want to go out with me."

"But—" Yep, brain and mouth still muddling.

"If you want to go, just say yes. Later, if it doesn't work, I'll do more jobs for you." He leaned closer, smiling down at me. "And if it does work, I'll do more jobs for you. Later."

I said the only thing I could think of.

"Yes."

The End

For announcements about upcoming books, as well as other titles and news, join Patricia McLinn's ReadHeads and receive her twice- monthly free newsletter.

patriciamclinn.com/readers-list

You can buy this book and all my others, including print editions and audiobooks, from my online store. I've added direct-to-you buying options to better control how my books reach you, while having lots more elbow room to give you special bundles, early offers, and exclusive bonuses.

Patricia's Bookstore

shop.patriciamclinn.com

Thank you for reading Sheila's latest adventure!

After helping to solve some startling murders in otherwise quiet North Bend County, Sheila, Clara and Teague, along with their canine friends, would be happy to have no crimes to solve in their neighborhood. But this time a cold case comes calling. A friend of Clara's has suspicions about the death of a cousin, and turns to Sheila and Clara to investigate.

Death on Shady Bridge

Sheila, Clara, Teague and friends ask if you'll help spread the word about them and the Secret Sleuth series. You have the power to do that in two quick ways:

Recommend the book and the series to your friends and/or the whole wide world on social media. Shouting from rooftops is particu-larly appreciated.

Review the book. Take a few minutes to write an honest review and it can make a huge difference. As you likely know, it's the single best way for your fellow readers to find books they'll enjoy, too.

To me—as an author and a reader—the goal is always to find a good author-reader match. By sharing your reading experience through recommendations and reviews, you become a vital matchmaker. ☺

More Secret Sleuth mysteries

DEATH ON THE DIVERSION

Final resting place? Deck chair.

DEATH ON TORRID AVENUE

A new love (canine), an ex-cop and a dog park discovery.

DEATH ON BEGUILING WAY

No zen in sight as Sheila untangles a yoga instructor's murder.

DEATH ON SHADY BRIDGE
A cold case homicide heats up.

DEATH ON CARRION LANE
A reunion for murder.

DEATH ON ZIGZAG TRAIL
A spooky legend twists grave matters.

DEATH ON PUZZLE PLACE
Season's greetings: Whodunit?

Caught Dead in Wyoming mysteries

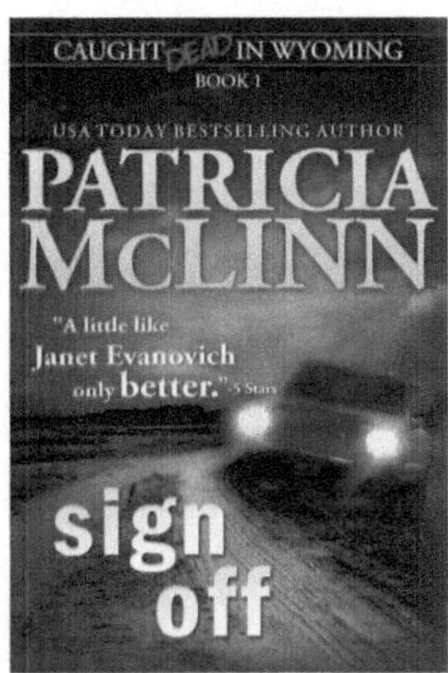

SIGN OFF

Divorce a husband, lose a career … grapple with a murder.

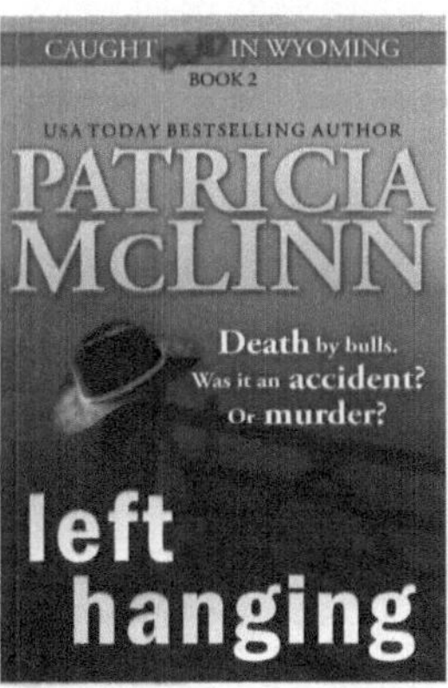

LEFT HANGING

Trampled by bulls—an accident? Elizabeth, Mike and friends dig into the world of rodeo.

SHOOT FIRST

For Elizabeth, death hits close to home. She and friends delve into old
Wyoming treasures and secrets to save lives.

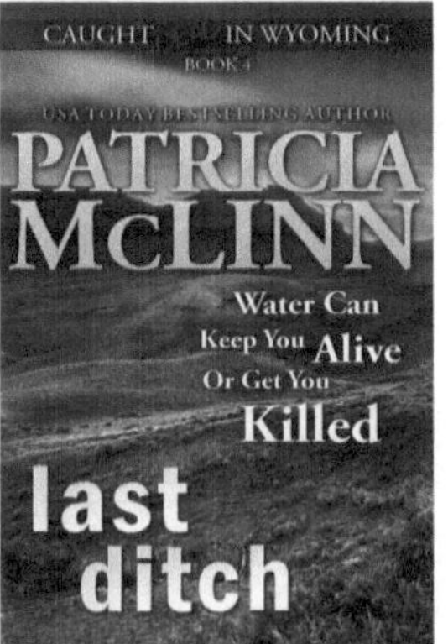

LAST DITCH

Elizabeth and Mike search after a man in a wheelchair goes missing in
dangerous, desolate country.

LOOK LIVE

Elizabeth and friends take on misleading murder with help—and hindrance—from intriguing out-of-towners.

BACK STORY

Murder never dies, but comes back to threaten Elizabeth and the team of investigators.

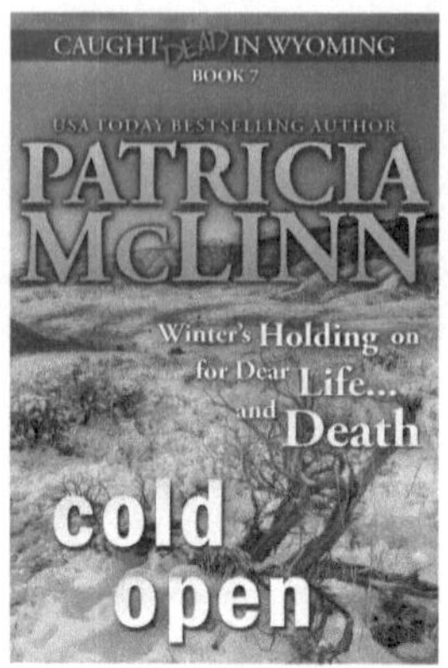

COLD OPEN

Elizabeth's search for a place of her own becomes an open house for murder.

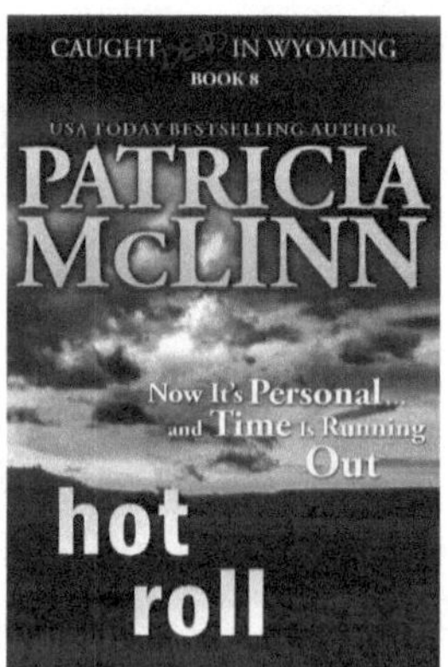

HOT ROLL

One of their own becomes a target—and time is running out.

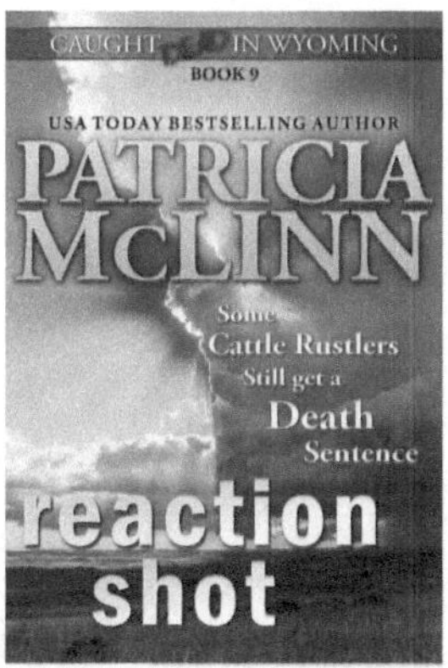

REACTION SHOT

Some cattle rustlers still get a death sentence.

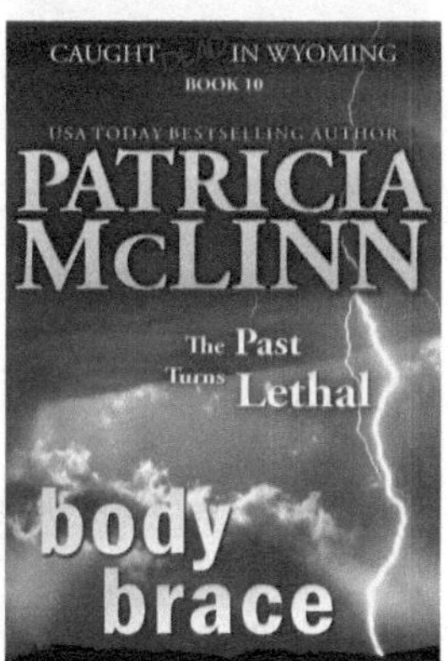

BODY BRACE

Everything can change … except murder.

AIR READY

Love and death decisions.

HOLIDAY BULLETS

A Christmas wish with Elizabeth's name on it.

CUE UP

On the trail of murder.

Mystery with romance
The Innocence Trilogy

PROOF OF INNOCENCE

She's a prosecutor chasing demons. He's wrestling them. Will they find proof of innocence?

PRICE OF INNOCENCE

She runs a foundation dedicated to forgiveness. He runs down criminals. If they don't work together, people will die.

PREMISE OF INNOCENCE

The last woman Detective Landis is prepared to see is the one
he must save.

"Evocative description, vivid characterization, and lots of twists and
turns." —*5-star review*

Explore a complete list of all Patricia's books
patriciamclinn.com/patricias-books

Or get a printable booklist
patriciamclinn.com/patricias-books/printable-booklist

Patricia's Bookstore (buy online directly from Patricia)
shop.patriciamclinn.com

About the Author

Patricia McLinn is the USA Today bestselling author of more than 60 published novels cited by readers and reviewers for their wit and vivid characterization. Her books include mysteries, romantic suspense, contemporary romance, historical romance, and women's fiction. They have topped bestseller lists and won numerous awards.

She has spoken about writing from London to Melbourne, Australia, to Washington, D.C., including being a guest speaker at the Smithsonian Institution.

McLinn spent more than 20 years as an editor at The Washington Post after stints as a sports writer (Rockford, Ill.) and assistant sports editor (Charlotte, N.C.). She received BA and MSJ degrees from Northwestern University.

Now living in northern Kentucky, McLinn loves to hear from readers through her website and social media.

Visit with Patricia:
Website: patriciamclinn.com
Facebook: facebook.com/PatriciaMcLinn
Pinterest: pinterest.com/patriciamclinn
Instagram: instagram.com/patriciamclinnauthor